The Wife

and other stories

Anton Chekhov

Translated by
Constance Garnett

1ˢᵗ WORLD
LIBRARY
Literary Society

The Wife and other stories

Anton Chekhov

© 1st World Library – Literary Society, 2004
PO Box 2211
Fairfield, IA 52556
www.1stworldlibrary.org
First Edition

LCCN: 2003099600

ISBN: 1-59540-004-4

Purchase *"The Wife"*
as a traditional bound book at:
www.1stWorldLibrary.org/purchase.asp?ISBN=1-59540-004-4

1st World Library Literary Society is a nonprofit
organization dedicated to promoting literacy by:

- Creating a free internet library accessible from any
computer worldwide.
- Hosting writing competitions and offering book
publishing scholarships.

Readers interested in supporting literacy
through sponsorship, donations or
membership please contact:
literacy@1stworldlibrary.org
Check us out at: www.1stworldlibrary.org

The Wife and other stories
contributed by Ed, Tim & Rodney
in support of
1st World Library Literary Society

CONTENTS

THE WIFE

I

I RECEIVED the following letter:

"DEAR SIR, PAVEL ANDREITCH!

"Not far from you - that is to say, in the village of
Pestrovo - very distressing incidents are taking place,
concerning which I feel it my duty to write to you. All
the peasants of that village sold their cottages and all
their belongings, and set off for the province of Tomsk,
but did not succeed in getting there, and have come
back. Here, of course, they have nothing now;
everything belongs to other people. They have settled
three or four families in a hut, so that there are no less
than fifteen persons of both sexes in each hut, not
counting the young children; and the long and the short
of it is, there is nothing to eat. There is famine and
there is a terrible pestilence of hunger, or spotted,
typhus; literally every one is stricken. The doctor's
assistant says one goes into a cottage and what does
one see? Every one is sick, every one delirious, some
laughing, others frantic; the huts are filthy; there is no
one to fetch them water, no one to give them a drink,
and nothing to eat but frozen potatoes. What can Sobol
(our Zemstvo doctor) and his lady assistant do when

more than medicine the peasants need bread which they have not? The District Zemstvo refuses to assist them, on the ground that their names have been taken off the register of this district, and that they are now reckoned as inhabitants of Tomsk; and, besides, the Zemstvo has no money.

"Laying these facts before you, and knowing your humanity, I beg you not to refuse immediate help.

"Your well-wisher."

Obviously the letter was written by the doctor with the animal name * or his lady assistant. Zemstvo doctors and their assistants go on for years growing more and more convinced every day that they can do *nothing*, and yet continue to receive their salaries from people who are living upon frozen potatoes, and consider they have a right to judge whether I am humane or not.

* Sobol in Russian means "sable-marten."- TRANSLATOR'S NOTE.

Worried by the anonymous letter and by the fact that peasants came every morning to the servants' kitchen and went down on their knees there, and that twenty sacks of rye had been stolen at night out of the barn, the wall having first been broken in, and by the general depression which was fostered by conversations, newspapers, and horrible weather - worried by all this, I worked listlessly and ineffectively. I was writing "A History of Railways"; I had to read a great number of Russian and foreign books, pamphlets, and articles in the magazines, to make calculations, to refer to logarithms, to think and to write; then again to read, calculate, and think; but as soon as I took up a book or began to think, my thoughts were in a muddle, my eyes began blinking, I would get up from the table with a sigh and begin walking about the big rooms of my deserted country-house. When I was tired of walking about I would stand still at my study window, and, looking across the wide courtyard, over the pond and the bare young birch-trees and the great fields covered with recently fallen, thawing snow, I saw on a low hill on the horizon a group of mud-coloured huts from which a black muddy road ran down in an irregular streak through the white field. That was Pestrovo, concerning which my anonymous correspondent had written to me. If it had not been for the crows who, foreseeing rain or snowy weather, floated cawing over the pond and the fields, and the tapping in the carpenter's shed, this bit of the world about which such a fuss was being made would have seemed like the Dead Sea; it was all so still, motionless, lifeless, and dreary!

My uneasiness hindered me from working and concentrating myself; I did not know what it was, and chose to believe it was disappointment. I had actually given up my post in the Department of Ways and Communications, and had come here into the country expressly to live in peace and to devote myself to writing on social questions. It had long been my cherished dream. And now I had to say good-bye both to peace and to literature, to give up everything and think only of the peasants. And that was inevitable, because I was convinced that there was absolutely nobody in the district except me to help the starving. The people surrounding me were uneducated, unintellectual, callous, for the most part dishonest, or if they were honest, they were unreasonable and unpractical like my wife, for instance. It was impossible to rely on such people, it was impossible to leave the peasants to their fate, so that the only thing left to do was to submit to necessity and see to setting the peasants to rights myself.

I began by making up my mind to give five thousand roubles to the assistance of the starving peasants. And that did not decrease, but only aggravated my uneasiness. As I stood by the window or walked about the rooms I was tormented by the question which had not occurred to me before: how this money was to be spent. To have bread bought and to go from hut to hut distributing it was more than one man could do, to say nothing of the risk that in your haste you might give twice as much to one who was well-fed or to one who was making. money out of his fellows as to the hungry. I had no faith in the local officials. All these district captains and tax inspectors were young men, and I distrusted them as I do all young people of today, who are materialistic and without ideals. The District Zemstvo, the Peasant Courts, and all the local institutions, inspired in me not the slightest desire to appeal to them for assistance. I knew that all these institutions who were busily engaged in picking out plums from the Zemstvo and the Government pie had their mouths always wide open for a bite at any other pie that might turn up.

The idea occurred to me to invite the neighbouring landowners and suggest to them to organize in my house something like a committee or a centre to which all subscriptions could be forwarded, and from which assistance and instructions could be distributed throughout the district; such an organization, which would render possible frequent consultations and free control on a big scale, would completely meet my views. But I imagined the lunches, the dinners, the suppers and the noise, the waste of time, the verbosity and the bad taste which that mixed provincial company would inevitably bring into my house, and I made haste to reject my idea.

As for the members of my own household, the last thing I could look for was help or support from them. Of my father's household, of the household of my childhood, once a big and noisy family, no one remained but the governess Mademoiselle Marie, or, as she was now called, Marya Gerasimovna, an absolutely insignificant person. She was a precise little old lady of seventy, who wore a light grey dress and a cap with white ribbons, and looked like a china doll. She always sat in the drawing-room reading.

Whenever I passed by her, she would say, knowing the reason for my brooding:

"What can you expect, Pasha? I told you how it would be before. You can judge from our servants."

My wife, Natalya Gavrilovna, lived on the lower storey, all the rooms of which she occupied. She slept, had her meals, and received her visitors downstairs in her own rooms, and took not the slightest interest in how I dined, or slept, or whom I saw. Our relations with one another were simple and not strained, but cold, empty, and dreary as relations are between people who have been so long estranged, that even living under the same roof gives no semblance of nearness. There was no trace now of the passionate and tormenting love - at one time sweet, at another bitter as wormwood - which I had once felt for NatalyaGavrilovna. There was nothing left, either, of the outbursts of the past - the loud altercations, upbraidings, complaints, and gusts of hatred which had usually ended in my wife's going abroad or to her own people, and in my sending money in small but frequent instalments that I might sting her pride oftener. (My proud and sensitive wife and her family live at my expense, and much as she would have liked to do so, my wife could not refuse my money: that afforded me satisfaction and was one comfort in my sorrow.) Now when we chanced to meet in the corridor downstairs or in the yard, I bowed, she smiled graciously. We spoke of the weather, said that it seemed time to put in the double windows, and that some one with bells on their harness had driven over the dam. And at such times I read in her face: "I am faithful to you and am not disgracing your good name which you think so much about; you are sensible and do not worry me; we are quits."

I assured myself that my love had died long ago, that I was too much absorbed in my work to think seriously of my relations with my wife. But, alas! that was only what I imagined. When my wife talked aloud downstairs I listened intently to her voice, though I could not distinguish one word. When she played the piano downstairs I stood up and listened. When her carriage or her saddlehorse was brought to the door, I went to the window and waited to see her out of the house; then I watched her get into her carriage or mount her horse and ride out of the yard. I felt that there was something wrong with me, and was afraid the expression of my eyes or my face might betray me. I looked after my wife and then watched for her to come back that I might see again from the window her face, her shoulders, her fur coat, her hat. I felt dreary, sad, infinitely regretful, and felt inclined in her absence to walk through her rooms, and longed that the problem that my wife and I had not been able to solve because our characters were incompatible, should solve itself in the natural way as soon as possible - that is, that this beautiful woman of twenty-seven might make haste and grow old, and that my head might be grey and bald.

One day at lunch my bailiff informed me that the Pestrovo peasants had begun to pull the thatch off the roofs to feed their cattle. Marya Gerasimovna looked at me in alarm and perplexity.

"What can I do?" I said to her. "One cannot fight single-handed, and I have never experienced such loneliness as I do now. I would give a great deal to find one man in the whole province on whom I could rely."

"Invite Ivan Ivanitch," said Marya Gerasimovna.

"To be sure!" I thought, delighted. "That is an idea! *C'est raison*," I hummed, going to my study to write to Ivan Ivanitch. "*C'est raison, c'est raison.*"

II

Of all the mass of acquaintances who, in this house twenty-five to thirty-five years ago, had eaten, drunk, masqueraded, fallen in love, married bored us with accounts of their splendid packs of hounds and horses, the only one still living was Ivan Ivanitch Bragin. At one time he had been very active, talkative, noisy, and given to falling in love, and had been famous for his extreme views and for the peculiar charm of his face, which fascinated men as well as women; now he was an old man, had grown corpulent, and was living out his days with neither views nor charm. He came the day after getting my letter, in the evening just as the samovar was brought into the dining-room and little Marya Gerasimovna had begun slicing the lemon.

"I am very glad to see you, my dear fellow," I said gaily, meeting him. "Why, you are stouter than ever. . . ."

"It isn't getting stout; it's swelling," he answered. "The bees must have stung me."

With the familiarity of a man laughing at his own fatness, he put his arms round my waist and laid on my breast his big soft head, with the hair combed down on the forehead like a Little Russian's, and went off into a thin, aged laugh.

"And you go on getting younger," he said through his laugh. "I wonder what dye you use for your hair and beard; you might let me have some of it." Sniffing and gasping, he embraced me and kissed me on the cheek.

Anton Chekhov

"You might give me some of it," he repeated. "Why, you are not forty, are you?"

"Alas, I am forty-six!" I said, laughing.

Ivan Ivanitch smelt of tallow candles and cooking, and that suited him. His big, puffy, slow-moving body was swathed in a long frock-coat like a coachman's full coat, with a high waist, and with hooks and eyes instead of buttons, and it would have been strange if he had smelt of eau-de-Cologne, for instance. In his long, unshaven, bluish double chin, which looked like a thistle, his goggle eyes, his shortness of breath, and in the whole of his clumsy, slovenly figure, in his voice, his laugh, and his words, it was difficult to recognize the graceful, interesting talker who used in old days to make the husbands of the district jealous on account of their wives.

"I am in great need of your assistance, my friend," I said, when we were sitting in the dining-room, drinking tea. "I want to organize relief for the starving peasants, and I don't know how to set about it. So perhaps you will be so kind as to advise me."

"Yes, yes, yes," said Ivan Ivanitch, sighing. "To be sure, to be sure, to be sure. . . ."

"I would not have worried you, my dear fellow, but really there is no one here but you I can appeal to. You know what people are like about here."

"To be sure, to be sure, to be sure. . . . Yes."

I thought that as we were going to have a serious, business consultation in which any one might take part, regardless of their position or personal relations, why should I not invite Natalya Gavrilovna.

"*Tres faciunt collegium*," I said gaily. "What if we were to ask Natalya Gavrilovna? What do you think? Fenya," I said, turning to the maid, "ask Natalya Gavrilovna to come upstairs to us, if possible at once. Tell her it's a very important matter."

A little later Natalya Gavrilovna came in. I got up to meet her and said:

"Excuse us for troubling you, Natalie. We are discussing a very important matter, and we had the happy thought that we might take advantage of your good advice, which you will not refuse to give us. Please sit down."

Ivan Ivanitch kissed her hand while she kissed his forehead; then, when we all sat down to the table, he, looking at her tearfully and blissfully, craned forward to her and kissed her hand again. She was dressed in black, her hair was carefully arranged, and she smelt of fresh scent. She had evidently dressed to go out or was expecting somebody. Coming into the dining-room, she held out her hand to me with simple friendliness, and smiled to me as graciously as she did to Ivan Ivanitch - that pleased me; but as she talked she moved her fingers, often and abruptly leaned back in her chair and talked rapidly, and this jerkiness in her words and movements irritated me and reminded me of her native town - Odessa, where the society, men and women alike, had wearied me by its bad taste.

"I want to do something for the famine-stricken peasants," I began, and after a brief pause I went on: "

Money, of course, is a great thing, but to confine oneself to subscribing money, and with that to be satisfied, would be evading the worst of the trouble. Help must take the form of money, but the most important thing is a proper and sound organization. Let us think it over, my friends, and do something."

Natalya Gavrilovna looked at me inquiringly and shrugged her shoulders as though to say, "What do I know about it?"

"Yes, yes, famine . . ." muttered Ivan Ivanitch. "Certainly . . .yes."

"It's a serious position," I said, "and assistance is needed as soon as possible. I imagine the first point among the principles which we must work out ought to be promptitude. We must act on the military principles of judgment, promptitude, and energy."

"Yes, promptitude . . ." repeated Ivan Ivanitch in a drowsy and listless voice, as though he were dropping asleep. "Only one can't do anything. The crops have failed, and so what's the use of all your judgment and energy? . . . It's the elements. . . .You can't go against God and fate."

"Yes, but that's what man has a head for, to conten d against the elements."

"Eh? Yes . . . that's so, to be sure. . . . Yes."

Ivan Ivanitch sneezed into his handkerchief, brightened up, and as though he had just woken up, looked round at my wife and me.

"My crops have failed, too." He laughed a thin little laugh and gave a sly wink as though this were really funny. "No money, no corn, and a yard full of labourers like Count Sheremetyev's. I want to kick them out, but I haven't the heart to."

Natalya Gavrilovna laughed, and began questioning him about his private affairs. Her presence gave me a pleasure such as I had not felt for a long time, and I was afraid to look at her for fear my eyes would betray my secret feeling. Our relations were such that that feeling might seem surprising and ridiculous.

She laughed and talked with Ivan Ivanitch without being in the least disturbed that she was in my room and that I was not laughing.

"And so, my friends, what are we to do?" I asked after waiting for a pause. "I suppose before we do anything else we had better immediately open a subscription-list. We will write to our friends in the capitals and in Odessa, Natalie, and ask them to subscribe. When we have got together a little sum we will begin buying corn and fodder for the cattle; and you, Ivan Ivanitch, will you be so kind as to undertake distributing the relief? Entirely relying on your characteristic tact and efficiency, we will only venture to express a desire that before you give any relief you make acquaintance with the details of the case on the spot, and also, which is very important, you should be careful that corn should be distributed only to those who are in genuine need, and not to the drunken, the idle, or the dishonest."

"Yes, yes, yes . . ." muttered Ivan Ivanitch. "To be sure, to be sure."

"Well, one won't get much done with that slobbering wreck," I thought, and I felt irritated.

"I am sick of these famine-stricken peasants, bother them! It's nothing but grievances with them!" Ivan Ivanitch went on, sucking the rind of the lemon. "The hungry have a grievance against those who have enough, and those who have enough have a grievance against the hungry. Yes . . . hunger stupefies and maddens a man and makes him savage; hunger is not a potato. When a man is starving he uses bad language, and steals, and may do worse. . . . One must realize that."

Ivan Ivanitch choked over his tea, coughed, and shook all over with a squeaky, smothered laughter.

" 'There was a battle at Pol . . . Poltava,' " he brought out, gesticulating with both hands in protest against the laughter and coughing which prevented him from speaking. " 'There was a battle at Poltava!' When three years after the Emancipation we had famine in two districts here, Fyodor Fyodoritch came and invited me to go to him. 'Come along, come along,' he persisted, and nothing else would satisfy him. 'Very well, let us go,' I said. And, so we set off. It was in the evening; there was snow falling. Towards night we were getting near his place, and suddenly from the wood came 'bang!' and another time 'bang!' 'Oh, damn it all!' . . . I jumped out of the sledge, and I saw in the darkness a man running up to me, knee-deep in the snow. I put my arm round his shoulder, like this, and knocked the gun out of his hand. Then another one turned up; I fetched him a knock on the back of his head so that he grunted and flopped with his nose in the snow. I was a sturdy chap then, my fist was heavy; I disposed of two of them, and when I turned round Fyodor was sitting astride of a third. We did not let our three fine fellows go; we tied their hands behind their backs so that they might not do us or themselves any harm, and took the fools into the kitchen. We were angry with them and at the same time ashamed to look at them; they were peasants we knew, and were good fellows; we were sorry for them. They were quite stupid with terror. One was crying and begging our pardon, the second looked like a wild beast and kept swearing, the third knelt down and began to pray. I said to Fedya: 'Don't bear them a grudge; let them go, the rascals!' He fed them, gave them a bushel of flour each, and let them go: 'Get along with you,' he said. So that's what he did.. . . The Kingdom of Heaven be his and everlasting peace! He understood and did not bear them a grudge; but there were some who did, and how many people they ruined! Yes. . . Why, over the affair at the Klotchkovs' tavern eleven men were sent to the disciplinary battalion. Yes. . . . And now, look, it's the same thing. Anisyin, the investigating magistrate, stayed the night with me last Thursday, and he told me about some landowner. . . .Yes. . . . They took the wall of his barn to pieces at night and carried off twenty sacks of rye. When the gentleman heard that such a crime had been committed, he sent a telegram to the Governor and another to the police captain, another to the investigating magistrate! . . . Of course, every one is afraid of a man who is fond of litigation. The authorities were in a flutter and there was a general hubbub. Two villages were searched."

"Excuse me, Ivan Ivanitch," I said. "Twenty sacks of rye were stolen from me, and it was I who telegraphed to the Governor. I telegraphed to Petersburg, too. But it was by no means out of love for litigation, as you are pleased to express it, and not because I bore them a grudge. I look at every subject from the point of view of principle. From the point of view of the law, theft is the same whether a man is hungry or not."

"Yes, yes. . ." muttered Ivan Ivanitch in confusion. "Of course. . . To be sure, yes."

Natalya Gavrilovna blushed.

"There are people. . ." she said and stopped; she made an effort to seem indifferent, but she could not keep it up, and looked into my eyes with the hatred that I know so well. "There are people," she said, "for whom famine and human suffering exist simply that they may vent their hateful and despicable temperaments upon them."

I was confused and shrugged my shoulders.

"I meant to say generally," she went on, "that there are people who are quite indifferent and completely devoid of all feeling of sympathy, yet who do not pass human suffering by, but insist on meddling for fear people should be able to do without them. Nothing is sacred for their vanity."

"There are people," I said softly, "who have an angelic character, but who express their glorious ideas in such a form that it is difficult to distinguish the angel from an Odessa market-woman."

I must confess it was not happily expressed.

My wife looked at me as though it cost her a great effort to hold her tongue. Her sudden outburst, and then her inappropriate eloquence on the subject of my desire to help the famine-stricken peasants, were, to say the least, out of place; when I had invited her to come upstairs I had expected quite a different attitude to me and my intentions. I cannot say definitely what I had expected, but I had been agreeably agitated by the expectation. Now I saw that to go on speaking about the famine would be difficult and perhaps stupid.

"Yes . . ." Ivan Ivanitch muttered inappropriately. "Burov, the merchant, must have four hundred thousand at least. I said to him: 'Hand over one or two thousand to the famine. You can't take it with you when you die, anyway.' He was offended. But we all have to die, you know. Death is not a potato."

A silence followed again.

"So there's nothing left for me but to reconcile myself to loneliness," I sighed. "One cannot fight single-handed. Well, I will try single-handed. Let us hope that my campaign against the famine will be more successful than my campaign against indifference."

"I am expected downstairs," said Natalya Gavrilovna.

She got up from the table and turned to Ivan Ivanitch.

"So you will look in upon me downstairs for a minute? I won't say good-bye to you."

And she went away.

Ivan Ivanitch was now drinking his seventh glass of tea, choking, smacking his lips, and sucking sometimes his moustache, sometimes the lemon. He was muttering something drowsily and listlessly, and I did not listen but waited for him to go. At last, with an expression that suggested that he had only come to me to take a cup of tea, he got up and began to take leave. As I saw him out I said:

"And so you have given me no advice."

"Eh? I am a feeble, stupid old man," he answered. "What use would my advice be? You shouldn't worry yourself. . . . I really don't know why you worry yourself. Don't disturb yourself, my dear fellow! Upon my word, there's no need," he whispered genuinely and affectionately, soothing me as though I were a child. "Upon my word, there's no need."

"No need? Why, the peasants are pulling the thatch off their huts, and they say there is typhus somewhere already."

"Well, what of it? If there are good crops next year, they'll thatch them again, and if we die of typhus others will live after us. Anyway, we have to die - if not now, later. Don't worry yourself, my dear."

"I can't help worrying myself," I said irritably.

We were standing in the dimly lighted vestibule. Ivan Ivanitch suddenly took me by the elbow, and, preparing to say something evidently very important, looked at me in silence for a couple of minutes.

"Pavel Andreitch!" he said softly, and suddenly in his puffy, set face and dark eyes there was a gleam of the expression for which he had once been famous and which was truly charming. "Pavel Andreitch, I speak to you as a friend: try to be different! One is ill at ease with you, my dear fellow, one really is!"

He looked intently into my face; the charming expression faded away, his eyes grew dim again, and he sniffed and muttered feebly:

"Yes, yes. . . . Excuse an old man. . . . It's all nonsense . . .yes."

As he slowly descended the staircase, spreading out his hands to balance himself and showing me his huge, bulky back and red neck, he gave me the unpleasant impression of a sort of crab.

"You ought to go away, your Excellency," he muttered. "To Petersburg or abroad. . . . Why should you live here and waste your golden days? You are young, wealthy, and healthy. . . . Yes. . . . Ah, if I were younger I would whisk away like a hare, and snap my fingers at everything."

III

My wife's outburst reminded me of our married life together. In old days after every such outburst we felt irresistibly drawn to each other; we would meet and let off all the dynamite that had accumulated in our souls. And now after Ivan Ivanitch had gone away I had a strong impulse to go to my wife. I wanted to go downstairs and tell her that her behaviour at tea had been an insult to me, that she was cruel, petty, and that her plebeian mind had never risen to a comprehension of what *I* was saying and of what *I* was doing. I walked about the rooms a long time thinking of what I would say to her and trying to guess what she would say to me.

That evening, after Ivan Ivanitch went away, I felt in a peculiarly irritating form the uneasiness which had worried me of late. I could not sit down or sit still, but kept walking about in the rooms that were lighted up and keeping near to the one in which Marya Gerasimovna was sitting. I had a feeling very much like that which I had on the North Sea during a storm when every one thought that our ship, which had no freight nor ballast, would overturn. And that evening I understood that my uneasiness was not disappointment, as I had supposed, but a different feeling, though what exactly I could not say, and that irritated me more than ever.

"I will go to her," I decided. "I can think of a pretext. I shall say that I want to see Ivan Ivanitch; that will be all."

I went downstairs and walked without haste over the carpeted floor through the vestibule and the hall. Ivan Ivanitch was sitting on the sofa in the drawing-room; he was drinking tea again and muttering something. My wife was standing opposite to him and holding on to the back of a chair. There was a gentle, sweet, and docile expression on her face, such as one sees on the faces of people listening to crazy saints or holy men when a peculiar hidden significance is imagined in their vague words and mutterings. There was something morbid, something of a nun's exaltation, in my wife's expression and attitude; and her low-pitched, half-dark rooms with their old-fashioned furniture, with her birds asleep in their cages, and with a smell of geranium, reminded me of the rooms of some abbess or pious old lady.

I went into the drawing-room. My wife showed neither surprise nor confusion, and looked at me calmly and serenely, as though she had known I should come.

"I beg your pardon," I said softly. "I am so glad you have not gone yet, Ivan Ivanitch. I forgot to ask you, do you know the Christian name of the president of our Zemstvo?"

"Andrey Stanislavovitch. Yes. . . ."

"*Merci*," I said, took out my notebook, and wrote it down.

There followed a silence during which my wife and Ivan Ivanitch were probably waiting for me to go; my wife did not believe that I wanted to know the president's name - I saw that from her eyes.

"Well, I must be going, my beauty," muttered Ivan Ivanitch, after I had walked once or twice across the drawing-room and sat down by the fireplace.

"No," said Natalya Gavrilovna quickly, touching his hand. "Stay another quarter of an hour. . . . Please do!"

Evidently she did not wish to be left alone with me without a witness.

"Oh, well, I'll wait a quarter of an hour, too," I thought.

"Why, it's snowing!" I said, getting up and looking out of window. "A good fall of snow! Ivan Ivanitch" - I went on walking about the room - "I do regret not being a sportsman. I can imagine what a pleasure it must be coursing hares or hunting wolves in snow like this!"

My wife, standing still, watched my movements, looking out of the corner of her eyes without turning her head. She looked as though she thought I had a sharp knife or a revolver in my pocket.

"Ivan Ivanitch, do take me out hunting some day," I went on softly. "I shall be very, very grateful to you."

At that moment a visitor came into the room. He was a tall, thick-set gentleman whom I did not know, with a bald head, a big fair beard, and little eyes. From his baggy, crumpled clothes and his manners I took him to be a parish clerk or a teacher, but my wife introduced him to me as Dr. Sobol.

"Very, very glad to make your acquaintance," said the doctor in a loud tenor voice, shaking hands with me warmly, with a naïve smile. "Very glad!"

He sat down at the table, took a glass of tea, and said in a loud voice:

"Do you happen to have a drop of rum or brandy? Have pity on me, Olya, and look in the cupboard; I am frozen," he said, addressing the maid.

I sat down by the fire again, looked on, listened, and from time to time put in a word in the general conversation. My wife smiled graciously to the visitors and kept a sharp lookout on me, as though I were a wild beast. She was oppressed by my presence, and this aroused in me jealousy, annoyance, and an obstinate desire to wound her. "Wife, these snug rooms, the place by the fire," I thought, "are mine, have been mine for years, but some crazy Ivan Ivanitch or Sobol has for some reason more right to them than I. Now I see my wife, not out of window, but close at hand, in ordinary home surroundings that I feel the want of now I am growing older, and, in spite of her hatred for me, I miss her as years ago in my childhood I used to miss my mother and my nurse. And I feel that now, on the verge of old age, my love for her is purer and loftier than it was in the past; and that is why I want to go up to her, to stamp hard on her toe with my heel, to hurt her and smile as I do it."

"Monsieur Marten," I said, addressing the doctor, "how many hospitals have we in the district?"

"Sobol," my wife corrected.

"Two," answered Sobol.

"And how many deaths are there every year in each hospital?"

"Pavel Andreitch, I want to speak to you," said my wife.

She apologized to the visitors and went to the next room. I got up and followed her.

"You will go upstairs to your own rooms this minute," she said.

"You are ill-bred," I said to her.

"You will go upstairs to your own rooms this very minute," she repeated sharply, and she looked into my face with hatred.

She was standing so near that if I had stooped a lit tle my beard would have touched her face.

"What is the matter?" I asked. "What harm have I done all at once?"

Her chin quivered, she hastily wiped her eyes, and, with a cursory glance at the looking-glass, whispered:

"The old story is beginning all over again. Of course you won't go away. Well, do as you like. I'll go away myself, and you stay."

We returned to the drawing-room, she with a resolute face, while I shrugged my shoulders and tried to smile. There were some more visitors - an elderly lady and a young man in spectacles.

Without greeting the new arrivals or taking leave of the others, I went off to my own rooms.

After what had happened at tea and then again downstairs, it became clear to me that our "family happiness," which we had begun to forget about in the course of the last two years, was through some absurd and trivial reason beginning all over again, and that neither I nor my wife could now stop ourselves; and that next day or the day after, the outburst of hatred would, as I knew by experience of past years, be followed by something revolting which would upset the whole order of our lives. "So it seems that during these two years we have grown no wiser, colder, or calmer," I thought as I began walking about the rooms. "So there will again be tears, outcries, curses, packing up, going abroad, then the continual sickly fear that she will disgrace me with some coxcomb out there, Italian or Russian, refusing a passport, letters, utter loneliness, missing her, and in five years old age, grey hairs." I walked about, imagining what was really impossible - her, grown handsomer, stouter, embracing a man I did not know. By now convinced that that would certainly happen, "'Why," I asked myself, "Why, in one of our long past quarrels, had not I given her a divorce, or why had she not at that time left me altogether? I should not have had this yearning for her now, this hatred, this anxiety; and I should have lived out my life quietly, working and not worrying about anything."

A carriage with two lamps drove into the yard, then a big sledge with three horses. My wife was evidently having a party.

Till midnight everything was quiet downstairs and I heard nothing, but at midnight there was a sound of moving chairs and a clatter of crockery. So there was supper. Then the chairs moved again, and through the floor I heard a noise; they seemed to be shouting hurrah. Marya Gerasimovna was already asleep and I was quite alone in the whole upper storey; the portraits of my forefathers, cruel, insignificant people, looked at me from the walls of the drawing-room, and the reflection of my lamp in the window winked unpleasantly. And with a feeling of jealousy and envy for what was going on downstairs, I listened and thought: "I am master here; if I like, I can in a moment turn out all that fine crew." But I knew that all that was nonsense, that I could not turn out any one, and the word "master" had no meaning. One may think oneself master, married, rich, a kammer-junker, as much as one likes, and at the same time not know what it means.

After supper some one downstairs began singing in a tenor voice.

"Why, nothing special has happened," I tried to persuade myself. "Why am I so upset? I won't go downstairs tomorrow, that's all; and that will be the end of our quarrel."

At a quarter past one I went to bed.

"Have the visitors downstairs gone?" I asked Alexey as he was undressing me.

"Yes, sir, they've gone."

"And why were they shouting hurrah?"

"Alexey Dmitritch Mahonov subscribed for the famine

fund a thousand bushels of flour and a thousand roubles. And the old lady - I don't know her name - promised to set up a soup kitchen on her estate to feed a hundred and fifty people. Thank God . . . Natalya Gavrilovna has been pleased to arrange that all the gentry should assemble every Friday."

"To assemble here, downstairs?"

"Yes, sir. Before supper they read a list: since August up to today Natalya Gavrilovna has collected eight thousand roubles, besides corn. Thank God. . . . What I think is that if our mistress does take trouble for the salvation of her soul, she will soon collect a lot. There are plenty of rich people here."

Dismissing Alexey, I put out the light and drew the bedclothes over my head.

"After all, why am I so troubled?" I thought. "What force draws me to the starving peasants like a butterfly to a flame? I don't know them, I don't understand them; I have never seen them and I don't like them. Why this uneasiness?"

I suddenly crossed myself under the quilt.

"But what a woman she is!" I said to myself, thinking of my wife. "There's a regular committee held in the house without my knowing. Why this secrecy? Why this conspiracy? What have I done to them? Ivan Ivanitch is right - I must go away."

Next morning I woke up firmly resolved to go away. The events of the previous day - the conversation at tea, my wife, Sobol, the supper, my apprehensions -

worried me, and I felt glad to think of getting away from the surroundings which reminded me of all that. While I was drinking my coffee the bailiff gave me a long report on various matters. The most agreeable item he saved for the last.

"The thieves who stole our rye have been found," he announced with a smile. "The magistrate arrested three peasants at Pestrovo yesterday."

"Go away!" I shouted at him; and a propos of nothing, I picked up the cake-basket and flung it on the floor.

IV

After lunch I rubbed my hands, and thought I must go to my wife and tell her that I was going away. Why? Who cared? Nobody cares, I answered, but why shouldn't I tell her, especially as it would give her nothing but pleasure? Besides, to go away after our yesterday's quarrel without saying a word would not be quite tactful: she might think that I was frightened of her, and perhaps the thought that she has driven me out of my house may weigh upon her. It would be just as well, too, to tell her that I subscribe five thousand, and to give her some advice about the organization, and to warn her that her inexperience in such a complicated and responsible matter might lead to most lamentable results. In short, I wanted to see my wife, and while I thought of various pretexts for going to her, I had a firm conviction in my heart that I should do so.

It was still light when I went in to her, and the lamps had not yet been lighted. She was sitting in her study, which led from the drawing-room to her bedroom, and, bending low over the table, was writing something quickly. Seeing me, she started, got up from the table, and remained standing in an attitude such as to screen her papers from me.

"I beg your pardon, I have only come for a minute," I said, and, I don't know why, I was overcome with embarrassment. "I have learnt by chance that you are organizing relief for the famine, Natalie."

"Yes, I am. But that's my business," she answered.

"Yes, it is your business," I said softly. "I am glad of it, for it just fits in with my intentions. I beg your permission to take part in it."

"Forgive me, I cannot let you do it," she said in response, and looked away.

"Why not, Natalie?" I said quietly. "Why not? I, too, am well fed and I, too, want to help the hungry."

"I don't know what it has to do with you," she said with a contemptuous smile, shrugging her shoulders. "Nobody asks you."

"Nobody asks you, either, and yet you have got up a regular committee in *my* house," I said.

"I am asked, but you can have my word for it no one will ever ask you. Go and help where you are not known."

"For God's sake, don't talk to me in that tone." I tried to be mild, and besought myself most earnestly not to lose my temper. For the first few minutes I felt glad to be with my wife. I felt an atmosphere of youth, of home, of feminine softness, of the most refined elegance - exactly what was lacking on my floor and in my life altogether. My wife was wearing a pink flannel dressing-gown; it made her look much younger, and gave a softness to her rapid and sometimes abrupt movements. Her beautiful dark hair, the mere sight of which at one time stirred me to passion, had from sitting so long with her head bent c ome loose from the comb and was untidy, but, to my eyes, that only made it look more rich and luxuriant. All this, though is banal to the point of vulgarity. Before me stood an ordinary woman, perhaps neither beautiful nor elegant, but this was my wife with whom I had once lived, and with whom I should have been living to this day if it had not been for her unfortunate character; she was the one human being on the terrestrial globe whom I loved. At this moment, just before going away, when I knew that I should no longer see her even through the window, she seemed to me fascinating even as she was, cold and forbidding, answering me with a proud and contemptuous mockery. I was proud of her, and confessed to myself that to go away from her was terrible and impossible.

"Pavel Andreitch," she said after a brief silence, "for two years we have not interfered with each other but have lived quietly. Why do you suddenly feel it necessary to go back to the past? Yesterday you came to insult and humiliate me," she went on, raising her voice, and her face flushed and her eyes flamed with hatred; "but restrain yourself; do not do it, Pavel Andreitch! Tomorrow I will send in a petition and they will give me a passport, and I will go away; I will go! I will go! I'll go into a convent, into a widows' home, into an almshouse. . . ."

"Into a lunatic asylum!" I cried, not able to restrain myself.

"Well, even into a lunatic asylum! That would be better, that would be better," she cried, with flashing eyes. "When I was in Pestrovo today I envied the sick and starving peasant women because they are not living with a man like you. They are free and honest, while, thanks to you, I am a parasite, I am perishing in idleness, I eat your bread, I spend your money, and I repay you with my liberty and a fidelity which is of no use to any one. Because you won't give me a passport, I must respect your good name, though it doesn't exist."

I had to keep silent. Clenching my teeth, I walked quickly into the drawing-room, but turned back at once and said:

"I beg you earnestly that there should be no more assemblies, plots, and meetings of conspirators in my house! I only admit to my house those with whom I am acquainted, and let all your crew find another place to do it if they want to take up philanthropy. I can't allow people at midnight in my house to be shouting hurrah at successfully exploiting an hysterical woman like you!"

My wife, pale and wringing her hands, took a rapid stride across the room, uttering a prolonged moan as though she had toothache. With a wave of my hand, I went into the drawing-room. I was choking with rage, and at the same time I was trembling with terror that I might not restrain myself, and that I might say or do something which I might regret all my life. And I clenched my hands tight, hoping to hold myself in.

After drinking some water and recovering my calm a little, I went back to my wife. She was standing in the same attitude as before, as though barring my approach to the table with the papers. Tears were slowly trickling down her pale, cold face. I paused then and said to her bitterly but without anger:

"How you misunderstand me! How unjust you are to me! I swear upon my honour I came to you with the best of motives, with nothing but the desire to do good!"

"Pavel Andreitch!" she said, clasping her hands on her bosom, and her face took on the agonized, imploring expression with which frightened, weeping children beg not to be punished, "I know perfectly well that you will refuse me, but still I beg you. Force yourself to do one kind action in your life. I entreat you, go away from here! That's the only thing you can do for the starving peasants. Go away, and I will forgive you everything, everything!"

"There is no need for you to insult me, Natalie," I sighed, feeling a sudden rush of humility. "I had already made up my mind to go away, but I won't go until I have done something for the peasants. It's my duty!"

"Ach!" she said softly with an impatient frown. "You can make an excellent bridge or railway, but you can do nothing for the starving peasants. Do understand!"

"Indeed? Yesterday you reproached me with indifference and with being devoid of the feeling of compassion. How well you know me!" I laughed. "You believe in God - well, God is my witness that I am worried day and night. . . ."

"I see that you are worried, but the famine and compassion have nothing to do with it. You are worried because the starving peasants can get on without you, and because the Zemstvo, and in fact every one who is helping them, does not need your guidance."

I was silent, trying to suppress my irritation. Then

Anton Chekhov

I said:

"I came to speak to you on business. Sit down. Please sit down."

She did not sit down.

"I beg you to sit down," I repeated, and I motioned her to a chair.

She sat down. I sat down, too, thought a little, and said:

"I beg you to consider earnestly what I am saying. Listen. . . .Moved by love for your fellow-creatures, you have undertaken the organization of famine relief. I have nothing against that, of course; I am completely in sympathy with you, and am prepared to co-operate with you in every way, whatever our relations may be. But, with all my respect for your mind and your heart . . and your heart," I repeated, "I cannot allow such a difficult, complex, and responsible matter as the organization of relief to be left in your hands entirely. You are a woman, you are inexperienced, you know nothing of life, you are too confiding and expansive. You have surrounded yourself with assistants whom you know nothing about. I am not exaggerating if I say that under these conditions your work will inevitably lead to two deplorable consequences. To begin with, our district will be left unrelieved; and, secondly, you will have to pay for your mistakes and those of your assistants, not only with your purse, but with your reputation. The money deficit and other losses I could, no doubt, make good, but who could restore you your good name? When through lack of proper supervision and oversight there is a rumour that you, and consequently I, have made two hundred thousand over the famine fund, will your assistants come to your aid?"

She said nothing.

"Not from vanity, as you say," I went on, "but simply that the starving peasants may not be left unrelieved and your reputation may not be injured, I feel it my moral duty to take part in your work."

"Speak more briefly," said my wife.

"You will be so kind," I went on, "as to show me what has been subscribed so far and what you have spent. Then inform me daily of every fresh subscription in money or kind, and of every fresh outlay. You will also give me, Natalie, the list of your helpers. Perhaps they are quite decent people; I don't doubt it; but, still, it is absolutely necessary to make inquiries."

She was silent. I got up, and walked up and down the room.

"Let us set to work, then," I said, and I sat down to her table.

"Are you in earnest?" she asked, looking at me in alarm and bewilderment.

"Natalie, do be reasonable!" I said appealingly, seeing from her face that she meant to protest. "I beg you, trust my experience and my sense of honour."

"I don't understand what you want."

"Show me how much you have collected and how

much you have spent."

"I have no secrets. Any one may see. Look."

On the table lay five or six school exercise books, several sheets of notepaper covered with writing, a map of the district, and a number of pieces of paper of different sizes. It was getting dusk. I lighted a candle.

"Excuse me, I don't see anything yet," I said, turning over the leaves of the exercise books. "Where is the account of the receipt of money subscriptions?"

"That can be seen from the subscription lists."

"Yes, but you must have an account," I said, smiling at her naivete. "Where are the letters accompanying the subscriptions in money or in kind? *Pardon*, a little practical advice, Natalie: it's absolutely necessary to keep those letters. You ought to number each letter and make a special note of it in a special record. You ought to do the same with your own letters. But I will do all that myself."

"Do so, do so . . ." she said.

I was very much pleased with myself. Attracted by this living interesting work, by the little table, the naive exercise books and the charm of doing this work in my wife's society, I was afraid that my wife would suddenly hinder me and upset everything by some sudden whim, and so I was in haste and made an effort to attach no consequence to the fact that her lips were quivering, and that she was looking about her with a helpless and frightened air like a wild creature in a trap.

"I tell you what, Natalie," I said without looking at her; "let me take all these papers and exercise books upstairs to my study. There I will look through them and tell you what I think about it tomorrow. Have you any more papers?" I asked, arranging the exercise books and sheets of papers in piles.

"Take them, take them all!" said my wife, helping me to arrange them, and big tears ran down her cheeks. "Take it all! That's all that was left me in life. . . . Take the last."

"Ach! Natalie, Natalie!" I sighed reproachfully.

She opened the drawer in the table and began flinging the papers out of it on the table at random, poking me in the chest with her elbow and brushing my face with her hair; as she did so, copper coins kept dropping upon my knees and on the floor.

"Take everything!" she said in a husky voice.

When she had thrown out the papers she walked away from me, and putting both hands to her head, she flung herself on the couch. I picked up the money, put it back in the drawer, and locked it up that the servants might not be led into dishonesty; then I gathered up all the papers and went off with them. As I passed my wife I stopped. and, looking at her back and shaking shoulders, I said:

"What a baby you are, Natalie! Fie, fie! Listen, Natalie: when you realize how serious and responsible a business it is you will be the first to thank me. I assure you you will."

In my own room I set to work without haste. The exercise books were not bound, the pages were not numbered. The entries were put in all sorts of handwritings; evidently any one who liked had a hand in managing the books. In the record of the subscriptions in kind there was no note of their money value. But, excuse me, I thought, the rye which is now worth one rouble fifteen kopecks may be worth two roubles fifteen kopecks in two months' time! Was that the way to do things? Then, "Given to A. M. Sobol 32 roubles." When was it given? For what purpose was it given? Where was the receipt? There was nothing to show, and no making anything of it. In case of legal proceedings, these papers would only obscure the case.

"How naive she is!" I thought with surprise. "What a child!"

I felt both vexed and amused.

V

My wife had already collected eight thousand; with my five it would be thirteen thousand. For a start that was very good. The business which had so worried and interested me was at last in my hands; I was doing what the others would not and could not do; I was doing my duty, organizing the relief fund in a practical and businesslike way

Everything seemed to be going in accordance with my desires and intentions; but why did my feeling of uneasiness persist? I spent four hours over my wife's papers, making out their meaning and correcting her mistakes, but instead of feeling soothed, I felt as though some one were standing behind me and rubbing my back with a rough hand. What was it I wanted? The organization of the relief fund had come into trustworthy hands, the hungry would be fed - what more was wanted?

The four hours of this light work for some reason exhausted me, so that I could not sit bending over the table nor write. From below I heard from time to time a smothered moan; it was my wife sobbing. Alexey, invariably meek, sleepy, and sanctimonious, kept coming up to the table to see to the candles, and looked at me somewhat strangely.

"Yes, I must go away," I decided at last, feeling utterly exhausted. "As far as possible from these agreeable impressions! I will set off tomorrow."

I gathered together the papers and exercise books, and

went down to my wife. As, feeling quite worn out and shattered, I held the papers and the exercise books to my breast with both hands, and passing through my bedroom saw my trunks, the sound of weeping reached me through the floor.

"Are you a kammer-junker?" a voice whispered in my ear. "That's a very pleasant thing. But yet you are a reptile."

"It's all nonsense, nonsense, nonsense," I muttered as I went downstairs. "Nonsense . . . and it's nonsense, too, that I am actuated by vanity or a love of display. . . . What rubbish! Am I going to get a decoration for working for the peasants or be made the director of a department? Nonsense, nonsense! And who is there to show off to here in the country?"

I was tired, frightfully tired, and something kept whispering in my ear: "Very pleasant. But, still, you are a reptile." For some reason I remembered a line out of an old poem I knew as a child: "How pleasant it is to be good!"

My wife was lying on the couch in the same attitude, on her face and with her hands clutching her head. She was crying. A maid was standing beside her with a perplexed and frightened face. I sent the maid away, laid the papers on the table, thought a moment and said:

"Here are all your papers, Natalie. It's all in order, it's all capital, and I am very much pleased. I am going away tomorrow."

She went on crying. I went into the drawing-room and

sat there in the dark. My wife's sobs, her sighs, accused me of something, and to justify myself I remembered the whole of our quarrel, starting from my unhappy idea of inviting my wife to our consultation and ending with the exercise books and these tears. It was an ordinary attack of our conjugal hatred, senseless and unseemly, such as had been frequent during our married life, but what had the starving peasants to do with it? How could it have happened that they had become a bone of contention between us? It was just as though pursuing one another we had accidentally run up to the altar and had carried on a quarrel there.

"Natalie," I said softly from the drawing-room, "hush, hush!"

To cut short her weeping and make an end of this agonizing state of affairs, I ought to have gone up to my wife and comforted her, caressed her, or apologized; but how could I do it so that she would believe me? How could I persuade the wild duck, living in captivity and hating me, that it was dear to me, and that I felt for its sufferings? I had never known my wife, so I had never known how to talk to her or what to talk about. Her appearance I knew very well and appreciated it as it deserved, but her spiritual, moral world, her mind, her outlook on life, her frequent changes of mood, her eyes full of hatred, her disdain, the scope and variety of her reading which sometimes struck me, or, for instance, the nun-like expression I had seen on her face the day before - all that was unknown and incomprehensible to me. When in my collisions with her I tried to define what sort of a person she was, my psychology went no farther than deciding that she was giddy, impractical, ill-tempered, guided by feminine logic; and it seemed to me that that was quite sufficient. But now that she was crying I had a passionate desire to know more.

The weeping ceased. I went up to my wife. She sat up on the couch, and, with her head propped in both hands, looked fixedly and dreamily at the fire.

"I am going away tomorrow morning," I said.

She said nothing. I walked across the room, sighed, and said:

"Natalie, when you begged me to go away, you said: 'I will forgive you everything, everything' . . . . So you think I have wronged you. I beg you calmly and in brief terms to formulate the wrong I've done you."

"I am worn out. Afterwards, some time. . ." said my wife.

"How am I to blame?" I went on. "What have I done? Tell me: you are young and beautiful, you want to live, and I am nearly twice your age and hated by you, but is that my fault? I didn't marry you by force. But if you want to live in freedom, go; I'll give you your liberty. You can go and love who m you please. . . . I will give you a divorce."

"That's not what I want," she said. "You know I used to love you and always thought of myself as older than you. That's all nonsense. . . . You are not to blame for being older or for my being younger, or that I might be able to love some one else if I were free; but because you are a difficult person, an egoist, and hate every one."

"Perhaps so. I don't know," I said.

"Please go away. You want to go on at me till the morning, but I warn you I am quite worn out and cannot answer you. You promised me to go to town. I am very grateful; I ask nothing more."

My wife wanted me to go away, but it was not easy for me to do that. I was dispirited and I dreaded the big, cheerless, chill rooms that I was so weary of. Sometimes when I had an ache or a pain as a child, I used to huddle up to my mother or my nurse, and when I hid my face in the warm folds of their dress, it seemed to me as though I were hiding from the pain. And in the same way it seemed to me now that I could only hide from my uneasiness in this little room beside my wife. I sat down and screened away the light from my eyes with my hand. . . . There was a stillness.

"How are you to blame?" my wife said after a long silence, looking at me with red eyes that gleamed with tears. "You are very well educated and very well bred, very honest, just, and high-principled, but in you the effect of all that is that wherever you go you bring suffocation, oppression, something insulting and humiliating to the utmost degree. You have a straightforward way of looking at things, and so you hate the whole world. You hate those who have faith, because faith is an expression of ignorance and lack of culture, and at the same time you hate those who have no faith for having no faith and no ideals; you hate old people for being conservative and behind the times, and young people for free-thinking. The interests of the peasantry and of Russia are dear to you, and so you hate the peasants because you suspect every one of them of being a thief and a robber. You hate every one.

You are just, and always take your stand on your legal rights, and so you are always at law with the peasants and your neighbours. You have had twenty bushels of rye stolen, and your love of order has made you complain of the peasants to the Governor and all the local authorities, and to send a complaint of the local authorities to Petersburg. Legal justice!" said my wife, and she laughed. "On the ground of your legal rights and in the interests of morality, you refuse to give me a passport. Law and morality is such that a self-respecting healthy young woman has to spend her life in idleness, in depression, and in continual apprehension, and to receive in return board and lodging from a man she does not love. You have a thorough knowledge of the law, you are very honest and just, you respect marriage and family life, and the effect of all that is that all your life you have not done one kind action, that every one hates you, that you are on bad terms with every one, and the seven years that you have been married you've only lived seven months with your wife. You've had no wife and I've had no husband. To live with a man like you is impossible; there is no way of doing it. In the early years I was frightened with you, and now I am ashamed. . . . That's how my best years have been wasted. When I fought with you I ruined my temper, grew shrewish, coarse, timid, mistrustful. . . . Oh, but what's the use of talking! As though you wanted to understand! Go upstairs, and God be with you!"

My wife lay down on the couch and sank into thought.

"And how splendid, how enviable life might have been!" she said softly, looking reflectively into the fire. "What a life it might have been! There's no bringing it back now."

Any one who has lived in the country in winter and knows those long dreary, still evenings when even the dogs are too bored to bark and even the clocks seem weary of ticking, and any one who on such evenings has been troubled by awakening conscience and has moved restlessly about, trying now to smother his conscience, now to interpret it, will understand the distraction and the pleasure my wife's voice gave me as it sounded in the snug little room, telling me I was a bad man. I did not understand what was wanted of me by my conscience, and my wife, translating it in her feminine way, made clear to me in the meaning of my agitation. As often before in the moments of intense uneasiness, I guessed that the whole secret lay, not in the starving peasants, but in my not being the sort of a man I ought to be.

My wife got up with an effort and came up to me.

"Pavel Andreitch," she said, smiling mournfully, "forgive me, I don't believe you: you are not going away, but I will ask you one more favour. Call this" - she pointed to her papers - "self-deception, feminine logic, a mistake, as you like; but do not hinder me. It's all that is left me in life." She turned away and paused. "Before this I had nothing. I have wasted my youth in fighting with you. Now I have caught at this and am living; I am happy. . . . It seems to me that I have found in this a means of justifying my existence."

"Natalie, you are a good woman, a woman of ideas," I said, looking at my wife enthusiastically, and everything you say and do is intelligent and fine."

I walked about the room to conceal my emotion.

Anton Chekhov

"Natalie," I went on a minute later, "before I go away, I beg of you as a special favour, help me to do something for the starving peasants!"

"What can I do?" said my wife, shrugging her shoulders. "Here's the subscription list."

She rummaged among the papers and found the subscription list.

"Subscribe some money," she said, and from her tone I could see that she did not attach great importance to her subscription list; "that is the only way in which you can take part in the work."

I took the list and wrote: "Anonymous, 5,000."

In this "anonymous" there was something wrong, false, conceited, but I only realized that when I noticed that my wife flushed very red and hurriedly thrust the list into the heap of papers. We both felt ashamed; I felt that I must at all costs efface this clumsiness at once, or else I should feel ashamed afterwards, in the train and at Petersburg. But how efface it? What was I to say?

"I fully approve of what you are doing, Natalie," I said genuinely, "and I wish you every success. But allow me at parting to give you one piece of advice, Natalie; be on your guard with Sobol, and with your assistants generally, and don't trust them blindly. I don't say they are not honest, but they are not gentlefolks; they are people with no ideas, no ideals, no faith, with no aim in life, no definite principles, and the whole object of their life is comprised in the rouble. Rouble, rouble, rouble!" I sighed. "They are fond of getting money easily, for nothing, and in that respect the better educated they are the more they are to be dreaded."

My wife went to the couch and lay down.

"Ideas," she brought out, listlessly and reluctantly, "ideas, ideals, objects of life, principles . . . .you always used to use those words when you wanted to insult or humiliate some one, or say something unpleasant. Yes, that's your way: if with your views and such an attitude to people you are allowed to take part in anything, you would destroy it from the first day. It's time you understand that."

She sighed and paused.

"It's coarseness of character, Pavel Andreitch," she said. "You are well-bred and educated, but what a . . . Scythian you are in reality! That's because you lead a cramped life full of hatred, see no one, and read nothing but your engineering books. And, you know, there are good people, good books! Yes . . . but I am exhausted and it wearies me to talk. I ought to be in bed."

"So I am going away, Natalie," I said.

"Yes . . . yes. . . . *Merci.* . . ."

I stood still for a little while, then went upstairs. An hour later - it was half-past one - I went downstairs again with a candle in my hand to speak to my wife. I didn't know what I was going to say to her, but I felt that I must say some thing very important and necessary. She was not in her study, the door leading to her bedroom was closed.

"Natalie, are you asleep?" I asked softly.

There was no answer.

I stood near the door, sighed, and went into the drawing-room. There I sat down on the sofa, put out the candle, and remained sitting in the dark till the dawn.

VI

I went to the station at ten o'clock in the morning. There was no frost, but snow was falling in big wet flakes and an unpleasant damp wind was blowing.

We passed a pond and then a birch copse, and then began going uphill along the road which I could see from my window. I turned round to take a last look at my house, but I could see nothing for the snow. Soon afterwards dark huts came into sight ahead of us as in a fog. It was Pestrovo.

"If I ever go out of my mind, Pestrovo will be the cause of it," I thought. "It persecutes me."

We came out into the village street. All the roofs were intact, not one of them had been pulled to pieces; so my bailiff had told a lie. A boy was pulling along a little girl and a baby in a sledge. Another boy of three, with his head wrapped up like a peasant woman's and with huge mufflers on his hands, was trying to catch the flying snowflakes on his tongue, and laughing. Then a wagon loaded with fagots came toward us and a peasant walking beside it, and there was no telling whether his beard was white or whether it was covered with snow. He recognized my coachman, smiled at him and said something, and mechanically took off his hat to me. The dogs ran out of the yards and looked inquisitively at my horses. Everything was quiet, ordinary, as usual. The emigrants had returned, there was no bread; in the huts "some were laughing, some were delirious"; but it all looked so ordinary that one could not believe it really was so. There were no

Anton Chekhov

distracted faces, no voices whining for help, no weeping, nor abuse, but all around was stillness, order, life, children, sledges, dogs with dishevelled tails. Neither the children nor the peasant we met were troubled; why was I so troubled?

Looking at the smiling peasant, at the boy with the huge mufflers, at the huts, remembering my wife, I realized there was no calamity that could daunt this people; I felt as though there were already a breath of victory in the air. I felt proud and felt ready to cry out that I was with them too; but the horses were carrying us away from the village into the open country, the snow was whirling, the wind was howling, and I was left alone with my thoughts. Of the million people working for the peasantry, life itself had cast me out as a useless, incompetent, bad man. I was a hindrance, a part of the people's calamity; I was vanquished, cast out, and I was hurrying to the station to go away and hide myself in Petersburg in a hotel in Bolshaya Morskaya.

An hour later we reached the station. The coachman and a porter with a disc on his breast carried my trunks into the ladies' room. My coachman Nikanor, wearing high felt boots and the skirt of his coat tucked up through his belt, all wet with the snow and glad I was going away, gave me a friendly smile and said:

"A fortunate journey, your Excellency. God give you luck."

Every one, by the way, calls me "your Excellency," though I am only a collegiate councillor and a kammer-junker. The porter told me the train had not yet left the next station; I had to wait. I went outside, and with my head heavy from my sleepless night, and so exhausted I could hardly move my legs, I walked aimlessly towards the pump. There was not a soul anywhere near.

"Why am I going?" I kept asking myself. "What is there awaiting me there? The acquaintances from whom I have come away, loneliness, restaurant dinners, noise, the electric light, which makes my eyes ache. Where am I going, and what am I going for? What am I going for?"

And it seemed somehow strange to go away without speaking to my wife. I felt that I was leaving her in uncertainty. Going away, I ought to have told that she was right, that I really was a bad man.

When I turned away from the pump, I saw in the doorway the station-master, of whom I had twice made complaints to his superiors, turning up the collar of his coat, shrinking from the wind and the snow. He came up to me, and putting two fingers to the peak of his cap, told me with an expression of helpless confusion, strained respectfulness, and hatred on his face, that the train was twenty minutes late, and asked me would I not like to wait in the warm?

"Thank you," I answered, "but I am probably not going. Send word to my coachman to wait; I have not made up my mind."

I walked to and fro on the platform and thought, should I go away or not? When the train came in I decided not to go. At home I had to expect my wife's amazement and perhaps her mockery, the dismal upper storey and my uneasiness; but, still, at my age that was easier and as it were more homelike than travelling for two days and nights with strangers to Petersburg, where I should be conscious every minute that my life was of no use to any one or to anything, and that it was approaching its end. No, better at home whatever awaited me there. . . . I went out of the station. It was awkward by daylight to return home, where every one was so glad at my going. I might spend the rest of the day till evening at some neighbour's, but with whom? With some of them I was on strained relations, others I did not know at all. I considered and thought of Ivan Ivanitch.

"We are going to Bragino!" I said to the coachman, getting into the sledge.

"It's a long way," sighed Nikanor; "it will be twenty miles, or maybe twenty-five."

"Oh, please, my dear fellow," I said in a tone as though Nikanor had the right to refuse. "Please let us go!"

Nikanor shook his head doubtfully and said slowly that we really ought to have put in the shafts, not Circassian, but Peasant or Siskin; and uncertainly, as though expecting I should change my mind, took the reins in his gloves, stood up, thought a moment, and then raised his whip.

"A whole series of inconsistent actions . . ." I thought, screening my face from the snow. "I must have gone out of my mind. Well, I don't care. . . ."

In one place, on a very high and steep slope, Nikanor carefully held the horses in to the middle of the descent, but in the middle the horses suddenly bolted and dashed downhill at a fearful rate; he raised his elbows and shouted in a wild, frantic voice such as I had never heard from him before:

"Hey! Let's give the general a drive! If you come to grief he'll buy new ones, my darlings! Hey! look out! We'll run you down!"

Only now, when the extraordinary pace we were going at took my breath away, I noticed that he was very drunk. He must have been drinking at the station. At the bottom of the descent there was the crash of ice; a piece of dirty frozen snow thrown up from the road hit me a painful blow in the face.

The runaway horses ran up the hill as rapidly as they had downhill, and before I had time to shout to Nikanor my sledge was flying along on the level in an old pine forest, and the tall pines were stretching out their shaggy white paws to me from all directions.

"I have gone out of my mind, and the coachman's drunk," I thought. "Good!"

I found Ivan Ivanitch at home. He laughed till he coughed, laid his head on my breast, and said what he always did say on meeting me:

"You grow younger and younger. I don't know what dye you use for your hair and your beard; you might give me some of it."

"I've come to return your call, Ivan Ivanitch," I said untruthfully. "Don't be hard on me; I'm a townsman, conventional; I do keep count of calls."

"I am delighted, my dear fellow. I am an old man; I like respect. . . . Yes."

From his voice and his blissfully smiling face, I could see that he was greatly flattered by my visit. Two peasant women helped me off with my coat in the entry, and a peasant in a red shirt hung it on a hook, and when Ivan Ivanitch and I went into his little study, two barefooted little girls were sitting on the floor looking at a picture-book; when they saw us they jumped up and ran away, and a tall, thin old woman in specta cles came in at once, bowed gravely to me, and picking up a pillow from the sofa and a picture-book from the floor, went away. From the adjoining rooms we heard incessant whispering and the patter of bare feet.

"I am expecting the doctor to dinner," said Ivan Ivanitch. "He promised to come from the relief centre. Yes. He dines with me every Wednesday, God bless him." He craned towards me and kissed me on the neck. "You have come, my dear fellow, so you are not vexed," he whispered, sniffing. "Don't be vexed, my dear creature. Yes. Perhaps it is annoying, but don't be cross. My only prayer to God before I die is to live in peace and harmony with all in the true way. Yes."

"Forgive me, Ivan Ivanitch, I will put my feet on a chair," I said, feeling that I was so exhausted I could not be myself; I sat further back on the sofa and put up my feet on an arm-chair. My face was burning from the snow and the wind, and I felt as though my whole body were basking in the warmth and growing weaker from it.

"It's very nice here," I went on - "warm, soft, snug . . .

and goose-feather pens," I laughed, looking at the writing-table; "sand instead of blotting-paper."

"Eh? Yes . . . yes. . . . The writing-table and the mahogany cupboard here were made for my father by a self-taught cabinet-maker - Glyeb Butyga, a serf of General Zhukov's. Yes . . . a great artist in his own way."

Listlessly and in the tone of a man dropping asleep, he began telling me about cabinet-maker Butyga. I listened. Then Ivan Ivanitch went into the next room to show me a polisander wood chest of drawers remarkable for its beauty and cheapness. He tapped the chest with his fingers, then called my attention to a stove of patterned tiles, such as one never sees now. He tapped the stove, too, with his fingers. There was an atmosphere of good-natured simplicity and well-fed abundance about the chest of drawers, the tiled stove, the low chairs, the pictures embroidered in wool and silk on canvas in solid, ugly frames. When one remembers that all those objects were standing in the same places and precisely in the same order when I was a little child, and used to come here to name-day parties with my mother, it is simply unbelievable that they could ever cease to exist.

I thought what a fearful difference between Butyga and me! Butyga who made things, above all, solidly and substantially, and seeing in that his chief object, gave to length of life peculiar significance, had no thought of death, and probably hardly believed in its possibility; I, when I built my bridges of iron and stone which would last a thousand years, could not keep from me the thought, "It's not for long . . . .it's no use." If in time Butyga's cupboard and my bridge should come under the notice of some sensible historian of art, he would say: "These were two men remarkable in their own way: Butyga loved his fellow-creatures and would not admit the thought that they might die and be annihilated, and so when he made his furniture he had the immortal man in his mind. The engineer Asorin did not love life or his fellow-creatures; even in the happy moments of creation, thoughts of death, of finiteness and dissolution, were not alien to him, and we see how insignificant and finite, how timid and poor, are these lines of his. . . ."

"I only heat these rooms," muttered Ivan Ivanitch, showing me his rooms. "Ever since my wife died and my son was killed in the war, I have kept the best rooms shut up. Yes . . . see. . ."

He opened a door, and I saw a big room with four columns, an old piano, and a heap of peas on the floor; it smelt cold and damp.

"The garden seats are in the next room . . ." muttered Ivan Ivanitch. "There's no one to dance the mazurka now. . . . I've shut them up."

We heard a noise. It was Dr. Sobol arriving. While he was rubbing his cold hands and stroking his wet beard, I had time to notice in the first place that he had a very dull life, and so was pleased to see Ivan Ivanitch and me; and, secondly, that he was a naive and simple-hearted man. He looked at me as though I were very glad to see him and very much interested in him.

"I have not slept for two nights," he said, looking at me naively and stroking his beard. "One night with a confinement, and the next I stayed at a peasant's with the bugs biting me all night. I am as sleepy as Satan, do you know."

With an expression on his face as though it could not afford me anything but pleasure, he took me by the arm and led me to the dining-room. His naive eyes, his crumpled coat, his cheap tie and the smell of iodoform made an unpleasant impression upon me; I felt as though I were in vulgar company. When we sat down to table he filled my glass with vodka, and, smiling helplessly, I drank it; he put a piece of ham on my plate and I ate it submissively.

"*Repetitia est mater studiorum*," said Sobol, hastening to drink off another wineglassful. "Would you believe it, the joy of seeing good people has driven away my sleepiness? I have turned into a peasant, a savage in the wilds; I've grown coarse, but I am still an educated man, and I tell you in good earnest, it's tedious without company."

They served first for a cold course white sucking-pig with horse-radish cream, then a rich and very hot cabbage soup with pork on it, with boiled buckwheat, from which rose a column of steam. The doctor went on talking, and I was soon convinced that he was a weak, unfortunate man, disorderly in external life. Three glasses of vodka made him drunk; he grew unnaturally lively, ate a great deal, kept clearing his throat and smacking his lips, and already addressed me in Italian, "Eccellenza." Looking naively at me as though he were convinced that I was very glad to see and hear him, he informed me that he had long been separated from his wife and gave her three-quarters of his salary; that she lived in the town with his children, a boy and a girl, whom he adored; that he loved another woman, a widow, well educated, with an estate in the country, but was rarely able to see her, as he was busy with his work from morning till night and had not a free moment.

"The whole day long, first at the hospital, then on my rounds," he told us; "and I assure you, Eccellenza, I have not time to read a book, let alone going to see the woman I love. I've read nothing for ten years! For ten years, Eccellenza. As for the financial side of the question, ask Ivan Ivanitch: I have often no money to buy tobacco."

"On the other hand, you have the moral satisfaction of your work," I said.

"What?" he asked, and he winked. "No," he said, "better let us drink."

I listened to the doctor, and, after my invariable habit, tried to take his measure by my usual classification - materialist, idealist, filthy lucre, gregarious instincts, and so on; but no classification fitted him even approximately; and strange to say, while I simply listened and looked at him, he seemed perfectly clear to me as a person, but as soon as I began trying to classify him he became an exceptionally complex, intricate, and incomprehensible character in spite of all his candour and simplicity. "Is that man," I asked myself, "capable of wasting other people's money, abusing their confidence, being disposed to sponge on them?" And now this question, which had once seemed to me grave and important, struck me as crude, petty, and coarse.

Pie was served; then, I remember, with long intervals

between, during which we drank home-made liquors, they gave us a stew of pigeons, some dish of giblets, roast sucking-pig, partridges, cauliflower, curd dumplings, curd cheese and milk, jelly, and finally pancakes and jam. At first I ate with great relish, especially the cabbage soup and the buckwheat, but afterwards I munched and swallowed mechanically, smiling helplessly and unconscious of the taste of anything. My face was burning from the hot cabbage soup and the heat of the room. Ivan Ivanitch and Sobol, too, were crimson.

"To the health of your wife," said Sobol. "She likes me. Tell her her doctor sends her his respects."

"She's fortunate, upon my word," sighed Ivan Ivanitch. "Though she takes no trouble, does not fuss or worry herself, she has become the most important person in the whole district. Almost the whole business is in her hands, and they all gather round her, the doctor, the District Captains, and the ladies. With people of the right sort that happens of itself. Yes. . . . The apple-tree need take no thought for the apple to grow on it; it will grow of itself."

"It's only people who don't care who take no thought," said I.

"Eh? Yes . . . " muttered Ivan Ivanitch, not catching what I said, "that's true. . . . One must not worry oneself. Just so, just so. . . . Only do your duty towards God and your neighbour, and then never mind what happens."

"Eccellenza," said Sobol solemnly, "just look at nature about us: if you poke your nose or your ear out of your fur collar it will be frost-bitten; stay in the fields for one hour, you'll be buried in the snow; while the village is just the same as in the days of Rurik, the same Petchenyegs and Polovtsi. It's nothing but being burnt down, starving, and struggling against nature in every way. What was I saying? Yes! If one thinks about it, you know, looks into it and analyses all this hotchpotch, if you will allow me to call it so, it's not life but more like a fire in a theatre! Any one who falls down or screams with terror, or rushes about, is the worst enemy of good order; one must stand up and look sharp, and not stir a hair! There's no time for whimpering and busying oneself with trifles. When you have to deal with elemental forces you must put out force against them, be firm and as unyielding as a stone. Isn't that right, grandfather?" He turned to Ivan Ivanitch and laughed. "I am no better than a woman myself; I am a limp rag, a flabby creature, so I hate flabbiness. I can't endure petty feelings! One mopes, another is frightened, a third will come straight in here and say: 'Fie on you! Here you've guzzled a dozen courses and you talk about the starving!' That's petty and stupid! A fourth will reproach you, Eccellenza, for being rich. Excuse me, Eccellenza," he went on in a loud voice, laying his hand on his heart, "but your having set our magistrate the task of hunting day and night for your thieves - excuse me, that's also petty on your part. I am a little drunk, so that's why I say this now, but you know, it is petty!"

"Who's asking him to worry himself? I don't understand!" I said, getting up.

I suddenly felt unbearably ashamed and mortified, and I walked round the table.

"Who asks him to worry himself? I didn't ask him to. . . . Damn him!"

"They have arrested three men and let them go again. They turned out not to be the right ones, and now they are looking for a fresh lot," said Sobol, laughing. "It's too bad!"

"I did not ask him to worry himself," said I, almost crying with excitement. "What's it all for? What's it all for? Well, supposing I was wrong, supposing I have done wrong, why do they try to put me more in the wrong?"

"Come, come, come, come!" said Sobol, trying to soothe me. "Come! I have had a drop, that is why I said it. My tongue is my enemy. Come," he sighed, "we have eaten and drunk wine, and now for a nap."

He got up from the table, kissed Ivan Ivanitch on the head, and staggering from repletion, went out of the dining-room. Ivan Ivanitch and I smoked in silence.

I don't sleep after dinner, my dear," said Ivan Ivanitch, "but you have a rest in the lounge-room."

I agreed. In the half-dark and warmly heated room they called the lounge-room, there stood against the walls long, wide sofas, solid and heavy, the work of Butyga the cabinet maker; on them lay high, soft, white beds, probably made by the old woman in spectacles. On one of them Sobol, without his coat and boots, already lay asleep with his face to the back of the sofa; another bed was awaiting me. I took off my coat and boots, and, overcome by fatigue, by the spirit of Butyga which hovered over the quiet lounge-room, and by the light, caressing snore of Sobol, I lay down submissively.

And at once I began dreaming of my wife, of her room, of the station-master with his face full of hatred, the heaps of snow, a fire in the theatre. I dreamed of the peasants who had stolen twenty sacks of rye out of my barn.

"Anyway, it's a good thing the magistrate let them go," I said.

I woke up at the sound of my own voice, looked for a moment in perplexity at Sobol's broad back, at the buckles of his waistcoat, at his thick heels, then lay down again and fell asleep.

When I woke up the second time it was quite dark. Sobol was asleep. There was peace in my heart, and I longed to make haste home. I dressed and went out of the lounge-room. Ivan Ivanitch was sitting in a big arm-chair in his study, absolutely motionless, staring at a fixed point, and it was evident that he had been in the same state of petrifaction all the while I had been asleep.

"Good!" I said, yawning. "I feel as though I had woken up after breaking the fast at Easter. I shall often come and see you now. Tell me, did my wife ever dine here?"

"So-ome-ti-mes . . . sometimes,"' muttered Ivan Ivanitch, making an effort to stir. "She dined here last Saturday. Yes. . . . She likes me."

After a silence I said:

"Do you remember, Ivan Ivanitch, you told me I had a disagreeable character and that it was difficult to get on with me? But what am I to do to make my character different?"

"I don't know, my dear boy. . . . I'm a feeble old man, I can't advise you. . . . Yes. . . . But I said that to you at the time because I am fond of you and fond of your wife, and I was fond of your father. . . . Yes. I shall soon die, and what need have I to conceal things from you or to tell you lies? So I tell you: I am very fond of you, but I don't respect you. No, I don't respect you."

He turned towards me and said in a breathless whisper:

"It's impossible to respect you, my dear fellow. You look like a real man. You have the figure and deportment of the French President Carnot - I saw a portrait of him the other day in an illustrated paper . . . yes. . . . You use lofty language, and you are clever, and you are high up in the service beyond all reach, but haven't real soul, my dear boy . . . there's no strength in it."

"A Scythian, in fact," I laughed. "But what about my wife? Tell me something about my wife; you know her better."

I wanted to talk about my wife, but Sobol came in and prevented me.

"I've had a sleep and a wash," he said, looking at me naively. "I'll have a cup of tea with some rum in it and go home."

Anton Chekhov

VII

It was by now past seven. Besides Ivan Ivanitch, women servants, the old dame in spectacles, the little girls and the peasant, all accompanied us from the hall out on to the steps, wishing us good-bye and all sorts of blessings, while near the horses in the darkness there were standing and moving about men with lanterns, telling our coachmen how and which way to drive, and wishing us a lucky journey. The horses, the men, and the sledges were white.

"Where do all these people come from?" I asked as my three horses and the doctor's two moved at a walking pace out of the yard.

"They are all his serfs," said Sobol. "The new order has not reached him yet. Some of the old servants are living out their lives with him, and then there are orphans of all sorts who have nowhere to go; there are some, too, who insist on living there, there's no turning them out. A queer old man!"

Again the flying horses, the strange voice of drunken Nikanor, the wind and the persistent snow, which got into one's eyes, one's mouth, and every fold of one's fur coat. . . .

"Well, I am running a rig," I thought, while my bells chimed in with the doctor's, the wind whistled, the coachmen shouted; and while this frantic uproar was going on, I recalled all the details of that strange wild day, unique in my life, and it seemed to me that I really had gone out of my mind or become a different man. It was as though the man I had been till that day were already a stranger to me.

The doctor drove behind and kept talking loudly with his coachman. From time to time he overtook me, drove side by side, and always, with the same naive confidence that it was very pleasant to me, offered me a ci garette or asked for the matches. Or, overtaking me, he would lean right out of his sledge, and waving about the sleeves of his fur coat, which were at least twice as long as his arms, shout:

"Go it, Vaska! Beat the thousand roublers! Hey, my kittens!"

And to the accompaniment of loud, malicious laughter from Sobol and his Vaska the doctor's kittens raced ahead. My Nikanor took it as an affront, and held in his three horses, but when the doctor's bells had passed out of hearing, he raised his elbows, shouted, and our horses flew like mad in pursuit. We drove into a village, there were glimpses of lights, the silhouettes of huts. Some one shouted:

"Ah, the devils!" We seemed to have galloped a mile and a half, and still it was the village street and there seemed no end to it. When we caught up the doctor and drove more quietly, he asked for matches and said:

"Now try and feed that street! And, you know, there are five streets like that, sir. Stay, stay," he shouted. "Turn in at the tavern! We must get warm and let the horses rest."

They stopped at the tavern.

"I have more than one village like that in my district," said the doctor, opening a heavy door with a squeaky block, and ushering me in front of him. "If you look in broad daylight you can't see to the end of the street, and there are side-streets, too, and one can do nothing but scratch one's head. It's hard to do anything."

We went into the best room where there was a strong smell of table-cloths, and at our entrance a sleepy peasant in a waistcoat and a shirt worn outside his trousers jumped up from a bench. Sobol asked for some beer and I asked for tea.

"It's hard to do anything," said Sobol. "Your wife has faith; I respect her and have the greatest reverence for her, but I have no great faith myself. As long as our relations to the people continue to have the character of ordinary philanthropy, as shown in orphan asylums and almshouses, so long we shall only be shuffling, shamming, and deceiving ourselves, and nothing more. Our relations ought to be businesslike, founded on calculation, knowledge, and justice. My Vaska has been working for me all his life; his crops have failed, he is sick and starving. If I give him fifteen kopecks a day, by so doing I try to restore him to his former condition as a workman; that is, I am first and foremost looking after my own interests, and yet for some reason I call that fifteen kopecks relief, charity, good works. Now let us put it like this. On the most modest computation, reckoning seven kopecks a soul and five souls a family, one needs three hundred and fifty roubles a day to feed a thousand families. That sum is fixed by our practical duty to a thousand families. Meanwhile we give not three hundred and fifty a day, but only ten, and say that that is relief, charity, that that makes your wife and all of us exceptionally good people and hurrah for our humaneness. That is it, my dear soul! Ah! if we would talk less of being humane and calculated more, reasoned, and took a conscientious attitude to our duties! How many such humane, sensitive people there are among us who tear about in all good faith with subscription lists, but don't pay their tailors or their cooks. There is no logic in our life; that's what it is! No logic!"

We were silent for a while. I was making a mental calculation and said:

"I will feed a thousand families for two hundred days. Come and see me tomorrow to talk it over."

I was pleased that this was said quite simply, and was glad that Sobol answered me still more simply:

"Right."

We paid for what we had and went out of the tavern.

"I like going on like this," said Sobol, getting into the sledge. "Eccellenza, oblige me with a match. I've forgotten mine in the tavern."

A quarter of an hour later his horses fell behind, and the sound of his bells was lost in the roar of the snowstorm. Reaching home, I walked about my rooms, trying to think things over and to define my position clearly to myself; I had not one word, one phrase, ready for my wife. My brain was not working.

But without thinking of anything, I went downstairs to my wife. She was in her room, in the same pink dressing-gown, and standing in the same attitude as though screening her papers from me. On her face was an expression of perplexity and irony, and it was evident that having heard of my arrival, she had prepared herself not to cry, not to entreat me, not to defend herself, as she had done the day before, but to laugh at me, to answer me contemptuously, and to act with decision. Her face was saying: "If that's how it is, good-bye."

"Natalie, I've not gone away," I said, "but it's not deception. I have gone out of my mind; I've grown old, I'm ill, I've become a different man - think as you like . . . . I've shaken off my old self with horror, with horror; I despise him and am ashamed of him, and the new man who has been in me since yesterday will not let me go away. Do not drive me away, Natalie!"

She looked intently into my face and believed me, and there was a gleam of uneasiness in her eyes. Enchanted by her presence, warmed by the warmth of her room, I muttered as in delirium, holding out my hands to her:

"I tell you, I have no one near to me but you. I have never for one minute ceased to miss you, and only obstinate vanity prevented me from owning it. The past, when we lived as husband and wife, cannot be brought back, and there's no need; but make me your servant, take all my property, and give it away to any one you like. I am at peace, Natalie, I am content. . . . I am at peace."

My wife, looking intently and with curiosity into my face, suddenly uttered a faint cry, burst into tears, and ran into the next room. I went upstairs to my own storey.

An hour later I was sitting at my table, writing my "History of Railways," and the starving peasants did not now hinder me from doing so. Now I feel no uneasiness. Neither the scenes of disorder which I saw when I went the round of the huts at Pestrovo with my wife and Sobol the other day, nor malignant rumours, nor the mistakes of the people around me, nor old ageclose upon me - nothing disturbs me. Just as the flying bullets do not hinder soldiers from talking of their own affairs, ating and cleaning their boots, so the starving peasants do not hinder me from sleeping quietly and looking after my personal affairs. In my house and far around it there is in full swing the work which Dr. Sobol calls "an orgy of philanthropy." My wife often comes up to me and looks about my rooms uneasily, as though looking for what more she can give to the starving peasants "to justify her existence," and I see that, thanks to her, there will soon be nothing of our property left and we shall be poor; but that does not trouble me, and I smile at her gaily. What will happen in the future I don't know.

DIFFICULT PEOPLE

YEVGRAF IVANOVITCH SHIRYAEV, a small farmer, whose father, a parish priest, now deceased, had received a gift of three hundred acres of land from Madame Kuvshinnikov, a general's widow, was standing in a corner before a copper washing-stand, washing his hands. As usual, his face looked anxious and ill-humoured, and his beard was uncombed.

"What weather!" he said. "It's not weather, but a curse laid upon us. It's raining again!"

He grumbled on, while his family sat waiting at table for him to have finished washing his hands before beginning dinner. Fedosya Semyonovna, his wife, his son Pyotr, a student, his eldest daughter Varvara, and three small boys, had been sitting waiting a long time. The boys - Kolka, Vanka, and Arhipka - grubby, snub-nosed little fellows with chubby faces and tousled hair that wanted cutting, moved their chairs impatiently, while their elders sat without stirring, and apparently did not care whether they ate their dinner or waited. . .

As though trying their patience, Shiryaev deliberately dried his hands, deliberately said his prayer, and sat down to the table without hurrying himself. Cabbage-soup was served immediately. The sound of carpenters' axes (Shiryaev was having a new barn built) and the laughter of Fomka, their labourer, teasing the turkey, floated in from the courtyard.

Big, sparse drops of rain pattered on the window.

Pyotr, a round-shouldered student in spectacles, kept exchanging glances with his mother as he ate his dinner. Several times he laid down his spoon and cleared his throat, meaning to begin to speak, but after an intent look at his father he fell to eating again. At last, when the porridge had been served, he cleared his throat resolutely and said:

"I ought to go tonight by the evening train. I out to have gone before; I have missed a fortnight as it is. The lectures begin on the first of September."

"Well, go," Shiryaev assented; "why are you lingering on here? Pack up and go, and good luck to you."

A minute passed in silence.

"He must have money for the journey, Yevgraf Ivanovitch," the mother observed in a low voice.

"Money? To be sure, you can't go without money. Take it at once, since you need it. You could have had it long ago!"

The student heaved a faint sigh and looked with relief at his mother. Deliberately Shiryaev took a pocket-book out of his coat-pocket and put on his spectacles.

"How much do you want?" he asked.

"The fare to Moscow is eleven roubles forty-two kopecks. . . ."

"Ah, money, money!" sighed the father. (He always sighed when he saw money, even when he was receiving it.) "Here are twelve roubles for you. You will have change out of that which will be of use to you on the journey."

"Thank you."

After waiting a little, the student said:

"I did not get lessons quite at first last year. I don't know how it will be this year; most likely it will take me a little time to find work. I ought to ask you for fifteen roubles for my lodging and dinner."

Shiryaev thought a little and heaved a sigh.

"You will have to make ten do," he said. "Here, take it."

The student thanked him. He ought to have asked him for something more, for clothes, for lecture fees, for books, but after an intent look at his father he decided not to pester him further.

The mother, lacking in diplomacy and prudence, like all mothers, could not restrain herself, and said:

"You ought to give him another six roubles, Yevgraf Ivanovitch, for a pair of boots. Why, just see, how can he go to Moscow in such wrecks?"

"Let him take my old ones; they are still quite good."

"He must have trousers, anyway; he is a disgrace to look at."

And immediately after that a storm-signal showed itself, at the sight of which all the family trembled.

Shiryaev's short, fat neck turned suddenly red as a beetroot. The colour mounted slowly to his ears, from his ears to his temples, and by degrees suffused his whole face. Yevgraf Ivanovitch shifted in his chair and unbuttoned his shirt-collar to save himself from choking. He was evidently struggling with the feeling that was mastering him. A deathlike silence followed. The children held their breath. Fedosya Semyonovna, as though she did not grasp what was happening to her husband, went on:

"He is not a little boy now, you know; he is ashamed to go about without clothes."

Shiryaev suddenly jumped up, and with all his might flung down his fat pocket-book in the middle of the table, so that a hunk of bread flew off a plate. A revolting expression of anger, resentment, avarice - all mixed together - flamed on his face.

"Take everything!" he shouted in an unnatural voice; "plunder me! Take it all! Strangle me!"

He jumped up from the table, clutched at his head, and ran staggering about the room.

"Strip me to the last thread!" he shouted in a shrill voice. "Squeeze out the last drop! Rob me! Wring my neck!"

The student flushed and dropped his eyes. He could not go on eating. Fedosya Semyonovna, who had not after twenty-five years grown used to her husband's difficult character, shrank into herself and muttered something in self-defence. An expression of amazement and dull terror came into her wasted and birdlike face, which at all times looked dull and scared. The little boys and the elder daughter Varvara, a girl in her teens, with a pale ugly face, laid down their spoons and sat mute.

Shiryaev, growing more and more ferocious, uttering words each more terrible than the one before, dashed up to the table and began shaking the notes out of his pocket-book.

"Take them!" he muttered, shaking all over. "You've eaten and drunk your fill, so here's money for you too! I need nothing! Order yourself new boots and uniforms!"

The student turned pale and got up.

"Listen, papa," he began, gasping for breath. "I . . . I beg you to end this, for . . ."

"Hold your tongue!" the father shouted at him, and so loudly that the spectacles fell off his nose; "hold your tongue!"

"I used . . . I used to be able to put up with such scenes, but . . . but now I have got out of the way of it. Do you understand? I have got out of the way of it!"

"Hold your tongue!" cried the father, and he stamped with his feet. "You must listen to what I say! I shall say what I like, and you hold your tongue. At your age I was earning my living, while you . . . Do you know what you cost me, you scoundrel? I'll turn you out! Wastrel!"

"Yevgraf Ivanovitch," muttered Fedosya Semyonovna, moving her fingers nervously; "you know he. . . you know Petya . . . !"

"Hold your tongue!" Shiryaev shouted out to her, and tears actually came into his eyes from anger. "It is you who have spoilt them - you! It's all your fault! He has no respect for us, does not say his prayers, and earns nothing! I am only one against the ten of you! I'll turn you out of the house!"

The daughter Varvara gazed fixedly at her mother with her mouth open, moved her vacant-looking eyes to the window, turned pale, and, uttering a loud shriek, fell back in her chair. The father, with a curse and a wave of the hand, ran out into the yard.

This was how domestic scenes usually ended at the Shiryaevs'. But on this occasion, unfortunately, Pyotr the student was carried away by overmastering anger. He was just as hasty and ill-tempered as his father and his grandfather the priest, who used to beat his parishioners about the head with a stick. Pale and clenching his fists, he went up to his mother and shouted in the very highest tenor note his voice could reach:

"These reproaches are loathsome! sickening to me! I want nothing from you! Nothing! I would rather die of hunger than eat another mouthful at your expense! Take your nasty money back! take it!"

Anton Chekhov

The mother huddled against the wall and waved her hands, as though it were not her son, but some phantom before her. "What have I done?" she wailed. "What?"

Like his father, the boy waved his hands and ran into the yard. Shiryaev's house stood alone on a ravine which ran like a furrow for four miles along the steppe. Its sides were overgrown with oak saplings and alders, and a stream ran at the bottom. On one side the house looked towards the ravine, on the other towards the open country, there were no fences nor hurdles. Instead there were farm-buildings of all sorts close to one another, shutting in a small space in front of the house which was regarded as the yard, and in which hens, ducks, and pigs ran about.

Going out of the house, the student walked along the muddy road towards the open country. The air was full of a penetrating autumn dampness. The road was muddy, puddles gleamed here and there, and in the yellow fields autumn itself seemed looking out from the grass, dismal, decaying, dark. On the right-hand side of the road was a vegetable-garden cleared of its crops and gloomy-looking, with here and there sunflowers standing up in it with hanging heads already black.

Pyotr thought it would not be a bad thing to walk to Moscow on foot; to walk just as he was, with holes in his boots, without a cap, and without a farthing of money. When he had gone eighty miles his father, frightened and aghast, would overtake him, would begin begging him to turn back or take the money, but he would not even look at him, but would go on and on. . . . Bare forests would be followed by desolate fields, fields by forests again; soon the earth would be white with the first snow, and the streams would be coated with ice. . . . Somewhere near Kursk or near Serpuhovo, exhausted and dying of hunger, he would sink down and die. His corpse would be found, and there would be a paragraph in all the papers saying that a student called Shiryaev had died of hunger. . . .

A white dog with a muddy tail who was wandering about the vegetable-garden looking for something gazed at him and sauntered after him.

He walked along the road and thought of death, of the grief of his family, of the moral sufferings of his father, and then pictured all sorts of adventures on the road, each more marvellous than the one before - picturesque places, terrible nights, chance encounters. He imagined a string of pilgrims, a hut in the forest with one little window shining in the darkness; he stands before the window, begs for a night's lodging. . . They let him in, and suddenly he sees that they are robbers. Or, better still, he is taken into a big manor-house, where, learning who he is, they give him food and drink, play to him on the piano, listen to his complaints, and the daughter of the house, a beauty, falls in love with him.

Absorbed in his bitterness and such thoughts, young Shiryaev walked on and on. Far, far ahead he saw the inn, a dark patch against the grey background of cloud. Beyond the inn, on the very horizon, he could see a little hillock; this was the railway-station. That hillock reminded him of the connection existing between the place where he was now standing and Moscow, where street-lamps were burning and carriages were rattling in the streets, where lectures were being given. And he almost wept with depression and impatience. The solemn landscape, with its order and beauty, the death-like stillness all around, revolted him and moved him to despair and hatred!

"Look out!" He heard behind him a loud voice.

An old lady of his acquaintance, a landowner of the neighbourhood, drove past him in a light, elegant landau. He bowed to her, and smiled all over his face. And at once he caught himself in that smile, which was so out of keeping with his gloomy mood. Where did it come from if his whole heart was full of vexation and misery? And he thought nature itself had given man this capacity for lying, that even in difficult moments of spiritual strain he might be able to hide the secrets of his nest as the fox and the wild duck do. Every family has its joys and its horrors, but however great they may be, it's hard for an outsider's eye to see them; they are a secret. The father of the old lady who had just driven by, for instance, had for some offence lain for half his lifetime under the ban of the wrath of Tsar Nicolas I.; her husband had been a gambler; of her four sons, not one had turned out well. One could imagine how many terrible scenes there must have been in her life, how many tears must have been shed. And yet the old lady seemed happy and satisfied, and she had answered his smile by smiling too. The student thought of his comrades, who did not like talking about their families; he thought of his mother, who almost always lied when she had to speak of her husband and children. . . .

Pyotr walked about the roads far from home till dusk, abandoning himself to dreary thoughts. When it began to drizzle with rain he turned homewards. As he walked back he made up his mind at all costs to talk to his father, to explain to him, once and for all, that it was dreadful and oppressive to live with him.

He found perfect stillness in the house. His sister Varvara was lying behind a screen with a headache, moaning faintly. His mother, with a look of amazement and guilt upon her face, was sitting beside her on a box, mending Arhipka's trousers. Yevgraf Ivanovitch was pacing from one window to another, scowling at the weather. From his walk, from the way he cleared his throat, and even from the back of his head, it was evident he felt himself to blame.

"I suppose you have changed your mind about going today?" he asked.

The student felt sorry for him, but immediately suppressing that feeling, he said:

"Listen . . . I must speak to you seriously. . . yes, seriously. I have always respected you, and . . . and have never brought myself to speak to you in such a tone, but your behaviour . . .your last action . . ."

The father looked out of the window and did not speak. The student, as though considering his words, rubbed his forehead and went on in great excitement:

"Not a dinner or tea passes without your making an uproar. Your bread sticks in our throat. . . nothing is more bitter, more humiliating, than bread that sticks in one's throat. . . . Though you are my father, no one, neither God nor nature, has given you the right to insult and humiliate us so horribly, to vent your ill-humour on the weak. You have worn my mother out

Anton Chekhov

and made a slave of her, my sister is hopelessly crushed, while I . . ."

"It's not your business to teach me," said his father.

"Yes, it is my business! You can quarrel with me as much as you like, but leave my mother in peace! I will not allow you to torment my mother!" the student went on, with flashing eyes. "You are spoilt because no one has yet dared to oppose you. They tremble and are mute towards you, but now that is over! Coarse, ill-bred man! You are coarse . . . do you understand? You are coarse, ill-humoured, unfeeling. And the peasants can't endure you!"

The student had by now lost his thread, and was not so much speaking as firing off detached words. Yevgraf Ivanovitch listened in silence, as though stunned; but suddenly his neck turned crimson, the colour crept up his face, and he made a movement.

"Hold your tongue!" he shouted.

"That's right!" the son persisted; "you don't like to hear the truth! Excellent! Very good! begin shouting! Excellent!"

"Hold your tongue, I tell you!" roared Yevgraf Ivanovitch.

Fedosya Semyonovna appeared in the doorway, very pale, with an astonished face; she tried to say something, but she could not, and could only move her fingers.

"It's all your fault!" Shiryaev shouted at her. "You have

brought him up like this!"

"I don't want to go on living in this house!" shouted the student, crying, and looking angrily at his mother. "I don't want to live with you!"

Varvara uttered a shriek behind the screen and broke into loud sobs. With a wave of his hand, Shiryaev ran out of the house.

The student went to his own room and quietly lay down. He lay till midnight without moving or opening his eyes. He felt neither anger nor shame, but a vague ache in his soul. He neither blamed his father nor pitied his mother, nor was he tormented by stings of conscience; he realized that every one in the house was feeling the same ache, and God only knew which was most to blame, which was suffering most. . . .

At midnight he woke the labourer, and told him to have the horse ready at five o'clock in the morning for him to drive to the station; he undressed and got into bed, but could not get to sleep. He heard how his father, still awake, paced slowly from window to window, sighing, till early morning. No one was asleep; they spoke rarely, and only in whispers. Twice his mother came to him behind the screen. Always with the same look of vacant wonder, she slowly made the cross over him, shaking nervously.

At five o'clock in the morning he said good-bye to them all affectionately, and even shed tears. As he passed his father's room, he glanced in at the door. Yevgraf Ivanovitch, who had not taken off his clothes or gone to bed, was standing by the window, drumming on the panes.

"Good-bye; I am going," said his son.

"Good-bye . . . the money is on the round table . . ." his father answered, without turning round.

A cold, hateful rain was falling as the labourer drove him to the station. The sunflowers were drooping their heads still lower, and the grass seemed darker than ever.

THE GRASSHOPPER

I

ALL Olga Ivanovna's friends and acquaintances were at her wedding.

"Look at him; isn't it true that there is something in him?" she said to her friends, with a nod towards her husband, as though she wanted to explain why she was marrying a simple, very ordinary, and in no way remarkable man.

Her husband, Osip Stepanitch Dymov, was a doctor, and only of the rank of a titular councillor. He was on the staff of two hospitals: in one a ward-surgeon and in the other a dissecting demonstrator. Every day from nine to twelve he saw patients and was busy in his ward, and after twelve o'clock he went by tram to the other hospital, where he dissected. His private practice was a small one, not worth more than five hundred roubles a year. That was all. What more could one say about him? Meanwhile, Olga Ivanovna and her friends and acquaintances were not quite ordinary people. Every one of them was remarkable in some way, and more or less famous; already had made a reputation and was looked upon as a celebrity; or if not yet a celebrity, gave brilliant promise of becoming one.

There was an actor from the Dramatic Theatre, who was a great talent of established reputation, as well as an elegant, intelligent, and modest man, and a capital elocutionist, and who taught Olga Ivanovna to recite; there was a singer from the opera, a good-natured, fat man who assured Olga Ivanovna, with a sigh, that she was ruining herself, that if she would take herself in hand and not be lazy she might make a remarkable singer; then there were several artists, and chief among them Ryabovsky, a very handsome, fair young man of five-and-twenty who painted genre pieces, animal studies, and landscapes, was successful at exhibitions, and had sold his last picture for five hundred roubles. He touched up Olga Ivanovna's sketches, and used to say she might do something. Then a violoncellist, whose instrument used to sob, and who openly declared that of all the ladies of his acquaintance the only one who could accompany him was Olga Ivanovna; then there was a literary man, young but already well known, who had written stories, novels, and plays. Who else? Why, Vassily Vassilyitch, a landowner and amateur illustrator and vignettist, with a great feeling for the old Russian style, the old ballad and epic. On paper, on china, and on smoked plates, he produced literally marvels. In the midst of this free artistic company, spoiled by fortune, though refined and modest, who recalled the existence of doctors only in times of illness, and to whom the name of Dymov sounded in no way different from Sidorov or Tarasov - in the midst of this company Dymov seemed strange, not wanted, and small, though he was tall and broad-shouldered. He looked as though he had on somebody else's coat, and his beard was like a shopman's. Though if he had been a writer or an artist, they would have said that his beard reminded them of Zola.

An artist said to Olga Ivanovna that with her flaxen hair and in her wedding-dress she was very much like a graceful cherry-tree when it is covered all over with delicate white blossoms in spring.

"Oh, let me tell you," said Olga Ivanovna, taking his arm, "how it was it all came to pass so suddenly. Listen, listen! . . . I must tell you that my father was on the same staff at the hospital as Dymov. When my poor father was taken ill, Dymov watched for days and nights together at his bedside. Such self-sacrifice! Listen, Ryabovsky! You, my writer, listen; it is very interesting! Come nearer. Such self-sacrifice, such genuine sympathy! I sat up with my father, and did not sleep for nights, either. And all at once - the princess had won the hero's heart - my Dymov fell head over ears in love. Really, fate is so strange at times! Well, after my father's death he came to see me sometimes, met me in the street, and one fine evening, all at once he made me an offer . . . like snow upon my head. . . . I lay awake all night, crying, and fell hellishly in love myself. And here, as you see, I am his wife. There really is something strong, powerful, bearlike about him, isn't there? Now his face is turned three-quarters towards us in a bad light, but when he turns round look at his forehead. Ryabovsky, what do you say to that forehead? Dymov, we are talking about you!" she called to her husband. "Come here; hold out your honest hand to Ryabovsky . . . That's right, be friends."

Dymov, with a naive and good-natured smile, held out his hand to Ryabovsky, and said:

"Very glad to meet you. There was a Ryabovsky in my year at the medical school. Was he a relation of yours?"

Anton Chekhov

II

Olga Ivanovna was twenty-two, Dymov was thirty-one. They got on splendidly together when they were married. Olga Ivanovna hung all her drawing-room walls with her own and other people's sketches, in frames and without frames, and near the piano and furniture arranged picturesque corners with Japanese parasols, easels, daggers, busts, photographs, and rags of many colours. . . . In the dining-room she papered the walls with peasant woodcuts, hung up bark shoes and sickles, stood in a corner a scythe and a rake, and so achieved a dining-room in the Russian style. In her bedroom she draped the ceiling and the walls with dark cloths to make it like a cavern, hung a Venetian lantern over the beds, and at the door set a figure with a halberd. And every one thought that the young people had a very charming little home.

When she got up at eleven o'clock every morning, Olga Ivanovna played the piano or, if it were sunny, painted something in oils. Then between twelve and one she drove to her dressmaker's. As Dymov and she had very little money, only just enough, she and her dressmaker were often put to clever shifts to enable her to appear constantly in new dresses and make a sensation with them. Very often out of an old dyed dress, out of bits of tulle, lace, plush, and silk, costing nothing, perfect marvels were created, something bewitching - not a dress, but a dream. From the dressmaker's Olga Ivanovna usually drove to some actress of her acquaintance to hear the latest theatrical gossip, and incidentally to try and get hold of tickets for the first night of some new play or for a benefit performance. From the actress's she had to go to some artist's studio or to some exhibition or to see some celebrity - either to pay a visit or to give an invitation or simply to have a chat. And everywhere she met with a gay and friendly welcome, and was assured that she was good, that she was sweet, that she was rare. . . . Those whom she called great and famous received her as one of themselves, as an equal, and predicted with one voice that, with her talents, her taste, and her intelligence, she would do great things if she concentrated herself. She sang, she played the piano, she painted in oils, she carved, she took part in amateur performances; and all this not just anyhow, but all with talent, whether she made lanterns for an illumination or dressed up or tied somebody's cravat - everything she did was exceptionally graceful, artistic, and charming. But her talents showed themselves in nothing so clearly as in her faculty for quickly becoming acquainted and on intimate terms with celebrated people. No sooner did any one become ever so little celebrated, and set people talking about him, than she made his acquaintance, got on friendly terms the same day, and invited him to her house. Every new acquaintance she made was a veritable fete for her. She adored celebrated people, was proud of them, dreamed of them every night. She craved for them, and never could satisfy her craving. The old ones departed and were forgotten, new ones came to replace them, but to these, too, she soon grew accustomed or was disappointed in them, and began eagerly seeking for fresh great men, finding them and seeking for them again. What for?

Between four and five she dined at home with her husband. His simplicity, good sense, and kind-heartedness touched her and moved her up to enthusiasm. She was constantly jumping up, impulsively hugging his head and showering kisses on it.

"You are a clever, generous man, Dymov," she used to say, "but you have one very serious defect. You take absolutely no interest in art. You don't believe in music or painting."

"I don't understand them," he would say mildly. "I have spent all my life in working at natural science and medicine, and I have never had time to take an interest in the arts."

"But, you know, that's awful, Dymov!"

"Why so? Your friends don't know a nything of science or medicine, but you don't reproach them with it. Every one has his own line. I don't understand landscapes and operas, but the way I look at it is that if one set of sensible people devote their whole lives to them, and other sensible people pay immense sums for them, they must be of use. I don't understand them, but not understanding does not imply disbelieving in them."

"Let me shake your honest hand!"

After dinner Olga Ivanovna would drive off to see her friends, then to a theatre or to a concert, and she returned home after midnight. So it was every day.

On Wednesdays she had "At Homes." At these "At Homes" the hostess and her guests did not play cards and did not dance, but entertained themselves with various arts. An actor from the Dramatic Theatre recited, a singer sang, artists sketched in the albums of which Olga Ivanovna had a great number, the violoncellist played, and the hostess herself sketched, carved, sang, and played accompaniments. In the intervals between the recitations, music, and singing, they talked and argued about literature, the theatre, and painting. There were no ladies, for Olga Ivanovna considered all ladies wearisome and vulgar except actresses and her dressmaker. Not one of these entertainments passed without the hostess starting at every ring at the bell, and saying, with a triumphant expression, "It is he," meaning by "he," of course, some new celebrity. Dymov was not in the drawing-room, and no one remembered his existence. But exactly at half-past eleven the door leading into the dining-room opened, and Dymov would appear with his good-natured, gentle smile and say, rubbing his hands:

"Come to supper, gentlemen."

They all went into the dining-room, and every time found on the table exactly the same things: a dish of oysters, a piece of ham or veal, sardines, cheese, caviare, mushrooms, vodka, and two decanters of wine.

My dear *maitre d' hotel!*" Olga Ivanovna would say, clasping her hands with enthusiasm, "you are simply fascinating! My friends, look at his forehead! Dymov, turn your profile. Look! he has the face of a Bengal tiger and an expression as kind and sweet as a gazelle. Ah, the darling!"

The visitors ate, and, looking at Dymov, thought, "He really is a nice fellow"; but they soon forgot about him, and went on talking about the theatre, music, and painting.

The young people were happy, and their life flowed on without a hitch.

The third week of their honeymoon was spent, however, not quite happily - sadly, indeed. Dymov caught erysipelas in the hospital, was in bed for six days, and had to have his beautiful black hair cropped. Olga Ivanovna sat beside him and wept bitterly, but when he was better she put a white handkerchief on his shaven head and began to paint him as a Bedouin. And they were both in good spirits. Three days after he had begun to go back to the hospital he had another mischance.

"I have no luck, little mother," he said one day at dinner. "I had four dissections to do today, and I cut two of my fingers at one. And I did not notice it till I got home."

Olga Ivanovna was alarmed. He smiled, and told her that it did not matter, and that he often cut his hands when he was dissecting.

"I get absorbed, little mother, and grow careless."

Olga Ivanovna dreaded symptoms of blood-poisoning, and prayed about it every night, but all went well. And again life flowed on peaceful and happy, free from grief and anxiety. The present was happy, and to follow it spring was at hand, already smiling in the distance, and promising a thousand delights. There would be no end to their happiness. In April, May and June a summer villa a good distance out of town;

walks, sketching, fishing, nightingales; and then from July right on to autumn an artist's tour on the Volga, and in this tour Olga Ivanovna would take part as an indispensable member of the society. She had already had made for her two travelling dresses of linen, had bought paints, brushes, canvases, and a new palette for the journey. Almost every day Ryabovsky visited her to see what progress she was making in her painting; when she showed him her painting, he used to thrust his hands deep into his pockets, compress his lips, sniff, and say:

"Ye - es . . . ! That cloud of yours is screaming: it's not in the evening light. The foreground is somehow chewed up, and there is something, you know, not the thing. . . . And your cottage is weighed down and whines pitifully. That corner ought to have been taken more in shadow, but on the whole it is not bad; I like it."

And the more incomprehensible he talked, the more readily Olga Ivanovna understood him.

III

After dinner on the second day of Trinity week, Dymov bought some sweets and some savouries and went down to the villa to see his wife. He had not seen her for a fortnight, and missed her terribly. As he sat in the train and afterwards as he looked for his villa in a big wood, he felt all the while hungry and weary, and dreamed of how he would have supper in freedom with his wife, then tumble into bed and to sleep. And he was delighted as he looked at his parcel, in which there was caviare, cheese, and white salmon.

The sun was setting by the time he found his villa and recognized it. The old servant told him that her mistress was not at home, but that most likely she would soon be in. The villa, very uninviting in appearance, with low ceilings papered with writing-paper and with uneven floors full of crevices, consisted only of three rooms. In one there was a bed, in the second there were canvases, brushes, greasy papers, and men's overcoats and hats lying about on the chairs and in the windows, while in the third Dymov found three unknown men; two were dark-haired and had beards, the other was clean-shaven and fat, apparently an actor. There was a samovar boiling on the table.

"What do you want?" asked the actor in a bass voice, looking at Dymov ungraciously. "Do you want Olga Ivanovna? Wait a minute; she will be here directly."

Dymov sat down and waited. One of the dark-haired men, looking sleepily and listlessly at him, poured himself out a glass of tea, and asked:

"Perhaps you would like some tea?"

Dymov was both hungry and thirsty, but he refused tea for fear of spoiling his supper. Soon he heard footsteps and a familiar laugh; a door slammed, and Olga Ivanovna ran into the room, wearing a wide-brimmed hat and carrying a box in her hand; she was followed by Ryabovsky, rosy and good-humoured, carrying a big umbrella and a camp-stool.

"Dymov!" cried Olga Ivanovna, and she flushed crimson with pleasure. "Dymov!" she repeated, laying her head and both arms on his bosom. "Is that you? Why haven't you come for so long? Why? Why?"

"When could I, little mother? I am always busy, and whenever I am free it always happens somehow that the train does not fit."

"But how glad I am to see you! I have been dreaming about you the whole night, the whole night, and I was afraid you must be ill. Ah! if you only knew how sweet you are! You have come in the nick of time! You will be my salvation! You are the only person who can save me! There is to be a most original wedding here tomorrow," she went on, laughing, and tying her husband's cravat. "A young telegraph clerk at the station, called Tchikeldyeev, is going to be married. He is a handsome young man and - well, not stupid, and you know there is something strong, bearlike in his face . . . you might paint him as a young Norman. We summer visitors take a great interest in him, and have promised to be at his wedding. . . . He is a lonely, timid man, not well off, and of course it would be a shame not to be sympathetic to him. Fancy! the wedding will be after the service; then we shall all walk from the church to the bride's lodgings. . . you see the wood, the birds singing, patches of sunlight on the grass, and all of us spots of different colours against the bright green background - very original, in the style of the French impressionists. But, Dymov, what am I to go to the church in?" said Olga Ivanovna, and she looked as though she were going to cry. "I have nothing here, literally nothing! no dress, no flowers, no gloves . . . you must save me. Since you have come, fate itself bids you save me. Take the keys, my precious, go home and get my pink dress from the wardrobe. You remember it; it hangs in front. . . . Then, in the storeroom, on the floor, on the right side, you will see two cardboard boxes. When you open the top one you will see tulle, heaps of tulle and rags of all sorts, and under them flowers. Take out all the flowers carefully, try not to crush them, darling; I will choose among them later. . . . And buy me some gloves."

"Very well," said Dymov; "I will go tomorrow and send them to you."

"Tomorrow?" asked Olga Ivanovna, and she looked at him surprised. "You won't have time tomorrow. The first train goes tomorrow at nine, and the wedding's at eleven. No, darling, it must be today; it absolutely must be today. If you won't be able to come tomorrow, send them by a messenger. Come, you must run along. . . . The passenger train will be in directly; don't miss it, darling."

"Very well."

"Oh, how sorry I am to let you go!" said Olga Ivanovna, and tears came into her eyes. "And why did I promise that telegraph clerk, like a silly?"

Dymov hurriedly drank a glass of tea, took a cracknel, and, smiling gently, went to the station. And the caviare, the cheese, and the white salmon were eaten by the two dark gentlemen and the fat actor.

IV

On a still moonlight night in July Olga Ivanovna was standing on the deck of a Volga steamer and looking alternately at the water and at the picturesque banks. Beside her was standing Ryabovsky, telling her the black shadows on the water were not shadows, but a dream, that it would be sweet to sink into forgetfulness, to die, to become a memory in the sight of that enchanted water with the fantastic glimmer, in sight of the fathomless sky and the mournful, dreamy shores that told of the vanity of our life and of the existence of something higher, blessed, and eternal. The past was vulgar and uninteresting, the future was trivial, and that marvellous night, unique in a lifetime, would soon be over, would blend with eternity; then, why live?

And Olga Ivanovna listened alternately to Ryabovsky's voice and the silence of the night, and thought of her being immortal and never dying. The turquoise colour of the water, such as she had never seen before, the sky, the river-banks, the black shadows, and the unaccountable joy that flooded her soul, all told her that she would make a great artist, and that somewhere in the distance, in the infinite space beyond the moonlight, success, glory, the love of the people, lay awaiting her. . . . When she gazed steadily without blinking into the distance, she seemed to see crowds of people, lights, triumphant strains of music, cries of enthusiasm, she herself in a white dress, and flowers showered upon her from all sides. She thought, too, that beside her, leaning with his elbows on the rail of the steamer, there was standing a real great man, a genius, one of God's elect. . . . All that he had created up to the present was fine, new, and extraordinary, but what he would create in time, when with maturity his rare talent reached its full development, would be astounding, immeasurably sublime; and that could be seen by his face, by his manner of expressing himself and his attitude to nature. He talked of shadows, of the tones of evening, of the moonlight, in a special way, in a language of his own, so that one could not help feeling the fascination of his power over nature. He was very handsome, original, and his life, free, independent, aloof from all common cares, was like the life of a bird.

"It's growing cooler," said Olga Ivanovna, and she gave a shudder.

Ryabovsky wrapped her in his cloak, and said mournfully:

"I feel that I am in your power; I am a slave. Why are you so enchanting today?"

He kept staring intently at her, and his eyes were terrible. And she was afraid to look at him.

"I love you madly," he whispered, breathing on her cheek. "Say one word to me and I will not go on living; I will give up art . . ." he muttered in violent emotion. "Love me, love . . . ."

"Don't talk like that," said Olga Ivanovna, covering her eyes. "It's dreadful! How about Dymov?"

"What of Dymov? Why Dymov? What have I to do with Dymov? The Volga, the moon, beauty, my love, ecstasy, and there is no such thing as Dymov. . . . Ah! I don't know . . . I don't care about the past; give me one moment, one instant!"

Olga Ivanovna's heart began to throb. She tried to think about her husband, but all her past, with her wedding, with Dymov, and with her "At Homes," seemed to her petty, trivial, dingy, unnecessary, and far, far away. . . . Yes, really, what of Dymov? Why Dymov? What had she to do with Dymov? Had he any existence in nature, or was he only a dream?

"For him, a simple and ordinary man the happiness he has had already is enough," she thought, covering her face with her hands. "Let them condemn me, let them curse me, but in spite of them all I will go to my ruin; I will go to my ruin! . . . One must experience everything in life. My God! how terrible and how glorious!"

"Well? Well?" muttered the artist, embracing her, and greedily kissing the hands with which she feebly tried to thrust him from her. "You love me? Yes? Yes? Oh, what a night! marvellous night!"

"Yes, what a night!" she whispered, looking into his eyes, which were bright with tears.

Then she looked round quickly, put her arms round him, and kissed him on the lips.

"We are nearing Kineshmo!" said some one on the other side of the deck.

They heard heavy footsteps; it was a waiter from the refreshment-bar.

"Waiter," said Olga Ivanovna, laughing and crying with happiness, "bring us some wine."

The artist, pale with emotion, sat on the seat, looking at Olga Ivanovna with adoring, grateful eyes; then he closed his eyes, and said, smiling languidly:

"I am tired."

And he leaned his head against the rail.

V

On the second of September the day was warm and still, but overcast. In the early morning a light mist had hung over the Volga, and after nine o'clock it had begun to spout with rain. And there seemed no hope of the sky clearing. Over their morning tea Ryabovsky told Olga Ivanovna that painting was the most ungrateful and boring art, that he was not an artist, that none but fools thought that he had any talent, and all at once, for no rhyme or reason, he snatched up a knife and with it scraped over his very best sketch. After his tea he sat plunged in gloom at the window and gazed at the Volga. And now the Volga was dingy, all of one even colour without a gleam of light, cold-looking. Everything, everything recalled the approach of dreary, gloomy autumn. And it seemed as though nature had removed now from the Volga the sumptuous green covers from the banks, the brilliant reflections of the sunbeams, the transparent blue distance, and all its smart gala array, and had packed it away in boxes till the coming spring, and the crows were flying above the Volga and crying tauntingly, "Bare, bare!"

Ryabovsky heard their cawing, and thought he had already gone off and lost his talent, that everything in this world was relative, conditional, and stupid, and that he ought not to have taken up with this woman . . . .In short, he was out of humour and depressed.

Olga Ivanovna sat behind the screen on the bed, and, passing her fingers through her lovely flaxen hair, pictured herself first in the drawing-room, then in the bedroom, then in her husband's study; her imagination carried her to the theatre, to the dress-maker, to her distinguished friends. Were they getting something up now? Did they think of her? The season had begun by now, and it would be time to think about her "At Homes." And Dymov? Dear Dymov! with what gentleness and childlike pathos he kept begging her in his letters to make haste and come home! Every month he sent her seventy-five roubles, and when she wrote him that she had lent the artists a hundred roubles, he sent that hundred too. What a kind, generous-hearted man! The travelling wearied Olga Ivanovna; she was bored; and she longed to get away from the peasants, from the damp smell of the river, and to cast off the feeling of physical uncleanliness of which she was conscious all the time, living in the peasants' huts and wandering from village to village. If Ryabovsky had not given his word to the artists that he would stay with them till the twentieth of September, they might have gone away that very day. And how nice that would have been!

"My God!" moaned Ryabovsky. "Will the sun ever come out? I can't go on with a sunny landscape without the sun. . . ."

"But you have a sketch with a cloudy sky," said Olga Ivanovna, coming from behind the screen. "Do you remember, in the right foreground forest trees, on the left a herd of cows and geese? You might finish it now."

"Aie!" the artist scowled. "Finish it! Can you imagine I am such a fool that I don't know what I want to do?"

"How you have changed to me!" sighed Olga Ivanovna.

"Well, a good thing too!"

Olga Ivanovna's face quivered; she moved away to the stove and began to cry.

"Well, that's the last straw - crying! Give over! I have a thousand reasons for tears, but I am not crying."

"A thousand reasons!" cried Olga Ivanovna. "The chief one is that you are weary of me. Yes!" she said, and broke into sobs. "If one is to tell the truth, you are ashamed of our love. You keep trying to prevent the artists from noticing it, though it is impossible to conceal it, and they have known all about it for ever so long."

"Olga, one thing I beg you," said the artist in an imploring voice, laying his hand on his heart - "one thing; don't worry me! I want nothing else from you!"

"But swear that you love me still!"

"This is agony!" the artist hissed through his teeth, and he jumped up. "It will end by my throwing myself in the Volga or going out of my mind! Let me alone!"

"Come, kill me, kill me!" cried Olga Ivanovna. "Kill me!"

She sobbed again, and went behind the screen. There was a swish of rain on the straw thatch of the hut. Ryabovsky clutched his head and strode up and down the hut; then with a resolute face, as though bent on proving something to somebody, put on his cap, slung his gun over his shoulder, and went out of the hut.

After he had gone, Olga Ivanovna lay a long time on the bed, crying. At first she thought it would be a good thing to poison herself, so that when Ryabovsky came back he would find her dead; then her imagination carried her to her drawing-room, to her husband's study, and she imagined herself sitting motionless beside Dymov and enjoying the physical peace and cleanliness, and in the evening sitting in the theatre, listening to Mazini. And a yearning for civilization, for the noise and bustle of the town, for celebrated people sent a pang to her heart. A peasant woman came into the hut and began in a leisurely way lighting the stove to get the dinner. There was a smell of charcoal fumes, and the air was filled with bluish smoke. The artists came in, in muddy high boots and with faces wet with rain, examined their sketches, and comforted themselves by saying that the Volga had its charms even in bad weather. On the wall the cheap clock went "tic-tic-tic." . . . The flies, feeling chilled, crowded round the ikon in the corner, buzzing, and one could hear the cockroaches scurrying about among the thick portfolios under the seats. . . .

Ryabovsky came home as the sun was setting. He flung his cap on the table, and, without removing his muddy boots, sank pale and exhausted on the bench and closed his eyes.

"I am tired . . ." he said, and twitched his eyebrows, trying to raise his eyelids.

To be nice to him and to show she was not cross, Olga Ivanovna went up to him, gave him a silent kiss, and passed the comb through his fair hair. She meant to comb it for him.

"What's that?" he said, starting as though something cold had touched him, and he opened his eyes. "What is it? Please let me alone."

He thrust her off, and moved away. And it seemed to her that there was a look of aversion and annoyance on his face.

At that time the peasant woman cautiously carried him, in both hands, a plate of cabbage-soup. And Olga Ivanovna saw how she wetted her fat fingers in it. And the dirty peasant woman, standing with her body thrust forward, and the cabbage-soup which Ryabovsky began eating greedily, and the hut, and their whole way of life, which she at first had so loved for its simplicity and artistic disorder, seemed horrible to her now. She suddenly felt insulted, and said coldly:

"We must part for a time, or else from boredom we shall quarrel in earnest. I am sick of this; I am going today."

"Going how? Astride on a broomstick?"

"Today is Thursday, so the steamer will be here at half-past nine."

"Eh? Yes, yes. . . . Well, go, then . . ." Ryabovsky said softly, wiping his mouth with a towel instead of a dinner napkin. "You are dull and have nothing to do here, and one would have to be a great egoist to try and keep you. Go home, and we shall meet again after the twentieth."

Olga Ivanovna packed in good spirits. Her cheeks positively glowed with pleasure. Could it really be true, she asked herself, that she would soon be writing in her drawing-room and sleeping in her bedroom, and dining with a cloth on the table? A weight was lifted from her heart, and she no longer felt angry with the artist.

"My paints and brushes I will leave with you, Ryabovsky," she said. "You can bring what's left. . . . Mind, now, don't be lazy here when I am gone; don't mope, but work. You are such a splendid fellow, Ryabovsky!"

At ten o'clock Ryabovsky gave her a farewell kiss, in order, as she thought, to avoid kissing her on the steamer before the artists, and went with her to the landing-stage. The steamer soon came up and carried her away.

She arrived home two and a half days later. Breathless with excitement, she went, without taking off her hat or waterproof, into the drawing-room and thence into the dining-room. Dymov, with his waistcoat unbuttoned and no coat, was sitting at the table sharpening a knife on a fork; before him lay a grouse on a plate. As Olga Ivanovna went into the flat she was convinced that it was essential to hide everything from her husband, and that she would have the strength and skill to do so; but now, when she saw his broad, mild, happy smile, and shining, joyful eyes, she felt that to deceive this man was as vile, as revolting, and as impossible and out of her power as to bear false witness, to steal, or to kill, and in a flash she resolved to tell him all that had happened. Letting him kiss and embrace her, she sank down on her knees before him and hid her face.

"What is it, what is it, little mother?" he asked tenderly. "Were you homesick?"

She raised her face, red with shame, and gazed at him with a guilty and imploring look, but fear and shame prevented her from telling him the truth.

"Nothing," she said; "it's just nothing. . . ."

"Let us sit down," he said, raising her and seating her at the table. "That's right, eat the grouse. You are starving, poor darling."

She eagerly breathed in the atmosphere of home and ate the grouse, while he watched her with tenderness and laughed with delight.

VI

Apparently, by the middle of the winter Dymov began to suspect that he was being deceived. As though his conscience was not clear, he could not look his wife straight in the face, did not smile with delight when he met her, and to avoid being left alone with her, he often brought in to dinner his colleague, Korostelev, a little close-cropped man with a wrinkled face, who kept buttoning and unbuttoning his reefer jacket with embarrassment when he talked with Olga Ivanovna, and then with his right hand nipped his left moustache. At dinner the two doctors talked about the fact that a displacement of the diaphragm was sometimes accompanied by irregularities of the heart, or that a great number of neurotic complaints were met with of late, or that Dymov had the day before found a cancer of the lower abdomen while dissecting a corpse with the diagnosis of pernicious anaemia. And it seemed as though they were talking of medicine to give Olga Ivanovna a chance of being silent - that is, of not lying. After dinner Korostelev sat down to the piano, while Dymov sighed and said to him:

"Ech, brother - well, well! Play something melancholy."

Hunching up his shoulders and stretching his fingers wide apart, Korostelev played some chords and began singing in a tenor voice, "Show me the abode where the Russian peasant would not groan," while Dymov sighed once more, propped his head on his fist, and sank into thought.

Olga Ivanovna had been extremely imprudent in her conduct of late. Every morning she woke up in a very bad humour and with the thought that she no longer cared for Ryabovsky, and that, thank God, it was all over now. But as she drank her coffee she reflected that Ryabovsky had robbed her of her husband, and that now she was left with neither her husband nor Ryabovsky; then she remembered talks she had heard among her acquaintances of a picture Ryabovsky was preparing for the exhibition, something striking, a mixture of genre and landscape, in the style of Polyenov, about which every one who had been into his studio went into raptures; and this, of course, she mused, he had created under her influence, and altogether, thanks to her influence, he had greatly changed for the better. Her influence was so beneficent and essential that if she were to leave him he might perhaps go to ruin. And she remembered, too, that the last time he had come to see her in a great-coat with flecks on it and a new tie, he had asked her languidly:

"Am I beautiful?"

And with his elegance, his long curls, and his blue eyes, he really was very beautiful (or perhaps it only seemed so), and he had been affectionate to her.

Considering and remembering many things Olga Ivanovna dressed and in great agitation drove to Ryabovsky's studio. She found him in high spirits, and enchanted with his really magnificent picture. He was dancing about and playing the fool and answering serious questions with jokes. Olga Ivanovna was jealous of the picture and hated it, but from politeness she stood before the picture for five minutes in silence, and, heaving a sigh, as though before a holy shrine, said softly:

"Yes, you have never painted anything like it before. Do you know, it is positively awe-inspiring?"

And then she began beseeching him to love her and not to cast her off, to have pity on her in her misery and her wretchedness. She shed tears, kissed his hands, insisted on his swearing that he loved her, told him that without her good influence he would go astray and be ruined. And, when she had spoilt his good-humour, feeling herself humiliated, she would drive off to her dressmaker or to an actress of her acquaintance to try and get theatre tickets.

If she did not find him at his studio she left a letter in which she swore that if he did not come to see her that day she would poison herself. He was scared, came to see her, and stayed to dinner. Regardless of her husband's presence, he would say rude things to her, and she would answer him in the same way. Both felt they were a burden to each other, that they were tyrants and enemies, and were wrathful, and in their wrath did not notice that their behaviour was unseemly, and that even Korostelev, with his close-cropped head, saw it all. After dinner Ryabovsky made haste to say good-bye and get away.

"Where are you off to?" Olga Ivanovna would ask him in the hall, looking at him with hatred.

Scowling and screwing up his eyes, he mentioned some lady of their acquaintance, and it was evident that he was laughing at her jealousy and wanted to annoy her. She went to her bedroom and lay down on her bed; from jealousy, anger, a sense of humiliation and shame, she bit the pillow and began sobbing aloud. Dymov left Korostelev in the drawing-room, went into the bedroom, and with a desperate and embarrassed face said softly:

"Don't cry so loud, little mother; there's no need. You must be quiet about it. You must not let people see. . . . You know what is done is done, and can't be mended."

Not knowing how to ease the burden of her jealousy, which actually set her temples throbbing with pain, and thinking still that things might be set right, she would wash, powder her tear-stained face, and fly off to the lady mentioned.

Not finding Ryabovsky with her, she would drive off to a second, then to a third. At first she was ashamed to go about like this, but afterwards she got used to it, and it would happen that in one evening she would make the round of all her female acquaintances in search of Ryabovsky, and they all understood it.

One day she said to Ryabovsky of her husband:

"That man crushes me with his magnanimity."

This phrase pleased her so much that when she met the artists who knew of her affair with Ryabovsky she said every time of her husband, with a vigorous movement of her arm:

"That man crushes me with his magnanimity."

Their manner of life was the same as it had been the year before. On Wednesdays they were "At Home"; an actor recited, the artists sketched. The violoncellist played, a singer sang, and invariably at half-past eleven the door leading to the dining-room opened and Dymov, smiling, said:

"Come to supper, gentlemen."

As before, Olga Ivanovna hunted celebrities, found them, was not satisfied, and went in pursuit of fresh ones. As before she came back late every night; but now Dymov was not, as last year, asleep, but sitting in his study at work of some sort. He went to bed at three o'clock and got up at eight.

One evening when she was getting ready to go to the theatre and standing before the pier glass, Dymov came into her bedroom, wearing his dress-coat and a white tie. He was smiling gently and looked into his wife's face joyfully, as in old days; his face was radiant.

"I have just been defending my thesis," he said, sitting down and smoothing his knees.

"Defending?" asked Olga Ivanovna.

"Oh, oh!" he laughed, and he craned his neck to see his wife's face in the mirror, for she was still standing with her back to him, doing up her hair. "Oh, oh," he repeated, "do you know it's very possible they may offer me the Readership in General Pathology? It seems like it."

It was evident from his beaming, blissful face that if Olga Ivanovna had shared with him his joy and triumph he would have forgiven her everything, both the present and the future, and would have forgotten

Anton Chekhov

everything, but she did not understand what was meant by a "readership" or by "general pathology"; besides, she was afraid of being late for the theatre, and she said nothing.

He sat there another two minutes, and with a guilty smile went away.

VII

It had been a very troubled day.

Dymov had a very bad headache; he had no breakfast, and did not go to the hospital, but spent the whole time lying on his sofa in the study. Olga Ivanovna went as usual at midday to see Ryabovsky, to show him her still-life sketch, and to ask him why he had not been to see her the evening before. The sketch seemed to her worthless, and she had painted it only in order to have an additional reason for going to the artist.

She went in to him without ringing, and as she was taking off her goloshes in the entry she heard a sound as of something running softly in the studio, with a feminine rustle of skirts; and as she hastened to peep in she caught a momentary glimpse of a bit of brown petticoat, which vanished behind a big picture draped, together with the easel, with black calico, to the floor. There could be no doubt that a woman was hiding there. How often Olga Ivanovna herself had taken refuge behind that picture!

Ryabovsky, evidently much embarrassed, held out both hands to her, as though surprised at her arrival, and said with a forced smile:

"Aha! Very glad to see you! Anything nice to tell me?"

Olga Ivanovna's eyes filled with tears. She felt ashamed and bitter, and would not for a million roubles have consented to speak in the presence of the outsider, the rival, the deceitful woman who was

Anton Chekhov

standing now behind the picture, and probably giggling malignantly.

"I have brought you a sketch," she said timidly in a thin voice, and her lips quivered. "*Nature morte*."

"Ah - ah! . . . A sketch?"

The artist took the sketch in his hands, and as he examined it w alked, as it were mechanically, into the other room.

Olga Ivanovna followed him humbly.

"*Nature morte* . . . first-rate sort," he muttered, falling into rhyme. "Kurort . . . sport . . . port . . ."

From the studio came the sound of hurried footsteps and the rustle of a skirt.

So she had gone. Olga Ivanovna wanted to scream aloud, to hit the artist on the head with something heavy, but she could see nothing through her tears, was crushed by her shame, and felt herself, not Olga Ivanovna, not an artist, but a little insect.

"I am tired . . ." said the artist languidly, looking at the sketch and tossing his head as though struggling with drowsiness. "It's very nice, of course, but here a sketch today, a sketch last year, another sketch in a month . . . I wonder you are not bored with them. If I were you I should give up painting and work seriously at music or something. You're not an artist, you know, but a musician. But you can't think how tired I am! I'll tell them to bring us some tea, shall I?"

He went out of the room, and Olga Ivanovna heard him give some order to his footman. To avoid farewells and explanations, and above all to avoid bursting into sobs, she ran as fast as she could, before Ryabovsky came back, to the entry, put on her goloshes, and went out into the street; then she breathed easily, and felt she was free for ever from Ryabovsky and from painting and from the burden of shame which had so crushed her in the studio. It was all over!

She drove to her dressmaker's; then to see Barnay, who had only arrived the day before; from Barnay to a music-shop, and all the time she was thinking how she would write Ryabovsky a cold, cruel letter full of personal dignity, and how in the spring or the summer she would go with Dymov to the Crimea, free herself finally from the past there, and begin a new life.

On getting home late in the evening she sat down in the drawing-room, without taking off her things, to begin the letter. Ryabovsky had told her she was not an artist, and to pay him out she wrote to him now that he painted the same thing every year, and said exactly the same thing every day; that he was at a standstill, and that nothing more would come of him than had come already. She wanted to write, too, that he owed a great deal to her good influence, and that if he was going wrong it was only because her influence was paralysed by various dubious persons like the one who had been hiding behind the picture that day.

"Little mother!" Dymov called from the study, without opening the door.

"What is it?"

"Don't come in to me, but only come to the door - that's right. . . . The day before yesterday I must have caught diphtheria at the hospital, and now . . . I am ill. Make haste and send for Korostelev."

Olga Ivanovna always called her husband by his surname, as she did all the men of her acquaintance; she disliked his Christian name, Osip, because it reminded her of the Osip in Gogol and the silly pun on his name. But now she cried:

"Osip, it cannot be!"

"Send for him; I feel ill," Dymov said behind the door, and she could hear him go back to the sofa and lie down. "Send!" she heard his voice faintly.

"Good Heavens!" thought Olga Ivanovna, turning chill with horror. "Why, it's dangerous!"

For no reason she took the candle and went into the bedroom, and there, reflecting what she must do, glanced casually at herself in the pier glass. With her pale, frightened face, in a jacket with sleeves high on the shoulders, with yellow ruches on her bosom, and with stripes running in unusual directions on her skirt, she seemed to herself horrible and disgusting. She suddenly felt poignantly sorry for Dymov, for his boundless love for her, for his young life, and even for the desolate little bed in which he had not slept for so long; and she remembered his habitual, gentle, submissive smile. She wept bitterly, and wrote an imploring letter to Korostelev. It was two o'clock in the night.

VIII

When towards eight o'clock in the morning Olga Ivanovna, her head heavy from want of sleep and her hair unbrushed, came out of her bedroom, looking unattractive and with a guilty expression on her face, a gentleman with a black beard, apparently the doctor, passed by her into the entry. There was a smell of drugs. Korostelev was standing near the study door, twisting his left moustache with his right hand.

"Excuse me, I can't let you go in," he said surlily to Olga Ivanovna; "it's catching. Besides, it's no use, really; he is delirious, anyway."

"Has he really got diphtheria?" Olga Ivanovna asked in a whisper.

"People who wantonly risk infection ought to be hauled up and punished for it," muttered Korostelev, not answering Olga Ivanovna's question. "Do you know why he caught it? On Tuesday he was sucking up the mucus through a pipette from a boy with diphtheria. And what for? It was stupid. . . . Just from folly. .. ."

"Is it dangerous, very?" asked Olga Ivanovna.

"Yes; they say it is the malignant form. We ought to send for Shrek really."

A little red-haired man with a long nose and a Jewish accent arrived; then a tall, stooping, shaggy individual, who looked like a head deacon; then a stout young

Anton Chekhov

man with a red face and spectacles. These were doctors who came to watch by turns beside their colleague. Korostelev did not go home when his turn was over, but remained and wandered about the rooms like an uneasy spirit. The maid kept getting tea for the various doctors, and was constantly running to the chemist, and there was no one to do the rooms. There was a dismal stillness in the flat.

Olga Ivanovna sat in her bedroom and thought that God was punishing her for having deceived her husband. That silent, unrepining, uncomprehended creature, robbed by his mildness of all personality and will, weak from excessive kindness, had been suffering in obscurity somewhere on his sofa, and had not complained. And if he were to complain even in delirium, the doctors watching by his bedside would learn that diphtheria was not the only cause of his sufferings. They would ask Korostelev. He knew all about it, and it was not for nothing that he looked at his friend's wife with eyes that seemed to say that she was the real chief criminal and diphtheria was only her accomplice. She did not think now of the moonlight evening on the Volga, nor the words of love, nor their poetical life in the peasant's hut. She thought only that from an idle whim, from self-indulgence, she had sullied herself all over from head to foot in something filthy, sticky, which one could never wash off. . . .

"Oh, how fearfully false I've been!" she thought, recalling the troubled passion she had known with Ryabovsky. "Curse it all! . .."

At four o'clock she dined with Korostelev. He did nothing but scowl and drink red wine, and did not eat a morsel. She ate nothing, either. At one minute she was praying inwardly and vowing to God that if Dymov recovered she would love him again and be a faithful wife to him. Then, forgetting herself for a minute, she would look at Korostelev, and think: "Surely it must be dull to be a humble, obscure person, not remarkable in any way, especially with such a wrinkled face and bad manners!"

Then it seemed to her that God would strike her dead that minute for not having once been in her husband's study, for fear of infection. And altogether she had a dull, despondent feeling and a conviction that her life was spoilt, and that there was no setting it right anyhow. . . .

After dinner darkness came on. When Olga Ivanovna went into the drawing-room Korostelev was asleep on the sofa, with a gold-embroidered silk cushion under his head.

"Khee-poo-ah," he snored - "khee-poo-ah."

And the doctors as they came to sit up and went away again did not notice this disorder. The fact that a strange man was asleep and snoring in the drawing-room, and the sketches on the walls and the exquisite decoration of the room, and the fact that the lady of the house was dishevelled and untidy - all that aroused not the slightest interest now. One of the doctors chanced to laugh at something, and the laugh had a strange and timid sound that made one's heart ac he.

When Olga Ivanovna went into the drawing-room next time, Korostelev was not asleep, but sitting up and smoking.

"He has diphtheria of the nasal cavity," he said in a low voice, "and the heart is not working properly now. Things are in a bad way, really."

"But you will send for Shrek?" said Olga Ivanovna.

"He has been already. It was he noticed that the diphtheria had passed into the nose. What's the use of Shrek! Shrek's no use at all, really. He is Shrek, I am Korostelev, and nothing more."

The time dragged on fearfully slowly. Olga Ivanovna lay down in her clothes on her bed, that had not been made all day, and sank into a doze. She dreamed that the whole flat was filled up from floor to ceiling with a huge piece of iron, and that if they could only get the iron out they would all be light-hearted and happy. Waking, she realized that it was not the iron but Dymov's illness that was weighing on her.

"Nature morte, port . . ." she thought, sinking into forgetfulness again. "Sport . . . Kurort . . . and what of Shrek? Shrek. . . trek . . . wreck. . . . And where are my friends now? Do they know that we are in trouble? Lord, save . . . spare! Shrek. . . trek . . ."

And again the iron was there. . . . The time dragged on slowly, though the clock on the lower storey struck frequently. And bells were continually ringing as the doctors arrived. . . . The house-maid came in with an empty glass on a tray, and asked, "Shall I make the bed, madam?" and getting no answer, went away.

The clock below struck the hour. She dreamed of the rain on the Volga; and again some one came into her bedroom, she thought a stranger. Olga Ivanovna jumped up, and recognized Korostelev.

"What time is it?" she asked.

"About three."

"Well, what is it?"

"What, indeed! . . . I've come to tell you he is passing. . . ."

He gave a sob, sat down on the bed beside her, and wiped away the tears with his sleeve. She could not grasp it at once, but turned cold all over and began slowly crossing herself.

"He is passing," he repeated in a shrill voice, and again he gave a sob. "He is dying because he sacrificed himself. What a loss for science!" he said bitterly. "Compare him with all of us. He was a great man, an extraordinary man! What gifts! What hopes we all had of him!" Korostelev went on, wringing his hands: "Merciful God, he was a man of science; we shall never look on his like again. Osip Dymov, what have you done - aie, aie, my God!"

Korostelev covered his face with both hands in despair, and shook his head.

"And his moral force," he went on, seeming to grow more and more exasperated against some one. "Not a man, but a pure, good, loving soul, and clean as crystal. He served science and died for science. And he worked like an ox night and day - no one spared him - and with his youth and his learning he had to take a private practice and work at translations at night to pay for these . . . vile rags!"

Korostelev looked with hatred at Olga Ivanovna, snatched at the sheet with both hands and angrily tore it, as though it were to blame.

"He did not spare himself, and others did not spare him. Oh, what's the use of talking!"

"Yes, he was a rare man," said a bass voice in the drawing-room.

Olga Ivanovna remembered her whole life with him from the beginning to the end, with all its details, and suddenly she understood that he really was an extraordinary, rare, and, compared with every one else she knew, a great man. And remembering how her father, now dead, and all the other doctors had behaved to him, she realized that they really had seen in him a future celebrity. The walls, the ceiling, the lamp, and the carpet on the floor, seemed to be winking at her sarcastically, as though they would say, "You were blind! you were blind!" With a wail she flung herself out of the bedroom, dashed by some unknown man in the drawing-room, and ran into her husband's study. He was lying motionless on the sofa, covered to the waist with a quilt. His face was fearfully thin and sunken, and was of a greyish-yellow colour such as is never seen in the living; only from the forehead, from the black eyebrows and from the familiar smile, could he be recognized as Dymov. Olga Ivanovna hurriedly felt his chest, his forehead, and his hands. The chest was still warm, but the forehead and hands were unpleasantly cold, and the half-open eyes looked, not at Olga Ivanovna, but at the quilt.

"Dymov!" she called aloud, "Dymov!" She wanted to explain to him that it had been a mistake, that all was not lost, that life might still be beautiful and happy, that he was an extraordinary, rare, great man, and that she would all her life worship him and bow down in homage and holy awe before him. . . .

"Dymov!" she called him, patting him on the shoulder, unable to believe that he would never wake again. "Dymov! Dymov!"

In the drawing-room Korostelev was saying to the housemaid:

"Why keep asking? Go to the church beadle and enquire where they live. They'll wash the body and lay it out, and do everything that is necessary."

A DREARY STORY

FROM THE NOTEBOOK OF AN OLD MAN

I

THERE is in Russia an emeritus Professor Nikolay Stepanovitch, a chevalier and privy councillor; he has so many Russian and foreign decorations that when he has occasion to put them on the students nickname him "The Ikonstand." His acquaintances are of the most aristocratic; for the last twenty-five or thirty years, at any rate, there has not been one single distinguished man of learning in Russia with whom he has not been intimately acquainted. There is no one for him to make friends with nowadays; but if we turn to the past, the long list of his famous friends winds up with such names as Pirogov, Kavelin, and the poet Nekrasov, all of whom bestowed upon him a warm and sincere affection. He is a member of all the Russian and of three foreign universities. And so on, and so on. All that and a great deal more that might be said makes up what is called my "name."

That is my name as known to the public. In Russia it is known to every educated man, and abroad it is mentioned in the lecture-room with the addition "honoured and distinguished." It is one of those fortunate names to abuse which or to take which in vain, in public or in print, is considered a sign of bad taste. And that is as it should be. You see, my name is closely associated with the conception of a highly distinguished man of great gifts and unquestionable usefulness. I have the industry and power of endurance of a camel, and that is important, and I have talent, which is even more important. Moreover, while I am on this subject, I am a well-educated, modest, and honest fellow. I have never poked my nose into literature or politics; I have never sought popularity in polemics with the ignorant; I have never made speeches either at public dinners or at the funerals of my friends. . . . In fact, there is no slur on my learned name, and there is no complaint one can make against it. It is fortunate.

The bearer of that name, that is I, see myself as a man of sixty-two, with a bald head, with false teeth, and with an incurable tic douloureux. I am myself as dingy and unsightly as my name is brilliant and splendid. My head and my hands tremble with weakness; my neck, as Turgenev says of one of his heroines, is like the handle of a double bass; my chest is hollow; my shoulders narrow; when I talk or lecture, my mouth turns down at one corner; when I smile, my whole face is covered with aged-looking, deathly wrinkles. There is nothing impressive about my pitiful figure; only, perhaps, when I have an attack of tic douloureux my face wears a peculiar expression, the sight of which must have roused in every one the grim and impressive thought, "Evidently that man will soon die."

I still, as in the past, lecture fairly well; I can still, as in the past, hold the attention of my listeners for a couple of hours. My fervour, the literary skill of my exposition, and my humour, almost efface the defects of my voice, though it is harsh, dry, and monotonous as a praying beggar's. I write poorly. That bit of my brain which presides over the faculty of authorship refuses to work. My memory has grown weak; there is a lack of sequence in my ideas, and when I put them on paper it always seems to me that I have lost the instinct for their organic connection; my construction is monotonous; my language is poor and timid. Often I write what I do not mean; I have forgotten the beginning when I am writing the end. Often I forget ordinary words, and I always have to waste a great deal of energy in avoiding superfluous phrases and unnecessary parentheses in my letters, both unmistakable proofs of a decline in mental activity. And it is noteworthy that the simpler the letter the more painful the effort to write it. At a scientific article I feel far more intelligent and at ease than at a letter of congratulation or a minute of proceedings. Another point: I find it easier to write German or English than to write Russian.

As regards my present manner of life, I must give a foremost place to the insomnia from which I have suffered of late. If I were asked what constituted the chief and fundamental feature of my existence now, I should answer, Insomnia. As in the past, from habit I undress and go to bed exactly at midnight. I fall asleep quickly, but before two o'clock I wake up and feel as though I had not slept at all. Sometimes I get out of bed and light a lamp. For an hour or two I walk up and down the room looking at the familiar photographs and pictures. When I am weary of walking about, I sit down to my table. I sit motionless, thinking of nothing, conscious of no inclination; if a book is lying before me, I mechanically move it closer and read it without any interest - in that way not long ago I mechanically read through in one night a whole novel, with the strange title "The Song the Lark was Singing"; or to occupy my attention I force myself to count to a thousand; or I imagine the face of one of my colleagues and begin trying to remember in what year and under what circumstances he entered the service. I like listening to sounds. Two rooms away from me my daughter Liza says something rapidly in her sleep, or my wife crosses the drawing-room with a candle and invariably drops the matchbox; or a warped cupboard creaks; or the burner of the lamp suddenly begins to hum - and all these sounds, for some reason, excite me.

To lie awake at night means to be at every moment conscious of being abnormal, and so I look forward with impatience to the morning and the day when I have a right to be awake. Many wearisome hours pass before the cock crows in the yard. He is my first bringer of good tidings. As soon as he crows I know that within an hour the porter will wake up below, and, coughing angrily, will go upstairs to fetch something. And then a pale light will begin gradually glimmering at the windows, voices will sound in the street. . . .

The day begins for me with the entrance of my wife. She comes in to me in her petticoat, before she has done her hair, but after she has washed, smelling of flower-scented eau-de-Cologne, looking as though she had come in by chance. Every time she says exactly the same thing: "Excuse me, I have just come in for a minute. . . . Have you had a bad night again?"

Then she puts out the lamp, sits down near the table, and begins talking. I am no prophet, but I know what she will talk about. Every morning it is exactly the same thing. Usually, after anxious inquiries concerning my health, she suddenly mentions our son who is an officer serving at Warsaw. After the twentieth of each month we send him fifty roubles, and that serves as the chief topic of our conversation.

"Of course it is difficult for us," my wife would sigh, "but until he is completely on his own feet it is our duty to help him. The boy is among strangers, his pay is small. . . . However, if you like, next month we won't send him fifty, but forty. What do you think?"

Daily experience might have taught my wife that constantly talking of our expenses does not reduce them, but my wife refuses to learn by experience, and regularly every morning discusses our officer son, and tells me that bread, thank God, is cheaper, while sugar is a halfpenny dearer - with a tone and an air as though she were communicating interesting news.

I listen, mechanically assent, and probably because I have had a bad night, strange and inappropriate thoughts intrude themselves upon me. I gaze at my wife and wonder like a child. I ask myself in perplexity, is it possible that this old, very stout, ungainly woman, with her dull expression of petty anxiety and alarm about daily bread, with eyes dimmed by continual brooding over debts and money difficulties, who can talk of nothing but expenses and who smiles at nothing but things getting cheaper - is it possible that this woman is no other than the slender Varya whom I fell in love with so passionately for her fine, clear intelligence, for her pure soul, her beauty, and, as Othello his Desdemona, for her "sympathy" for my studies? Could that woman be no other than the Varya who had once borne me a son?

I look with strained attention into the face of this flabby, spiritless, clumsy old woman, seeking in her my Varya, but of her past self nothing is left but her anxiety over my health and her manner of calling my salary "our salary," and my cap "our cap." It is painful for me to look at her, and, to give her what little comfort I can, I let her say what she likes, and say nothing even when she passes unjust criticisms on other people or pitches into me for not having a private practice or not publishing text-books.

Our conversation always ends in the same way. My wife suddenly remembers with dismay that I have not had my tea.

"What am I thinking about, sitting here?" she says, getting up. "The samovar has been on the table ever so long, and here I stay gossiping. My goodness! how forgetful I am growing!"

She goes out quickly, and stops in the doorway to say:

"We owe Yegor five months' wages. Did you know it? You mustn't let the servants' wages run on; how many times I have said it! It's much easier to pay ten roubles a month than fifty roubles every five months!"

As she goes out, she stops to say:

"The person I am sorriest for is our Liza. The girl studies at the Conservatoire, always mixes with people of good position, and goodness knows how she is dressed. Her fur coat is in such a state she is ashamed to show herself in the street. If she were somebody else's daughter it wouldn't matter, but of course every one knows that her father is a distinguished professor,

Anton Chekhov

a privy councillor."

And having reproached me with my rank and reputation, she goes away at last. That is how my day begins. It does not improve as it goes on.

As I am drinking my tea, my Liza comes in wearing her fur coat and her cap, with her music in her hand, already quite ready to go to the Conservatoire. She is two-and-twenty. She looks younger, is pretty, and rather like my wife in her young days. She kisses me tenderly on my forehead and on my hand, and says:

"Good-morning, papa; are you quite well?"

As a child she was very fond of ice-cream, and I used often to take her to a confectioner's. Ice-cream was for her the type of everything delightful. If she wanted to praise me she would say: "You are as nice as cream, papa." We used to call one of her little fingers "pistachio ice," the next, "cream ice," the third "raspberry," and so on. Usually when she came in to say good-morning to me I used to sit her on my knee, kiss her little fingers, and say:

"Creamy ice . . . pistachio . . . lemon. . . ."

And now, from old habit, I kiss Liza's fingers and mutter: "Pistachio . . . cream . . . lemon. . ." but the effect is utterly different. I am cold as ice and I am ashamed. When my daughter comes in to me and touches my forehead with her lips I start as though a bee had stung me on the head, give a forced smile, and turn my face away. Ever since I have been suffering from sleeplessness, a question sticks in my brain like a nail. My daughter often sees me, an old man and a distinguished man, blush painfully at being in debt to my footman; she sees how often anxiety over petty debts forces me to lay aside my work and to walk u p and down the room for hours together, thinking; but why is it she never comes to me in secret to whisper in my ear: "Father, here is my watch, here are my bracelets, my earrings, my dresses. . . . Pawn them all; you want money . . ."? How is it that, seeing how her mother and I are placed in a false position and do our utmost to hide our poverty from people, she does not give up her expensive pleasure of music lessons? I would not accept her watch nor her bracelets, nor the sacrifice of her lessons - God forbid! That isn't what I want.

I think at the same time of my son, the officer at Warsaw. He is a clever, honest, and sober fellow. But that is not enough for me. I think if I had an old father, and if I knew there were moments when he was put to shame by his poverty, I should give up my officer's commission to somebody else, and should go out to earn my living as a workman. Such thoughts about my children poison me. What is the use of them? It is only a narrow-minded or embittered man who can harbour evil thoughts about ordinary people because they are not heroes. But enough of that!

At a quarter to ten I have to go and give a lecture to my dear boys. I dress and walk along the road which I have known for thirty years, and which has its history for me. Here is the big grey house with the chemist's shop; at this point there used to stand a little house, and in it was a beershop; in that beershop I thought out my thesis and wrote my first love-letter to Varya. I wrote it in pencil, on a page headed "Historia morbi." Here there is a grocer's shop; at one time it was kept by a little Jew, who sold me cigarettes on credit; then by a fat peasant woman, who liked the students because "every one of them has a mother"; now there is a red-haired shopkeeper sitting in it, a very stolid man who drinks tea from a copper teapot. And here are the gloomy gates of the University, which have long needed doing up; I see the bored porter in his sheep-skin, the broom, the drifts of snow. . . . On a boy coming fresh from the provinces and imagining that the temple of science must really be a temple, such gates cannot make a healthy impression. Altogether the dilapidated condition of the University buildings, the gloominess of the corridors, the griminess of the walls, the lack of light, the dejected aspect of the steps, the hat-stands and the benches, take a prominent position among predisposing causes in the history of Russian pessimism. . . . Here is our garden . . . I fancy it has grown neither better nor worse since I was a student. I don't like it. It would be far more sensible if there were tall pines and fine oaks growing here instead of sickly-looking lime-trees, yellow acacias, and skimpy pollard lilacs. The student whose state of mind is in the majority of cases created by his surroundings, ought in the place where he is studying to see facing him at every turn nothing but what is lofty, strong and elegant. . . . God preserve him from gaunt trees, broken windows, grey walls, and doors covered with torn American leather!

When I go to my own entrance the door is flung wide open, and I am met by my colleague, contemporary, and namesake, the porter Nikolay. As he lets me in he clears his throat and says:

"A frost, your Excellency!"

Or, if my great-coat is wet:

"Rain, your Excellency!"

Then he runs on ahead of me and opens all the doors on my way. In my study he carefully takes off my fur coat, and while doing so manages to tell me some bit of University news. Thanks to the close intimacy existing between all the University porters and beadles, he knows everything that goes on in the four faculties, in the office, in the rector's private room, in the library. What does he not know? When in an evil day a rector or dean, for instance, retires, I hear him in conversation with the young porters mention the candidates for the post, explain that such a one would not be confirmed by the minister, that another would himself refuse to accept it, then drop into fantastic details concerning mysterious papers received in the office, secret conversations alleged to have taken place between the minister and the trustee, and so on. With the exception of these details, he almost always turns out to be right. His estimates of the candidates, though original, are very correct, too. If one wants to know in what year some one read his thesis, entered the service, retired, or died, then summon to your assistance the vast memory of that soldier, and he will not only tell you the year, the month and the day, but will furnish you also with the details that accompanied this or that event. Only one who loves can remember like that.

He is the guardian of the University traditions. From the porters who were his predecessors he has inherited many legends of University life, has added to that wealth much of his own gained during his time of service, and if you care to hear he will tell you many long and intimate stories. He can tell one about extraordinary sages who knew *everything*, about remarkable students who did not sleep for weeks, about numerous martyrs and victims of science; with him good triumphs over evil, the weak always vanquishes the strong, the wise man the fool, the humble the proud, the young the old. There is no need to take all these fables and legends for sterling coin; but filter them, and you will have left what is wanted: our fine traditions and the names of real heroes, recognized as such by all.

In our society the knowledge of the learned world consists of anecdotes of the extraordinary absentmindedness of certain old professors, and two or three witticisms variously ascribed to Gruber, to me, and to Babukin. For the educated public that is not much. If it loved science, learned men, and students, as Nikolay does, its literature would long ago have contained whole epics, records of sayings and doings such as, unfortunately, it cannot boast of now.

After telling me a piece of news, Nikolay assumes a severe expression, and conversation about business begins. If any outsider could at such times overhear Nikolay's free use of our terminology, he might perhaps imagine that he was a learned man disguised as a soldier. And, by the way, the rumours of the erudition of the University porters are greatly exaggerated. It is true that Nikolay knows more than a hundred Latin words, knows how to put the skeleton together, sometimes prepares the apparatus and amuses the students by some long, learned quotation, but the by no means complicated theory of the circulation of the blood, for instance, is as much a mystery to him now as it was twenty years ago.

At the table in my study, bending low over some book or preparation, sits Pyotr Ignatyevitch, my demonstrator, a modest and industrious but by no means clever man of five-and-thirty, already bald and corpulent; he works from morning to night, reads a lot, remembers well everything he has read - and in that way he is not a man, but pure gold; in all else he is a carthorse or, in other words, a learned dullard. The carthorse characteristics that show his lack of talent are these: his outlook is narrow and sharply limited by his specialty; outside his special branch he is simple as a child.

"Fancy! what a misfortune! They say Skobelev is dead."

Nikolay crosses himself, but Pyotr Ignatyevitch turns to me and asks:

"What Skobelev is that?"

Another time - somewhat earlier - I told him that Professor Perov was dead. Good Pyotr Ignatyevitch asked:

"What did he lecture on?"

I believe if Patti had sung in his very ear, if a horde of Chinese had invaded Russia, if there had been an earthquake, he would not have stirred a limb, but screwing up his eye, would have gone on calmly looking through his microscope. What is he to Hecuba or Hecuba to him, in fact? I would give a good deal to see how this dry stick sleeps with his wife at night.

Another characteristic is his fanatical faith in the infallibility of science, and, above all, of everything written by the Germans. He believes in himself, in his preparations; knows the object of life, and knows nothing of the doubts and disappointments that turn the hair o f talent grey. He has a slavish reverence for authorities and a complete lack of any desire for independent thought. To change his convictions is difficult, to argue with him impossible. How is one to argue with a man who is firmly persuaded that medicine is the finest of sciences, that doctors are the best of men, and that the traditions of the medical profession are superior to those of any other? Of the evil past of medicine only one tradition has been preserved - the white tie still worn by doctors; for a learned - in fact, for any educated man the only traditions that can exist are those of the University as a whole, with no distinction between medicine, law, etc. But it would be hard for Pyotr Ignatyevitch to accept these facts, and he is ready to argue with you till the day of judgment.

I have a clear picture in my mind of his future. In the course of his life he will prepare many hundreds of chemicals of exceptional purity; he will write a number of dry and very accurate memoranda, will make some dozen conscientious translations, but he won't do anything striking. To do that one must have imagination, inventiveness, the gift of insight, and Pyotr Ignatyevitch has nothing of the kind. In short, he is not a master in science, but a journeyman.

Pyotr Ignatyevitch, Nikolay, and I, talk in subdued tones. We are not quite ourselves. There is always a peculiar feeling when one hears through the doors a murmur as of the sea from the lecture-theatre. In the course of thirty years I have not grown accustomed to this feeling, and I experience it every morning. I nervously button up my coat, ask Nikolay unnecessary questions, lose my temper. . . . It is just as though I were frightened; it is not timidity, though, but something different which I can neither describe nor find a name for.

Quite unnecessarily, I look at my watch and say: "Well, it's time to go in."

And we march into the room in the following order: foremost goes Nikolay, with the chemicals and apparatus or with a chart; after him I come; and then the carthorse follows humbly, with hanging head; or, when necessary, a dead body is carried in first on a stretcher, followed by Nikolay, and so on. On my entrance the students all stand up, then they sit down, and the sound as of the sea is suddenly hushed. Stillness reigns.

I know what I am going to lecture about, but I don't know how I am going to lecture, where I am going to begin or with what I am going to end. I haven't a single sentence ready in my head. But I have only to look round the lecture-hall (it is built in the form of an amphitheatre) and utter the stereotyped phrase, "Last lecture we stopped at . . ." when sentences spring up from my soul in a long string, and I am carried away by my own eloquence. I speak with irresistible rapidity and passion, and it seems as though there were no force which could check the flow of my words. To lecture well - that is, with profit to the listeners and without boring them - one must have, besides talent, experience and a special knack; one must possess a clear conception of one's own powers, of the audience to which one is lecturing, and of the subject of one's lecture. Moreover, one must be a man who knows what he is doing; one must keep a sharp lookout, and not for one second lose sight of what lies before one.

A good conductor, interpreting the thought of the composer, does twenty things at once: reads the score, waves his baton, watches the singer, makes a motion sideways, first to the drum then to the wind-instruments, and so on. I do just the same when I lecture. Before me a hundred and fifty faces, all unlike one another; three hundred eyes all looking straight into my face. My object is to dominate this many-headed monster. If every moment as I lecture I have a clear vision of the degree of its attention and its power of comprehension, it is in my power. The other foe I have to overcome is in myself. It is the infinite variety of forms, phenomena, laws, and the multitude of ideas of my own and other people's conditioned by them. Every moment I must have the skill to snatch out of that vast mass of material what is most important and necessary, and, as rapidly as my words flow, clothe my thought in a form in which it can be grasped by the monster's intelligence, and may arouse its attention, and at the same time one must keep a sharp lookout that one's thoughts are conveyed, not just as they come, but in a certain order, essential for the correct composition of the picture I wish to sketch. Further, I endeavour to make my diction literary, my definitions brief and precise, my wording, as far as possible, simple and eloquent. Every minute I have to pull myself up and remember that I have only an hour and forty minutes at my disposal. In short, one has one's work cut out. At one and the same minute one has to play the part of savant and teacher and orator, and it's a bad thing if the orator gets the upper hand of the savant or of the teacher in one, or *vice versa*.

You lecture for a quarter of an hour, for half an hour, when you notice that the students are beginning to look at the ceiling, at Pyotr Ignatyevitch; one is feeling for his handkerchief, another shifts in his seat, another smiles at his thoughts. . . . That means that their attention is flagging. Something must be done. Taking advantage of the first opportunity, I make some pun. A broad grin comes on to a hundred and fifty faces, the eyes shine brightly, the sound of the sea is audible for a brief moment. . . . I laugh too. Their attention is refreshed, and I can go on.

No kind of sport, no kind of game or diversion, has ever given me such enjoyment as lecturing. Only at lectures have I been able to abandon myself entirely to passion, and have understood that inspiration is not an invention of the poets, but exists in real life, and I imagine Hercules after the most piquant of his exploits felt just such voluptuous exhaustion as I experience after every lecture.

That was in old times. Now at lectures I feel nothing but torture. Before half an hour is over I am conscious of an overwhelming weakness in my legs and my shoulders. I sit down in my chair, but I am not accustomed to lecture sitting down; a minute later I get up and go on standing, then sit down again. There is a dryness in my mouth, my voice grows husky, my head begins to go round. . . . To conceal my condition from my audience I continually drink water, cough, often blow my nose as though I were hindered by a cold, make puns inappropriately, and in the end break off earlier than I ought to. But above all I am ashamed.

My conscience and my intelligence tell me that the very best thing I could do now would be to deliver a farewell lecture to the boys, to say my last word to them, to bless them, and give up my post to a man younger and stronger than me. But, God, be my judge, I have not manly courage enough to act according to my conscience.

Unfortunately, I am not a philosopher and not a theologian. I know perfectly well that I cannot live more than another six months; it might be supposed that I ought now to be chiefly concerned with the question of the shadowy life beyond the grave, and the visions that will visit my slumbers in the tomb. But for some reason my soul refuses to recognize these questions, though my mind is fully alive to their importance. Just as twenty, thirty years ago, so now, on the threshold of death, I am interested in nothing but science. As I yield up my last breath I shall still believe that science is the most important, the most splendid, the most essential thing in the life of man; that it always has been and will be the highest manifestation of love, and that only by means of it will man conquer himself and nature. This faith is perhaps naive and may rest on false assumptions, but it is not my fault that I believe that and nothing else; I cannot overcome in myself this belief.

But that is not the point. I only ask people to be indulgent to my weakness, and to realize that to tear from the lecture-theatre and his pupils a man who is more interested in the history of the development of the bone medulla than in the final object of creation would be equivalent to taking him and nailing him up in his coffin without waiting for him to be dead.

Sleeplessness and the consequent strain of combating increasing weakness leads to something strange in me.

In the middle of my lecture tears suddenly rise in my throat, my eyes begin to smart, and I feel a passionate, hysterical desire to stretch out my hands before me and break into loud lamentation. I want to cry out in a loud voice that I, a famous man, have been sentenced by fate to the death penalty, that within some six months another man will be in control here in the lecture-theatre. I want to shriek that I am poisoned; new ideas such as I have not known before have poisoned the last days of my life, and are still stinging my brain like mosquitoes. And at that moment my position seems to me so awful that I want all my listeners to be horrified, to leap up from their seats and to rush in panic terror, with desperate screams, to the exit.

It is not easy to get through such moments.

II

After my lecture I sit at home and work. I read journals
and monographs, or prepare my next lecture; sometimes I write something. I work with interruptions, as I
have from time to time to see visitors.

There is a ring at the bell. It is a colleague come to
discuss some business matter with me. He comes in to
me with his hat and his stick, and, holding out both
these objects to me, says:

"Only for a minute! Only for a minute! Sit down,
collega! Only a couple of words."

To begin with, we both try to show each other that we
are extraordinarily polite and highly delighted to see
each other. I make him sit down in an easy-chair, and
he makes me sit down; as we do so, we cautiously pat
each other on the back, touch each other's buttons, and
it looks as though we were feeling each other and
afraid of scorching our fingers. Both of us laugh,
though we say nothing amusing. When we are seated
we bow our heads towards each other and begin
talking in subdued voices. However affectionately
disposed we may be to one another, we cannot help
adorning our conversation with all sorts of Chinese
mannerisms, such as "As you so justly observed," or "I
have already had the honour to inform you"; we cannot
help laughing if one of us makes a joke, however
unsuccessfully. When we have finished with business
my colleague gets up impulsively and, waving his hat
in the direction of my work, begins to say good-bye.
Again we paw one another and laugh. I see him into

the hall; when I assist my colleague to put on his coat, while he does all he can to decline this high honour. Then when Yegor opens the door my colleague declares that I shall catch cold, while I make a show of being ready to go even into the street with him. And when at last I go back into my study my face still goes on smiling, I suppose from inertia.

A little later another ring at the bell. Somebody comes into the hall, and is a long time coughing and taking off his things. Yegor announces a student. I tell him to ask him in. A minute later a young man of agreeable appearance comes in. For the last year he and I have been on strained relations; he answers me disgracefully at the examinations, and I mark him one. Every year I have some seven such hopefuls whom, to express it in the students' slang, I "chivy" or "floor." Those of them who fail in their examination through incapacity or illness usually bear their cross patiently and do not haggle with me; those who come to the house and haggle with me are always youths of sanguine temperament, broad natures, whose failure at examinations spoils their appetites and hinders them from visiting the opera with their usual regularity. I let the first class off easily, but the second I chivy through a whole year.

"Sit down," I say to my visitor; "what have you to tell me?"

"Excuse me, professor, for troubling you," he begins, hesitating, and not looking me in the face. "I would not have ventured to trouble you if it had not been . . . I have been up for your examination five times, and have been ploughed. . . . I beg you, be so good as to mark me for a pass, because . . ."

The argument which all the sluggards bring forward on their own behalf is always the same; they have passed well in all their subjects and have only come to grief in mine, and that is the more surprising because they have always been particularly interested in my subject and knew it so well; their failure has always been entirely owing to some incomprehensible misunderstanding.

"Excuse me, my friend," I say to the visitor; "I cannot mark you for a pass. Go and read up the lectures and come to me again. Then we shall see."

A pause. I feel an impulse to torment the student a little for liking beer and the opera better than science, and I say, with a sigh:

"To my mind, the best thing you can do now is to give up medicine altogether. If, with your abilities, you cannot succeed in passing the examination, it's evident that you have neither the desire nor the vocation for a doctor's calling."

The sanguine youth's face lengthens.

"Excuse me, professor," he laughs, "but that would be odd of me, to say the least of it. After studying for five years, all at once to give it up."

"Oh, well! Better to have lost your five years than have to spend the rest of your life in doing work you do not care for."

But at once I feel sorry for him, and I hasten to add:

"However, as you think best. And so read a little more and come again."

"When?" the idle youth asks in a hollow voice.

"When you like. Tomorrow if you like."

And in his good-natured eyes I read:

"I can come all right, but of course you will plough me again, you beast!"

"Of course," I say, "you won't know more science for going in for my examination another fifteen times, but it is training your character, and you must be thankful for that."

Silence follows. I get up and wait for my visitor to go, but he stands and looks towards the window, fingers his beard, and thinks. It grows boring.

The sanguine youth's voice is pleasant and mellow, his eyes are clever and ironical, his face is genial, though a little bloated from frequent indulgence in beer and overlong lying on the sofa; he looks as though he could tell me a lot of interesting things about the opera, about his affairs of the heart, and about comrades whom he likes. Unluckily, it is not the thing to discuss these subjects, or else I should have been glad to listen to him.

"Professor, I give you my word of honour that if you mark me for a pass I . . . I'll . . ."

As soon as we reach the "word of honour" I wave my hands and sit down to the table. The student ponders a minute longer, and says dejectedly:

"In that case, good-bye. . . I beg your pardon."

"Good-bye, my friend. Good luck to you."

He goes irresolutely into the hall, slowly puts on his outdoor things, and, going out into the street, probably ponders for some time longer; unable to think of anything, except "old devil," inwardly addressed to me, he goes into a wretched restaurant to dine and drink beer, and then home to bed. "Peace be to thy ashes, honest toiler."

A third ring at the bell. A young doctor, in a pair of new black trousers, gold spectacles, and of course a white tie, walks in. He introduces himself. I beg him to be seated, and ask what I can do for him. Not without emotion, the young devotee of science begins telling me that he has passed his examination as a doctor of medicine, and that he has now only to write his dissertation. He would like to work with me under my guidance, and he would be greatly obliged to me if I would give him a subject for his dissertation.

"Very glad to be of use to you, colleague," I say, "but just let us come to an understanding as to the meaning of a dissertation. That word is taken to mean a composition which is a product of independent creative effort. Is that not so? A work written on another man's subject and under another man's guidance is called something different. . . ."

The doctor says nothing. I fly into a rage and jump up from my seat.

"Why is it you all come to me?" I cry angrily. "Do I keep a shop? I don't deal in subjects. For the tho usand and oneth time I ask you all to leave me in peace! Excuse my brutality, but I am quite sick of it!"

The doctor remains silent, but a faint flush is apparent on his cheek-bones. His face expresses a profound reverence for my fame and my learning, but from his eyes I can see he feels a contempt for my voice, my pitiful figure, and my nervous gesticulation. I impress him in my anger as a queer fish.

"I don't keep a shop," I go on angrily. "And it is a strange thing! Why don't you want to be independent? Why have you such a distaste for independence?"

I say a great deal, but he still remains silent. By degrees I calm down, and of course give in. The doctor gets a subject from me for his theme not worth a halfpenny, writes under my supervision a dissertation of no use to any one, with dignity defends it in a dreary discussion, and receives a degree of no use to him.

The rings at the bell may follow one another endlessly, but I will confine my description here to four of them. The bell rings for the fourth time, and I hear familiar footsteps, the rustle of a dress, a dear voice. . . .

Eighteen years ago a colleague of mine, an oculist, died leaving a little daughter Katya, a child of seven, and sixty thousand roubles. In his will he made me the child's guardian. Till she was ten years old Katya lived with us as one of the family, then she was sent to a boarding-school, and only spent the summer holidays with us. I never had time to look after her education. I only superintended it at leisure moments, and so I can say very little about her childhood.

The first thing I remember, and like so much in remembrance, is the extraordinary trustfulness with which she came into our house and let herself be treated by the doctors, a trustfulness which was always shining in her little face. She would sit somewhere out of the way, with her face tied up, invariably watching something with attention; whether she watched me writing or turning over the pages of a book, or watched my wife bustling about, or the cook scrubbing a potato in the kitchen, or the dog playing, her eyes invariably expressed the same thought - that is, "Everything that is done in this world is nice and sensible." She was curious, and very fond of talking to me. Sometimes she would sit at the table opposite me, watching my movements and asking questions. It interested her to know what I was reading, what I did at the University, whether I was not afraid of the dead bodies, what I did with my salary.

"Do the students fight at the University?" she would ask.

"They do, dear."

"And do you make them go down on their knees?"

"Yes, I do."

And she thought it funny that the students fought and I made them go down on their knees, and she laughed. She was a gentle, patient, good child. It happened not infrequently that I saw something taken away from her, saw her punished without reason, or her curiosity repressed; at such times a look of sadness was mixed with the invariable expression of trustfulness on her face - that was all. I did not know how to take her part; only when I saw her sad I had an inclination to draw her to me and to commiserate her like some old nurse: "My poor little orphan one!"

I remember, too, that she was fond of fine clothes and of sprinkling herself with scent. In that respect she was like me. I, too, am fond of pretty clothes and nice scent.

I regret that I had not time nor inclination to watch over the rise and development of the passion which took complete possession of Katya when she was fourteen or fifteen. I mean her passionate love for the theatre. When she used to come from boarding-school and stay with us for the summer holidays, she talked of nothing with such pleasure and such warmth as of plays and actors. She bored us with her continual talk of the theatre. My wife and children would not listen to her. I was the only one who had not the courage to refuse to attend to her. When she had a longing to share her transports, she used to come into my study and say in an imploring tone:

"Nikolay Stepanovitch, do let me talk to you about the theatre!"

I pointed to the clock, and said:

"I'll give you half an hour - begin."

Later on she used to bring with her dozens of portraits of actors and actresses which she worshipped; then she attempted several times to take part in private theatricals, and the upshot of it all was that when she left school she came to me and announced that she was born to be an actress.

I had never shared Katya's inclinations for the theatre. To my mind, if a play is good there is no need to trouble the actors in order that it may make the right impression; it is enough to read it. If the play is poor, no acting will make it good.

In my youth I often visited the theatre, and now my family takes a box twice a year and carries me off for a little distraction. Of course, that is not enough to give me the right to judge of the theatre. In my opinion the theatre has become no better than it was thirty or forty years ago. Just as in the past, I can never find a glass of clean water in the corridors or foyers of the theatre. Just as in the past, the attendants fine me twenty kopecks for my fur coat, though there is nothing reprehensible in wearing a warm coat in winter. As in the past, for no sort of reason, music is played in the intervals, which adds something new and uncalled-for to the impression made by the play. As in the past, men go in the intervals and drink spirits in the buffet. If no progress can be seen in trifles, I should look for it in vain in what is more important. When an actor wrapped from head to foot in stage traditions and conventions tries to recite a simple ordinary speech, "To be or not to be," not simply, but invariably with the accompaniment of hissing and convulsive movements all over his body, or when he tries to convince me at all costs that Tchatsky, who talks so much with fools and is so fond of folly, is a very clever man, and that "Woe from Wit" is not a dull play, the stage gives me the same feeling of conventionality which bored me so much forty years ago when I was regaled with the classical howling and beating on the breast. And every time I come out of the theatre more conservative than I go in.

The sentimental and confiding public may be persuaded that the stage, even in its present form, is a school; but any one who is familiar with a school in its true sense will not be caught with that bait. I cannot say what will happen in fifty or a hundred years, but in its actual condition the theatre can serve only as an entertainment. But this entertainment is too costly to be frequently enjoyed. It robs the state of thousands of healthy and talented young men and women, who, if they had not devoted themselves to the theatre, might have been good doctors, farmers, schoolmistresses, officers; it robs the public of the evening hours - the best time for intellectual work and social intercourse. I say nothing of the waste of money and the moral damage to the spectator when he sees murder, fornication, or false witness unsuitably treated on the stage.

Katya was of an entirely different opinion. She assured me that the theatre, even in its present condition, was superior to the lecture-hall, to books, or to anything in the world. The stage was a power that united in itself all the arts, and actors were missionaries. No art nor science was capable of producing so strong and so certain an effect on the soul of man as the stage, and it was with good reason that an actor of medium quality enjoys greater popularity than the greatest savant or artist. And no sort of public service could provide such enjoyment and gratification as the theatre.

And one fine day Katya joined a troupe of actors, and went off, I believe to Ufa, taking away with her a good supply of money, a store of rainbow hopes, and the most aristocratic views of her work.

Her first letters on the journey were marvellous. I read them, and was simply amazed that those small sheets of paper could contain so much youth, purity of spirit, holy innocence, and at the same time subtle and apt judgments which would have done credit to a fine mas culine intellect. It was more like a rapturous paean of praise she sent me than a mere description of the Volga, the country, the towns she visited, her companions, her failures and successes; every sentence was fragrant with that confiding trustfulness I was accustomed to read in her face - and at the same time there were a great many grammatical mistakes, and there was scarcely any punctuation at all.

Before six months had passed I received a highly poetical and enthusiastic letter beginning with the words, "I have come to love . . ." This letter was accompanied by a photograph representing a young man with a shaven face, a wide-brimmed hat, and a plaid flung over his shoulder. The letters that followed were as splendid as before, but now commas and stops made their appearance in them, the grammatical mistakes disappeared, and there was a distinctly masculine flavour about them. Katya began writing to me how splendid it would be to build a great theatre somewhere on the Volga, on a cooperative system, and to attract to the enterprise the rich merchants and the steamer owners; there would be a great deal of money in it; there would be vast audiences; the actors would play on co-operative terms. . . .Possibly all this was really excellent, but it seemed to me that such schemes could only originate from a man's mind.

However that may have been, for a year and a half everything seemed to go well: Katya was in love, believed in her work, and was happy; but then I began to notice in her letters unmistakable signs of falling off. It began with Katya's complaining of her companions - this was the first and most ominous symptom; if a young scientific or literary man begins his career with bitter complaints of scientific and literary men, it is a sure sign that he is worn out and not fit for his work. Katya wrote to me that her companions did not attend the rehearsals and never knew their parts; that one could see in every one of them an utter disrespect for the public in the production of absurd plays, and in their behaviour on the stage; that for the benefit of the Actors' Fund, which they only talked about, actresses of the serious drama demeaned themselves by singing chansonettes, while tragic actors sang comic songs making fun of deceived husbands and the pregnant condition of unfaithful wives, and so on. In fact, it was amazing that all this had not yet ruined the provincial stage, and that it could still maintain itself on such a rotten and unsubstantial footing.

In answer I wrote Katya a long and, I must confess, a very boring letter. Among other things, I wrote to her:

"I have more than once happened to converse with old actors, very worthy men, who showed a friendly disposition towards me; from my conversations with them I could understand that their work was controlled not so much by their own intelligence and free choice as by fashion and the mood of the public. The best of them had had to play in their day in tragedy, in operetta, in Parisian farces, and in extravaganzas, and they always seemed equally sure that they were on the right path and that they were of use. So, as you see, the cause of the evil must be sought, not in the actors, but, more deeply, in the art itself and in the attitude of the whole of society to it."

This letter of mine only irritated Katya. She answered me:

Anton Chekhov

"You and I are singing parts out of different operas. I wrote to you, not of the worthy men who showed a friendly disposition to you, but of a band of knaves who have nothing worthy about them. They are a horde of savages who have got on the stage simply because no one would have taken them elsewhere, and who call themselves artists simply because they are impudent. There are numbers of dull-witted creatures, drunkards, intriguing schemers and slanderers, but there is not one person of talent among them. I cannot tell you how bitter it is to me that the art I love has fallen into the hands of people I detest; how bitter it is that the best men look on at evil from afar, not caring to come closer, and, instead of intervening, write ponderous commonplaces and utterly useless sermons. . . ." And so on, all in the same style.

A little time passed, and I got this letter: "I have been brutally deceived. I cannot go on living. Dispose of my money as you think best. I loved you as my father and my only friend. Good-bye."

It turned out that *he*, too, belonged to the "horde of savages." Later on, from certain hints, I gathered that there had been an attempt at suicide. I believe Katya tried to poison herself. I imagine that she must have been seriously ill afterwards, as the next letter I got was from Yalta, where she had most probably been sent by the doctors. Her last letter contained a request to send her a thousand roubles to Yalta as quickly as possible, and ended with these words:

"Excuse the gloominess of this letter; yesterday I buried my child." After spending about a year in the Crimea, she returned home.

She had been about four years on her travels, and during those four years, I must confess, I had played a rather strange and unenviable part in regard to her. When in earlier days she had told me she was going on the stage, and then wrote to me of her love; when she was periodically overcome by extravagance, and I continually had to send her first one and then two thousand roubles; when she wrote to me of her intention of suicide, and then of the death of her baby, every time I lost my head, and all my sympathy for her sufferings found no expression except that, after prolonged reflection, I wrote long, boring letters which I might just as well not have written. And yet I took a father's place with her and loved her like a daughter!

Now Katya is living less than half a mile off. She has taken a flat of five rooms, and has installed herself fairly comfortably and in the taste of the day. If any one were to undertake to describe her surroundings, the most characteristic note in the picture would be indolence. For the indolent body there are soft lounges, soft stools; for indolent feet soft rugs; for indolent eyes faded, dingy, or flat colours; for the indolent soul the walls are hung with a number of cheap fans and trivial pictures, in which the originality of the execution is more conspicuous than the subject; and the room contains a multitude of little tables and shelves filled with utterly useless articles of no value, and shapeless rags in place of curtains. . . . All this, together with the dread of bright colours, of symmetry, and of empty space, bears witness not only to spiritual indolence, but also to a corruption of natural taste. For days together Katya lies on the lounge reading, principally novels and stories. She only goes out of the house once a day, in the afternoon, to see me.

I go on working while Katya sits silent not far from me on the sofa, wrapping herself in her shawl, as though she were cold. Either because I find her sympathetic or because I was used to her frequent visits when she was a little girl, her presence does not prevent me from concentrating my attention. From time to time I mechanically ask her some question; she gives very brief replies; or, to rest for a minute, I turn round and watch her as she looks dreamily at some medical journal or review. And at such moments I notice that her face has lost the old look of confiding trustfulness. Her expression now is cold, apathetic, and absent-minded, like that of passengers who had to wait too long for a train. She is dressed, as in old days, simply and beautifully, but carelessly; her dress and her hair show visible traces of the sofas and rocking-chairs in which she spends whole days at a stretch. And she has lost the curiosity she had in old days. She has ceased to ask me questions now, as though she had experienced everything in life and looked for nothing new from it.

Towards four o'clock there begins to be sounds of movement in the hall and in the drawing-room. Liza has come back from the Conservatoire, and has brought some girl-friends in with her. We hear them playing on the piano, trying their voices and laughing; in the dining-room Yegor is laying th e table, with the clatter of crockery.

"Good-bye," said Katya. "I won't go in and see your people today. They must excuse me. I haven't time. Come and see me."

While I am seeing her to the door, she looks me up and down grimly, and says with vexation:

"You are getting thinner and thinner! Why don't you consult a doctor? I'll call at Sergey Fyodorovitch's and ask him to have a look at you."

"There's no need, Katya."

"I can't think where your people's eyes are! They are a nice lot, I must say!"

She puts on her fur coat abruptly, and as she does so two or three hairpins drop unnoticed on the floor from her carelessly arranged hair. She is too lazy and in too great a hurry to do her hair up; she carelessly stuffs the falling curls under her hat, and goes away.

When I go into the dining-room my wife asks me:

"Was Katya with you just now? Why didn't she come in to see us? It's really strange . . . ."

"Mamma," Liza says to her reproachfully, "let her alone, if she doesn't want to. We are not going down on our knees to her."

"It's very neglectful, anyway. To sit for three hours in the study without remembering our existence! But of course she must do as she likes."

Varya and Liza both hate Katya. This hatred is beyond my comprehension, and probably one would have to be a woman in order to understand it. I am ready to stake my life that of the hundred and fifty young men I see every day in the lecture-theatre, and of the hundred elderly ones I meet every week, hardly one could be found capable of understanding their hatred and aversion for Katya's past - that is, for her having been a mother without being a wife, and for her having had an illegitimate child; and at the same time I cannot recall one woman or girl of my acquaintance who would not consciously or unconsciously harbour such feelings. And this is not because woman is purer or more virtuous than man: why, virtue and purity are not very different from vice if they are not free from evil feeling. I attribute this simply to the backwardness of woman. The mournful feeling of compassion and the pang of conscience experienced by a modern man at the sight of suffering is, to my mind, far greater proof of culture and moral elevation than hatred and aversion. Woman is as tearful and as coarse in her feelings now as she was in the Middle Ages, and to my thinking those who advise that she should be educated like a man are quite right.

My wife also dislikes Katya for having been an actress, for ingratitude, for pride, for eccentricity, and for the numerous vices which one woman can always find in another.

Besides my wife and daughter and me, there are dining with us two or three of my daughter's friends and Alexandr Adolfovitch Gnekker, her admirer and suitor. He is a fair-haired young man under thirty, of medium height, very stout and broad-shouldered, with red whiskers near his ears, and little waxed moustaches which make his plump smooth face look like a toy. He is dressed in a very short reefer jacket, a flowered waistcoat, breeches very full at the top and very narrow at the ankle, with a large check pattern on them, and yellow boots without heels. He has prominent eyes like a crab's, his cravat is like a crab's neck, and I even fancy there is a smell of crab-soup about the young man's whole person. He visits us every day, but no one in my family knows anything of his origin nor of the place of his education, nor of his means of livelihood. He neither plays nor sings, but has some connection with music and singing, sells somebody's pianos somewhere, is frequently at the Conservatoire, is acquainted with all the celebrities, and is a steward at the concerts; he criticizes music with great authority, and I have noticed that people are eager to agree with him.

Rich people always have dependents hanging about them; the arts and sciences have the same. I believe there is not an art nor a science in the world free from "foreign bodies" after the style of this Mr. Gnekker. I am not a musician, and possibly I am mistaken in regard to Mr. Gnekker, of whom, indeed, I know very little. But his air of authority and the dignity with which he takes his stand beside the piano when any one is playing or singing strike me as very suspicious.

You may be ever so much of a gentleman and a privy councillor, but if you have a daughter you cannot be secure of immunity from that petty bourgeois atmosphere which is so often brought into your house and into your mood by the attentions of suitors, by matchmaking and marriage. I can never reconcile myself, for instance, to the expression of triumph on my wife's face every time Gnekker is in our company, nor can I reconcile myself to the bottles of Lafitte, port and sherry which are only brought out on his account, that he may see with his own eyes the liberal and luxurious way in which we live. I cannot tolerate the habit of spasmodic laughter Liza has picked up at the Conservatoire, and her way of screwing up her eyes whenever there are men in the room. Above all, I cannot understand why a creature utterly alien to my habits, my studies, my whole manner of life, completely different from the people I like, should come and see me every day, and every day should dine with me. My wife and my servants mysteriously whisper that he is a suitor, but still I don't understand his presence; it rouses in me the same wonder and perplexity as if they were to set a Zulu beside me at the table. And it seems strange to me, too, that my daughter, whom I am used to thinking of as a child, should love that cravat, those eyes, those soft cheeks. . . .

In the old days I used to like my dinner, or at least was indifferent about it; now it excites in me no feeling but weariness and irritation. Ever since I became an "Excellency" and one of the Deans of the Faculty my family has for some reason found it necessary to make a complete change in our menu and dining habits. Instead of the simple dishes to which I was accustomed when I was a student and when I was in practice, now they feed me with a puree with little white things like circles floating about in it, and kidneys stewed in madeira. My rank as a general and my fame have robbed me for ever of cabbage-soup and savoury pies, and goose with apple-sauce, and bream with boiled grain. They have robbed me of our maid-servant Agasha, a chatty and laughter-loving old woman, instead of whom Yegor, a dull-witted and conceited fellow with a white glove on his right hand, waits at dinner. The intervals between the courses are short, but they seem immensely long because there is nothing to occupy them. There is none of the gaiety of the old days, the spontaneous talk, the jokes, the laughter; there is nothing of mutual affection and the joy which used to animate the children, my wife, and me when in old days we met together at meals. For me, the celebrated man of science, dinner was a time of rest and reunion, and for my wife and children a fete - brief indeed, but bright and joyous - in which they knew that for half an hour I belonged, not to science, not to students, but to them alone. Our real exhilaration from one glass of wine is gone for ever, gone is Agasha, gone the bream with boiled grain, gone the uproar that greeted every little startling incident at dinner, such as the cat and dog fighting under the table, or Katya's bandage falling off her face into her soup-plate.

To describe our dinner nowadays is as uninteresting as to eat it. My wife's face wears a look of triumph and affected dignity, and her habitual expression of anxiety. She looks at our plates and says, "I see you don't care for the joint. Tell me; you don't like it, do you?" and I am obliged to answer: "There is no need for you to trouble, my dear; the meat is very nice." And she will say: "You always stand up for me, Nikolay Stepanovitch, and you never tell the truth. Why is Alexandr Adolfovitch eating so little?" And so on in the same style all through dinner. Liza laughs spasmodically and screws up her eyes. I watch them both, and it is only now at dinner that it becomes absolutely evident to me that the inner life of these two has slipped away out of my ken. I have a feeling as though I had once lived at home with a real wife and children and that now I am dining with visitors, in the house of a sham wife who is not the real one, and am looking at a Liza who is not the real Liza. A startling change has taken place in both of them; I have missed the long process by which that change was effected, and it is no wonder that I can make nothing of it. Why did that change take place? I don't know. Perhaps the whole trouble is that God has not given my wife and daughter the same strength of character as me. From childhood I have been accustomed to resisting external influences, and have steeled myself pretty thoroughly. Such catastrophes in life as fame, the rank of a general, the transition from comfort to living beyond our means, acquaintance with celebrities, etc., have scarcely affected me, and I have remained intact and unashamed; but on my wife and Liza, who have not been through the same hardening process and are weak, all this has fallen like an avalanche of snow, overwhelming them. Gnekker and the young ladies talk of fugues, of counterpoint, of singers and pianists, of Bach and Brahms, while my wife, afraid of their suspecting her of ignorance of music, smiles to them sympathetically and mutters: "That's exquisite . . . really! You don't say so! . . . Gnekker eats with solid dignity, jests with solid dignity, and condescendingly listens to the remarks of the young ladies. From time to time he is moved to speak in bad French, and then, for some reason or other, he thinks it necessary to address me as *"Votre Excellence."*

And I am glum. Evidently I am a constraint to them and they are a constraint to me. I have never in my earlier days had a close knowledge of class antagonism, but now I am tormented by something of that sort. I am on the lookout for nothing but bad qualities in Gnekker; I quickly find them, and am fretted at the thought that a man not of my circle is sitting here as my daughter's suitor. His presence has a bad influence on me in other ways, too. As a rule, when I am alone or in the society of people I like, never think of my own achievements, or, if I do recall them, they seem to me as trivial as though I had only completed my studies yesterday; but in the presence of people like Gnekker my achievements in science seem to be a lofty mountain the top of which vanishes into the clouds, while at its foot Gnekkers are running about scarcely visible to the naked eye.

After dinner I go into my study and there smoke my pipe, the only one in the whole day, the sole relic of my old bad habit of smoking from morning till night. While I am smoking my wife comes in and sits down to talk to me. Just as in the morning, I know beforehand what our conversation is going to be about.

"I must talk to you seriously, Nikolay Stepanovitch," she begins. "I mean about Liza. . . . Why don't you pay attention to it?"

"To what?"

"You pretend to notice nothing. But that is not right. We can't shirk responsibility. . . . Gnekker has intentions in regard to Liza. . . . What do you say?"

"That he is a bad man I can't say, because I don't know him, but that I don't like him I have told you a thousand times already."

"But you can't . . . you can't!"

She gets up and walks about in excitement.

"You can't take up that attitude to a serious step," she says. "When it is a question of our daughter's happiness we must lay aside all personal feeling. I know you do not like him. . . . Very good . . . if we refuse him now, if we break it all off, how can you be sure that Liza will not have a grievance against us all her life? Suitors are not plentiful nowadays, goodness knows, and it may happen that no other match will turn up. . . . He is very much in love with Liza, and she seems to like him. . . . Of course, he has no settled position, but that can't be helped. Please God, in time he will get one. He is of good family and well off."

"Where did you learn that?"

"He told us so. His father has a large house in Harkov and an estate in the neighbourhood. In short, Nikolay Stepanovitch, you absolutely must go to Harkov."

"What for?"

"You will find out all about him there. . . . You know the professors there; they will help you. I would go myself, but I am a woman. I cannot. . . ."

"I am not going to Harkov," I say morosely.

My wife is frightened, and a look of intense suffering comes into her face.

"For God's sake, Nikolay Stepanovitch," she implores me, with tears in her voice -"for God's sake, take this burden off me! I am so worried!"

It is painful for me to look at her.

"Very well, Varya," I say affectionately, "if you wish it, then certainly I will go to Harkov and do all you want."

She presses her handkerchief to her eyes and goes off to her room to cry, and I am left alone.

A little later lights are brought in. The armchair and the lamp-shade cast familiar shadows that have long grown wearisome on the walls and on the floor, and when I look at them I feel as though the night had come and with it my accursed sleeplessness. I lie on my bed, then get up and walk about the room, then lie down again. As a rule it is after dinner, at the approach of evening, that my nervous excitement reaches its highest pitch. For no reason I begin crying and burying my head in the pillow. At such times I am afraid that some one may come in; I am afraid of suddenly dying; I am ashamed of my tears, and altogether there is something insufferable in my soul. I feel that I can no longer bear the sight of my lamp, of my books, of the shadows on the floor. I cannot bear the sound of the voices coming from the drawing-room. Some force unseen, uncomprehended, is roughly thrusting me out of my flat. I leap up hurriedly, dress, and cautiously, that my family may not notice, slip out into the street. Where am I to go?

The answer to that question has long been ready in my brain. To Katya.

III

As a rule she is lying on the sofa or in a lounge-chair reading. Seeing me, she raises her head languidly, sits up, and shakes hands.

"You are always lying down," I say, after pausing and taking breath. "That's not good for you. You ought to occupy yourself with something."

"What?"

"I say you ought to occupy yourself in some way."

"With what? A woman can be nothing but a simple workwoman or an actress."

"Well, if you can't be a workwoman, be an actress."

She says nothing.

"You ought to get married," I say, half in jest.

"There is no one to marry. There's no reason to, either."

"You can't live like this."

"Without a husband? Much that matters; I could have as many men as I like if I wanted to."

"That's ugly, Katya."

"What is ugly?"

"Why, what you have just said."

Noticing that I am hurt and wishing to efface the disagreeable impression, Katya says:

"Let us go; come this way."

She takes me into a very snug little room, and says, pointing to the writing-table:

"Look . . . I have got that ready for you. You shall work here. Come here every day and bring your work with you. They only hinder you there at home. Will you work here? Will you like to?"

Not to wound her by refusing, I answer that I will work here, and that I like the room very much. Then we both sit down in the snug little room and begin talking.

The warm, snug surroundings and the presence of a sympathetic person does not, as in old days, arouse in me a feeling of pleasure, but an intense impulse to complain and grumble. I feel for some reason that if I lament and complain I shall feel better.

"Things are in a bad way with me, my dear - very bad. . . ."

"What is it?"

"You see how it is, my dear; the best and holiest right of kings is the right of mercy. And I have always felt myself a king, since I have made unlimited use of that right. I have never judged, I have been indulgent, I have readily forgiven every one, right and left. Where others have protested and expressed indignation, I have only advised and persuaded. All my life it has been my endeavour that my society should not be a burden to my family, to my students, to my colleagues, to my servants. And I know that this attitude to people has had a good influence on all who have chanced to come into contact with me. But now I am not a king. Something is happening to me that is only excusable in a slave; day and night my brain is haunted by evil thoughts, and feelings such as I never knew before are brooding in my soul. I am full of hatred, and contempt, and indignation, and loathing, and dread. I have become excessively severe, exacting, irritable, ungracious, suspicious. Even things that in old days would have provoked me only to an unnecessary jest and a good-natured laugh now arouse an oppressive feeling in me. My reasoning, too, has undergone a change: in old days I despised money; now I harbour an evil feeling, not towards money, but towards the rich as though they were to blame: in old days I hated violence and tyranny, but now I hate the men who make use of violence, as though they were alone to blame, and not all of us who do not know how to educate each other. What is the meaning of it? If these new ideas and new feelings have come from a change of convictions, what is that change due to? Can the world have grown worse and I better, or was I blind before and indifferent? If this change is the result of a general decline of physical and intellectual powers - I am ill, you know, and every day I am losing weight - my position is pitiable; it means that my new ideas are morbid and abnormal; I ought to be ashamed of them and think them of no consequence. . . ."

"Illness has nothing to do with it," Katya interrupts me; "it's simply that your eyes are opened, that's all. You have seen what in old days, for some reason, you refused to see. To my thinking, what you ought to do first of all, is to break with your family for good, and go away."

"You are talking nonsense."

"You don't love them; why should you force your feelings? Can you call them a family? Nonentities! If they died today, no one would notice their absence tomorrow."

Katya despises my wife and Liza as much as they hate her. One can hardly talk at this date of people's having a right to despise one another. But if one looks at it from Katya's standpoint and recognizes such a right, one can see she has as much right to despise my wife and Liza as they have to hate her.

"Nonentities," she goes on. "Have you had dinner today? How was it they did not forget to tell you it was ready? How is it they still remember your existence?"

"Katya," I say sternly, "I beg you to be silent."

"You think I enjoy talking about them? I should be glad not to know them at all. Listen, my dear: give it all up and go away. Go abroad. The sooner the better."

"What nonsense! What about the University?"

"The University, too. What is it to you? There's no sense in it, anyway. You have been lecturing for thirty years, and where are your pupils? Are many of them celebrated scientific men? Count them up! And to multiply the doctors who exploit ignorance and pile up hundreds of thousands for themselves, there is no need to be a good and talented man. You are not wanted."

"Good heavens! how harsh you are!" I cry in horror. "How harsh you are! Be quiet or I will go away! I don't know how to answer the harsh things you say!"

The maid comes in and summons us to tea. At the samovar our conversation, thank God, changes. After having had my grumble out, I have a longing to give way to another weakness of old age, reminiscences. I tell Katya about my past, and to my great astonishment tell her incidents which, till then, I did not suspect of being still preserved in my memory, and she listens to me with tenderness, with pride, holding her breath. I am particularly fond of telling her how I was educated in a seminary and dreamed of going to the University.

"At times I used to walk about our seminary garden . ." I would tell her. "If from some faraway tavern the wind floated sounds of a song and the squeaking of an accordion, or a sledge with bells dashed by the garden-fence, it was quite enough to send a rush of happiness, filling not only my heart, but even my stomach, my legs, my arms. . . . I would listen to the accordion or the bells dying away in the distance and imagine myself a doctor, and paint pictures, one better than another. And here, as you see, my dreams have come true. I have had more than I dared to dream of. For thirty years I have been the favourite professor, I have had splendid comrades, I have enjoyed fame and honour. I have loved, married from passionate love, have had children. In fact, looking back upon it, I see my whole life as a fine composition arranged with talent. Now all that is left to me is not to spoil the end. For that I must die like a man. If death is really a thing to dread, I must meet it as a teacher, a man of science, and a citizen of a Christian country ought to meet it, with courage and untroubled soul. But I am spoiling the end; I am sinking, I fly to you, I beg for help, and you tell me 'Sink; that is what you ought to do.' "

But here there comes a ring at the front-door. Katya and I recognize it, and say:

"It must be Mihail Fyodorovitch."

And a minute later my colleague, the philologist Mihail Fyodorovitch, a tall, well-built man of fifty, clean-shaven, with thick grey hair and black eyebrows, walks in. He is a good-natured man and an excellent comrade. He comes of a fortunate and talented old noble family which has played a prominent part in the history of literature and enlightenment. He is himself intelligent, talented, and very highly educated, but has his oddities. To a certain extent we are all odd and all queer fish, but in his oddities there is something exceptional, apt to cause anxiety among his acquaintances. I know a good many people for whom his oddities completely obscure his good qualities.

Coming in to us, he slowly takes off his gloves and says in his velvety bass:

"Good-evening. Are you having tea? That's just right. It's diabolically cold."

Then he sits down to the table, takes a glass, and at once begins talking. What is most characteristic in his manner of talking is the continually jesting tone, a sort of mixture of philosophy and drollery as in Shakespeare's gravediggers. He is always talking about serious things, but he never speaks seriously. His judgments are always harsh and railing, but, thanks to his soft, even, jesting tone, the harshness and abuse do not jar upon the ear, and one soon grows used to them. Every evening he brings with him five or six anecdotes from the University, and he usually begins with them when he sits down to table.

"Oh, Lord!" he sighs, twitching his black eyebrows ironically. "What comic people there are in the world!"

"Well?" asks Katya.

"As I was coming from my lecture this morning I met that old idiot N. N - on the stairs. . . . He was going along as usual, sticking out his chin like a horse, looking for some one to listen to his grumblings at his migraine, at his wife, and his students who won't attend his lectures. 'Oh,' I thought, 'he has seen me - I am done for now; it is all up. . . .' "

And so on in the same style. Or he will begin like this:

"I was yesterday at our friend Z. Z - 's public lecture. I wonder how it is our alma mater - don't speak of it after dark - dare display in public such noodles and patent dullards as that Z. Z - Why, he is a European fool! Upon my word, you could not find another like him all over Europe! He lectures - can you imagine? - as though he were sucking a sugar-stick - sue, sue, sue; . . . he is in a nervous funk; he can hardly decipher his own manuscript; his poor little thoughts crawl along like a bishop on a bicycle, and, what's worse, you can never make out what he is trying to say. The deadly dulness is awful, the very flies expire. It can only be compared with the boredom in the assembly-hall at the yearly meeting when the traditional address is read -

damn it!"

And at once an abrupt transition:

"Three years ago - Nikolay Stepanovitch here will remember it - I had to deliver that address. It was hot, stifling, my uniform cut me under the arms - it was deadly! I read for half an hour, for an hour, for an hour and a half, for two hours. . . . 'Come,' I thought; 'thank God, there are only ten pages left!' And at the end there were four pages that there was no need to read, and I reckoned to leave them out. 'So there are only six really,' I thought; 'that is, only six pages left to read.' But, only fancy, I chanced to glance before me, and, sitting in the front row, side by side, were a general with a ribbon on his breast and a bishop. The poor beggars were numb with boredom; they were staring with their eyes wide open to keep awake, and yet they were trying to put on an expression of attention and to pretend that they understood what I was saying and liked it. 'Well,' I thought, 'since you like it you shall have it! I'll pay you out;' so I just gave them those four pages too."

As is usual with ironical people, when he talks nothing in his face smiles but his eyes and eyebrows. At such times there is no trace of hatred or spite in his eyes, but a great deal of humour, and that peculiar fox-like slyness which is only to be noticed in very observant people. Since I am speaking about his eyes, I notice another peculiarity in them. When he takes a glass from Katya, or listens to her speaking, or looks after her as she goes out of the room for a moment, I notice in his eyes something gentle, beseeching, pure. . . .

The maid-servant takes away the samovar and puts on

the table a large piece of cheese, some fruit, and a bottle of Crimean champagne - a rather poor wine of which Katya had grown fond in the Crimea. Mihail Fyodorovitch takes two packs of cards off the whatnot and begins to play patience. According to him, some varieties of patience require great concentration and attention, yet while he lays out the cards he does not leave off distracting his attention with talk. Katya watches his cards attentively, and more by gesture than by words helps him in his play. She drinks no more than a couple of wine-glasses of wine the whole evening; I drink four glasses, and the rest of the bottle falls to the share of Mihail Fyodorovitch, who can drink a great deal and never get drunk.

Over our patience we settle various questions, principally of the higher order, and what we care for most of all - that is, science and learning - is more roughly handled than anything. "Science, thank God, has outlived its day," says Mihail Fyodorovitch emphatically. "Its song is sung. Yes, indeed. Mankind begins to feel impelled to replace it by something different. It has grown on the soil of superstition, been nourished by superstition, and is now just as much the quintessence of superstition as its defunct granddames, alchemy, metaphysics, and philosophy. And, after all, what has it given to mankind? Why, the difference between the learned Europeans and the Chinese who have no science is trifling, purely external. The Chinese know nothing of science, but what have they lost thereby?"

"Flies know nothing of science, either," I observe, "but what of that?"

"There is no need to be angry, Nikolay Stepanovitch. I

only say this here between ourselves. . . I am more careful than you think, and I am not going to say this in public - God forbid! The superstition exists in the multitude that the arts and sciences are superior to agriculture, commerce, superior to handicrafts. Our sect is maintained by that superstition, and it is not for you and me to destroy it. God forbid!"

After patience the younger generation comes in for a dressing too.

"Our audiences have degenerated," sighs Mihail Fyodorovitch. "Not to speak of ideals and all the rest of it, if only they were capable of work and rational thought! In fact, it's a case of 'I look with mournful eyes on the young men of today.' "

"Yes; they have degenerated horribly," Katya agrees. "Tell me, have you had one man of distinction among them for the last five or ten years?"

"I don't know how it is with the other professors, but I can't remember any among mine."

"I have seen in my day many of your students and young scientific men and many actors - well, I have never once been so fortunate as to meet - I won't say a hero or a man of talent, but even an interesting man. It's all the same grey mediocrity, puffed up with self-conceit."

All this talk of degeneration always affects me as though I had accidentally overheard offensive talk about my own daughter. It offends me that these charges are wholesale, and rest on such worn-out commonplaces, on such wordy vapourings as degeneration and absence of ideals, or on references to the splendours of the past. Every accusation, even if it is uttered in ladies' society, ought to be formulated with all possible definiteness, or it is not an accusation, but idle disparagement, unworthy of decent people.

I am an old man, I have been lecturing for thirty years, but I notice neither degeneration nor lack of ideals, and I don't find that the present is worse than the past. My porter Nikolay, whose experience of this subject has its value, says that the students of today are neither better nor worse than those of the past.

If I were asked what I don't like in my pupils of today, I should answer the question, not straight off and not at length, but with sufficient definiteness. I know their failings, and so have no need to resort to vague generalities. I don't like their smoking, using spirituous beverages, marrying late, and often being so irresponsible and careless that they will let one of their number be starving in their midst while they neglect to pay their subscriptions to the Students' Aid Society. They don't know modern languages, and they don't express themselves correctly in Russian; no longer ago than yesterday my colleague, the professor of hygiene, complained to me that he had to give twice as many lectures, because the students had a very poor knowledge of physics and were utterly ignorant of meteorology. They are readily carried away by the influence of the last new writers, even when they are not first-rate, but they take absolutely no interest in classics such as Shakespeare, Marcus Aurelius, Epictetus, or Pascal, and this inability to distinguish the great from the small betrays their ignorance of practical life more than anything. All difficult questions that have more or less a social character (for instance the migration question) they settle by studying monographs on the subject, but not by way of scientific investigation or experiment, though that method is at their disposal and is more in keeping with their calling. They gladly become ward-surgeons, assistants, demonstrators, external teachers, and are ready to fill such posts until they are forty, though independence, a sense of freedom and personal initiative, are no less necessary in science than, for instance, in art or commerce. I have pupils and listeners, but no successors and helpers, and so I love them and am touched by them, but am not proud of them. And so on, and so on. . . .

Such shortcomings, however numerous they may be, can only give rise to a pessimistic or fault-finding temper in a faint-hearted and timid man. All these failings have a casual, transitory character, and are completely dependent on conditions of life; in some ten years they will have disappeared or given place to other fresh defects, which are all inevitable and will in their turn alarm the faint-hearted. The students' sins often vex me, but that vexation is nothing in comparison with the joy I have been experiencing now for the last thirty years when I talk to my pupils, lecture to them, watch their relations, and compare them with people not of their circle.

Mihail Fyodorovitch speaks evil of everything. Katya listens, and neither of them notices into what depths the apparently innocent diversion of finding fault with their neighbours is gradually drawing them. They are not conscious how by degrees simple talk passes into malicious mockery and jeering, and how they are both beginning to drop into the habits and methods of slander.

Anton Chekhov

"Killing types one meets with," says Mihail Fyodorovitch. "I went yesterday to our friend Yegor Petrovitch's, and there I found a studious gentleman, one of your medicals in his third year, I believe. Such a face! . . . in the Dobrolubov style, the imprint of profound thought on his brow; we got into talk. 'Such doings, young man,' said I. 'I've read,' said I, 'that some German - I've forgotten his name - has created from the human brain a new kind of alkaloid, idiotine.' What do you think? He believed it, and there was positively an expression of respect on his face, as though to say, 'See what we fellows can do!' And the other day I went to the theatre. I took my seat. In the next row directly in front of me were sitting two men: one of 'us fellows' and apparently a law student, the other a shaggy-looking figure, a medical student. The latter was as drunk as a cobbler. He did not look at the stage at all. He was dozing with his nose on his shirt-front. But as soon as an actor begins loudly reciting a monologue, or simply raises his voice, our friend starts, pokes his neighbour in the ribs, and asks, 'What is he saying? Is it elevating?' 'Yes,' answers one of our fellows. 'B-r-r-ravo!' roars the medical student. 'Elevating! Bravo!' He had gone to the theatre, you see, the drunken blockhead, not for the sake of art, the play, but for elevation! He wanted noble sentiments."

Katya listens and laughs. She has a strange laugh; she catches her breath in rhythmically regular gasps, very much as though she were playing the accordion, and nothing in her face is laughing but her nostrils. I grow depressed and don't know what to say. Beside myself, I fire up, leap up from my seat, and cry:

"Do leave off! Why are you sitting here like two toads, poisoning the air with your breath? Give over!"

And without waiting for them to finish their gossip I prepare to go home. And, indeed, it is high time: it is past ten.

"I will stay a little longer," says Mihail Fyodorovitch. "Will you allow me, Ekaterina Vladimirovna?"

"I will," answers Katya.

"*Bene!* In that case have up another little bottle."

They both accompany me with candles to the hall, and while I put on my fur coat, Mihail Fyodorovitch says:

"You have grown dreadfully thin and older looking, Nikolay Stepanovitch. What's the matter with you? Are you ill?"

"Yes; I am not very well."

"And you are not doing anything for it. . ." Katya puts in grimly.

"Why don't you? You can't go on like that! God helps those who help themselves, my dear fellow. Remember me to your wife and daughter, and make my apologies for not having been to see them. In a day or two, before I go abroad, I shall come to say good-bye. I shall be sure to. I am going away next week."

I come away from Katya, irritated and alarmed by what has been said about my being ill, and dissatisfied with myself. I ask myself whether I really ought not to consult one of my colleagues. And at once I imagine how my colleague, after listening to me, would walk away to the window without speaking, would think a moment, then would turn round to me and, trying to prevent my reading the truth in his face, would say in a careless tone: "So far I see nothing serious, but at the same time, *collega*, I advise you to lay aside your work. . . ." And that would deprive me of my last hope.

Who is without hope? Now that I am diagnosing my illness and prescribing for myself, from time to time I hope that I am deceived by my own illness, that I am mistaken in regard to the albumen and the sugar I find, and in regard to my heart, and in regard to the swellings I have twice noticed in the mornings; when with the fervour of the hypochondriac I look through the textbooks of therapeutics and take a different medicine every day, I keep fancying that I shall hit upon something comforting. All that is petty.

Whether the sky is covered with clouds or the moon and the stars are shining, I turn my eyes towards it every evening and think that death is taking me soon. One would think that my thoughts at such times ought to be deep as the sky, brilliant, striking. . . . But no! I think about myself, about my wife, about Liza, Gnekker, the students, people in general; my thoughts are evil, petty, I am insincere with myself, and at such times my theory of life may be expressed in the words the celebrated Araktcheev said in one of his intimate letters: "Nothing good can exist in the world without evil, and there is more evil than good." That is, everything is disgusting; there is nothing to live for, and the sixty-two years I have already lived must be reckoned as wasted.

I catch myself in these thoughts, and try to persuade myself that they are accidental, temporary, and not deeply rooted in me, but at once I think:

"If so, what drives me every evening to those two toads?"

And I vow to myself that I will never go to Katya's again, though I know I shall go next evening.

Ringing the bell at the door and going upstairs, I feel that I have no family now and no desire to bring it back again. It is clear that the new Araktcheev thoughts are not casual, temporary visitors, but have possession of my whole being. With my conscience ill at ease, dejected, languid, hardly able to move my limbs, feeling as though tons were added to my weight, I get into bed and quickly drop asleep.

And then - insomnia!

IV

Summer comes on and life is changed.

One fine morning Liza comes in to me and says in a jesting tone:

"Come, your Excellency! We are ready."

My Excellency is conducted into the street, and seated in a cab. As I go along, having nothing to do, I read the signboards from right to left. The word "Traktir" reads " Ritkart"; that would just suit some baron's family: Baroness Ritkart. Farther on I drive through fields, by the graveyard, which makes absolutely no impression on me, though I shall soon lie in it; then I drive by forests and again by fields. There is nothing of interest. After two hours of driving, my Excellency is conducted into the lower storey of a summer villa and installed in a small, very cheerful little room with light blue hangings.

At night there is sleeplessness as before, but in the morning I do not put a good face upon it and listen to my wife, but lie in bed. I do not sleep, but lie in the drowsy, half-conscious condition in which you know you are not asleep, but dreaming. At midday I get up and from habit sit down at my table, but I do not work now; I amuse myself with French books in yellow covers, sent me by Katya. Of course, it would be more patriotic to read Russian authors, but I must confess I cherish no particular liking for them. With the exception of two or three of the older writers, all our literature of today strikes me as not being literature, but a special sort of home industry, which exists simply in order to be encouraged, though people do not readily make use of its products. The very best of these home products cannot be called remarkable and cannot be sincerely praised without qualification. I must say the same of all the literary novelties I have read during the last ten or fifteen years; not one of them is remarkable, and not one of them can be praised without a "but." Cleverness, a good tone, but no talent; talent, a good tone, but no cleverness; or talent, cleverness, but not a good tone.

I don't say the French books have talent, cleverness, and a good tone. They don't satisfy me, either. But they are not so tedious as the Russian, and it is not unusual to find in them the chief element of artistic creation - the feeling of personal freedom which is lacking in the Russian authors. I don't remember one new book in which the author does not try from the first page to entangle himself in all sorts of conditions and contracts with his conscience. One is afraid to speak of the naked body; another ties himself up hand and foot in psychological analysis; a third must have a "warm attitude to man"; a fourth purposely scrawls whole descriptions of nature that he may not be suspected of writing with a purpose. . . . One is bent upon being middle-class in his work, another must be a nobleman, and so on. There is intentionalness, circumspection, and self-will, but they have neither the independence nor the manliness to write as they like, and therefore there is no creativeness.

All this applies to what is called belles-lettres.

As for serious treatises in Russian on sociology, for instance, on art, and so on, I do not rea d them simply from timidity. In my childhood and early youth I had for some reason a terror of doorkeepers and attendants at the theatre, and that terror has remained with me to this day. I am afraid of them even now. It is said that we are only afraid of what we do not understand. And, indeed, it is very difficult to understand why door-keepers and theatre attendants are so dignified, haughty, and majestically rude. I feel exactly the same terror when I read serious articles. Their extraordinary dignity, their bantering lordly tone, their familiar manner to foreign authors, their ability to split straws with dignity - all that is beyond my understanding; it is intimidating and utterly unlike the quiet, gentlemanly tone to which I am accustomed when I read the works of our medical and scientific writers. It oppresses me to read not only the articles written by serious Russians, but even works translated or edited by them. The pretentious, edifying tone of the preface; the redundancy of remarks made by the translator, which prevent me from concentrating my attention; the question marks and "sic" in parenthesis scattered all over the book or article by the liberal translator, are to my mind an outrage on the author and on my independence as a reader.

Once I was summoned as an expert to a circuit court; in an interval one of my fellow-experts drew my attention to the rudeness of the public prosecutor to the defendants, among whom there were two ladies of good education. I believe I did not exaggerate at all when I told him that the prosecutor s manner was no ruder than that of the authors of serious articles to one another. Their manners are, indeed, so rude that I cannot speak of them without distaste. They treat one another and the writers they criticize either with superfluous respect, at the sacrifice of their own dignity, or, on the contrary, with far more ruthlessness than I have shown in my notes and my thoughts in regard to my future son-in-law Gnekker. Accusations of irrationality, of evil intentions, and, indeed, of every sort of crime, form an habitual ornament of serious articles. And that, as young medical men are fond of saying in their monographs, is the *ultima ratio!* Such ways must infallibly have an effect on the morals of the younger generation of writers, and so I am not at all surprised that in the new works with which our literature has been enriched during the last ten or fifteen years the heroes drink too much vodka and the heroines are not over-chaste.

I read French books, and I look out of the window which is open; I can see the spikes of my garden-fence, two or three scraggy trees, and beyond the fence the road, the fields, and beyond them a broad stretch of pine-wood. Often I admire a boy and girl, both flaxen-headed and ragged, who clamber on the fence and laugh at my baldness. In their shining little eyes I read, "Go up, go up, thou baldhead!" They are almost the only people who care nothing for my celebrity or my rank.

Visitors do not come to me every day now. I will only mention the visits of Nikolay and Pyotr Ignatyevitch. Nikolay usually comes to me on holidays, with some pretext of business, though really to see me. He arrives very much exhilarated, a thing which never occurs to him in the winter.

"What have you to tell me?" I ask, going out to him in the hall.

"Your Excellency!" he says, pressing his hand to his

heart and looking at me with the ecstasy of a lover -
"your Excellency! God be my witness! Strike me dead
on the spot! *Gaudeamus egitur juventus!*"

And he greedily kisses me on the shoulder, on the
sleeve, and on the buttons.

"Is everything going well?" I ask him.

"Your Excellency! So help me God! . . ."

He persists in grovelling before me for no sort of
reason, and soon bores me, so I send him away to the
kitchen, where they give him dinner.

Pyotr Ignatyevitch comes to see me on holidays, too,
with the special object of seeing me and sharing his
thoughts with me. He usually sits down near my table,
modest, neat, and reasonable, and does not venture to
cross his legs or put his elbows on the table. All the
time, in a soft, even, little voice, in rounded bookish
phrases, he tells me various, to his mind, very
interesting and piquant items of news which he has
read in the magazines and journals. They are all alike
and may be reduced to this type: "A Frenchman has
made a discovery; some one else, a German, has
denounced him, proving that the discovery was made
in 1870 by some American; while a third person, also a
German, trumps them both by proving they both had
made fools of themselves, mistaking bubbles of air for
dark pigment under the microscope. Even when he
wants to amuse me, Pyotr Ignatyevitch tells me things
in the same lengthy, circumstantial manner as though
he were defending a thesis, enumerating in detail the
literary sources from which he is deriving his narrative,
doing his utmost to be accurate as to the date and

number of the journals and the name of every one concerned, invariably mentioning it in full - Jean Jacques Petit, never simply Petit. Sometimes he stays to dinner with us, and then during the whole of dinner-time he goes on telling me the same sort of piquant anecdotes, reducing every one at table to a state of dejected boredom. If Gnekker and Liza begin talking before him of fugues and counterpoint, Brahms and Bach, he drops his eyes modestly, and is overcome with embarrassment; he is ashamed that such trivial subjects should be discussed before such serious people as him and me.

In my present state of mind five minutes of him is enough to sicken me as though I had been seeing and hearing him for an eternity. I hate the poor fellow. His soft, smooth voice and bookish language exhaust me, and his stories stupefy me. . . . He cherishes the best of feelings for me, and talks to me simply in order to give me pleasure, and I repay him by looking at him as though I wanted to hypnotize him, and think, "Go, go, go! . . ." But he is not amenable to thought-suggestion, and sits on and on and on. . . .

While he is with me I can never shake off the thought, "It's possible when I die he will be appointed to succeed me," and my poor lecture-hall presents itself to me as an oasis in which the spring is died up; and I am ungracious, silent, and surly with Pyotr Ignatyevitch, as though he were to blame for such thoughts, and not I myself. When he begins, as usual, praising up the German savants, instead of making fun of him good-humouredly, as I used to do, I mutter sullenly:

"Asses, your Germans! . . ."

That is like the late Professor Nikita Krylov, who once, when he was bathing with Pirogov at Revel and vexed at the water's being very cold, burst out with, "Scoundrels, these Germans!" I behave badly with Pyotr Ignatyevitch, and only when he is going away, and from the window I catch a glimpse of his grey hat behind the garden-fence, I want to call out and say, "Forgive me, my dear fellow!"

Dinner is even drearier than in the winter. Gnekker, whom now I hate and despise, dines with us almost every day. I used to endure his presence in silence, now I aim biting remarks at him which make my wife and daughter blush. Carried away by evil feeling, I often say things that are simply stupid, and I don't know why I say them. So on one occasion it happened that I stared a long time at Gnekker, and, *a propos* of nothing, I fired off:

"An eagle may perchance swoop down below a cock, But never will the fowl soar upwards to the clouds. .

And the most vexatious thing is that the fowl Gnekker shows himself much cleverer than the eagle professor. Knowing that my wife and daughter are on his side, he takes up the line of meeting my gibes with condescending silence, as though to say:

"The old chap is in his dotage; what's the use of talking to him?"

Or he makes fun of me good-naturedly. It is wonderful how petty a man may become! I am capable of dreaming all dinner-time of how Gnekker will turn out to be an adventurer, how my wife and Liza will come to see their mistake, and how I will taunt them - and such absurd thoughts at the time when I am standing with one foot in th e grave!

There are now, too, misunderstandings of which in the old days I had no idea except from hearsay. Though I am ashamed of it, I will describe one that occurred the other day after dinner.

I was sitting in my room smoking a pipe; my wife came in as usual, sat down, and began saying what a good thing it would be for me to go to Harkov now while it is warm and I have free time, and there find out what sort of person our Gnekker is.

"Very good; I will go," I assented.

My wife, pleased with me, got up and was going to the door, but turned back and said:

"By the way, I have another favour to ask of you. I know you will be angry, but it is my duty to warn you. . . . Forgive my saying it, Nikolay Stepanovitch, but all our neighbours and acquaintances have begun talking about your being so often at Katya's. She is clever and well-educated; I don't deny that her company may be agreeable; but at your age and with your social position it seems strange that you should find pleasure in her society. . . . Besides, she has such a reputation that . . ."

All the blood suddenly rushed to my brain, my eyes flashed fire, I leaped up and, clutching at my head and stamping my feet, shouted in a voice unlike my own:

"Let me alone! let me alone! let me alone!"

Probably my face was terrible, my voice was strange, for my wife suddenly turned pale and began shrieking aloud in a despairing voice that was utterly unlike her own. Liza, Gnekker, then Yegor, came running in at our shouts. . . .

"Let me alone!" I cried; "let me alone! Go away!"

My legs turned numb as though they had ceased to exist; I felt myself falling into someone's arms; for a little while I still heard weeping, then sank into a swoon which lasted two or three hours.

Now about Katya; she comes to see me every day towards evening, and of course neither the neighbours nor our acquaintances can avoid noticing it. She comes in for a minute and carries me off for a drive with her. She has her own horse and a new chaise bought this summer. Altogether she lives in an expensive style; she has taken a big detached villa with a large garden, and has taken all her town retinue with her - two maids, a coachman . . . I often ask her:

"Katya, what will you live on when you have spent your father's money?"

"Then we shall see," she answers.

"That money, my dear, deserves to be treated more seriously. It was earned by a good man, by honest labour."

"You have told me that already. I know it."

At first we drive through the open country, then through the pine-wood which is visible from my window. Nature seems to me as beautiful as it always has been, though some evil spirit whispers to me that these pines and fir trees, birds, and white clouds on the sky, will not notice my absence when in three or four months I am dead. Katya loves driving, and she is pleased that it is fine weather and that I am sitting beside her. She is in good spirits and does not say harsh things.

"You are a very good man, Nikolay Stepanovitch," she says. "You are a rare specimen, and there isn't an actor who would understand how to play you. Me or Mihail Fyodorovitch, for instance, any poor actor could do, but not you. And I envy you, I envy you horribly! Do you know what I stand for? What?"

She ponders for a minute, and then asks me:

"Nikolay Stepanovitch, I am a negative phenomenon! Yes?"

"Yes," I answer.

"H'm! what am I to do?"

What answer was I to make her? It is easy to say "work," or "give your possessions to the poor," or "know yourself," and because it is so easy to say that, I don't know what to answer.

My colleagues when they teach therapeutics advise "the individual study of each separate case." One has but to obey this advice to gain the conviction that the methods recommended in the textbooks as the best and as providing a safe basis for treatment turn out to be quite unsuitable in individual cases. It is just the same

Anton Chekhov

in moral ailments.

But I must make some answer, and I say:

"You have too much free time, my dear; you absolutely must take up some occupation. After all, why shouldn't you be an actress again if it is your vocation?"

"I cannot!"

"Your tone and manner suggest that you are a victim. I don't like that, my dear; it is your own fault. Remember, you began with falling out with people and methods, but you have done nothing to make either better. You did not struggle with evil, but were cast down by it, and you are not the victim of the struggle, but of your own impotence. Well, of course you were young and inexperienced then; now it may all be different. Yes, really, go on the stage. You will work, you will serve a sacred art."

"Don't pretend, Nikolay Stepanovitch," Katya interrupts me. "Let us make a compact once for all; we will talk about actors, actresses, and authors, but we will let art alone. You are a splendid and rare person, but you don't know enough about art sincerely to think it sacred. You have no instinct or feeling for art. You have been hard at work all your life, and have not had time to acquire that feeling. Altogether . . . I don't like talk about art," she goes on nervously. "I don't like it! And, my goodness, how they have vulgarized it!"

"Who has vulgarized it?"

"They have vulgarized it by drunkenness, the newspapers by their familiar attitude, clever people by philosophy."

"Philosophy has nothing to do with it."

"Yes, it has. If any one philosophizes about it, it shows he does not understand it."

To avoid bitterness I hasten to change the subject, and then sit a long time silent. Only when we are driving out of the wood and turning towards Katya's villa I go back to my former question, and say:

"You have still not answered me, why you don't want to go on the stage."

"Nikolay Stepanovitch, this is cruel!" she cries, and suddenly flushes all over. "You want me to tell you the truth aloud? Very well, if . . . if you like it! I have no talent! No talent and . . . and a great deal of vanity! So there!"

After making this confession she turns her face away from me, and to hide the trembling of her hands tugs violently at the reins.

As we are driving towards her villa we see Mihail Fyodorovitch walking near the gate, impatiently awaiting us.

"That Mihail Fyodorovitch again!" says Katya with vexation. "Do rid me of him, please! I am sick and tired of him . . . bother him!"

Mihail Fyodorovitch ought to have gone abroad long

ago, but he puts off going from week to. week. Of late there have been certain changes in him. He looks, as it were, sunken, has taken to drinking until he is tipsy, a thing which never used to happen to him, and his black eyebrows are beginning to turn grey. When our chaise stops at the gate he does not conceal his joy and his impatience. He fussily helps me and Katya out, hurriedly asks questions, laughs, rubs his hands, and that gentle, imploring, pure expression, which I used to notice only in his eyes, is now suffused all over his face. He is glad and at the same time he is ashamed of his gladness, ashamed of his habit of spending every evening with Katya. And he thinks it necessary to explain his visit by some obvious absurdity such as: "I was driving by, and I thought I would just look in for a minute."

We all three go indoors; first we drink tea, then the familiar packs of cards, the big piece of cheese, the fruit, and the bottle of Crimean champagne are put upon the table. The subjects of our conversation are not new; they are just the same as in the winter. We fall foul of the University, the students, and literature and the theatre; the air grows thick and stifling with evil speaking, and poisoned by the breath, not of two toads as in the winter, but of three. Besides the velvety baritone laugh and the giggle like the gasp of a concertina, the maid who waits upon us hears an unpleasant cracked "He, he!" like the chuckle of a general in a vaudeville.

V

There are terrible nights with thunder, lightning, rain, and wind, such as are called among the people "sparrow nights." There has been one such night in my personal life.

I woke up after midnight and leaped suddenly out of bed. It seemed to me for some reason that I was just immedi ately going to die. Why did it seem so? I had no sensation in my body that suggested my immediate death, but my soul was oppressed with terror, as though I had suddenly seen a vast menacing glow of fire.

I rapidly struck a light, drank some water straight out of the decanter, then hurried to the open window. The weather outside was magnificent. There was a smell of hay and some other very sweet scent. I could see the spikes of the fence, the gaunt, drowsy trees by the window, the road, the dark streak of woodland, there was a serene, very bright moon in the sky and not a single cloud, perfect stillness, not one leaf stirring. I felt that everything was looking at me and waiting for me to die. . ..

It was uncanny. I closed the window and ran to my bed. I felt for my pulse, and not finding it in my wrist, tried to find it in my temple, then in my chin, and again in my wrist, and everything I touched was cold and clammy with sweat. My breathing came more and more rapidly, my body was shivering, all my inside was in commotion; I had a sensation on my face and on my bald head as though they were covered with

Anton Chekhov

spiders' webs.

What should I do? Call my family? No; it would be no use. I could not imagine what my wife and Liza would do when they came in to me.

I hid my head under the pillow, closed my eyes, and waited and waited. . . . My spine was cold; it seemed to be drawn inwards, and I felt as though death were coming upon me stealthily from behind

"Kee-vee! kee-vee!" I heard a sudden shriek in the night's stillness, and did not know where it was - in my breast or in the street - "Kee-vee! kee-vee!"

"My God, how terrible!" I would have drunk some more water, but by then it was fearful to open my eyes and I was afraid to raise my head. I was possessed by unaccountable animal terror, and I cannot understand why I was so frightened: was it that I wanted to live, or that some new unknown pain was in store for me?

Upstairs, overhead, some one moaned or laughed. I listened. Soon afterwards there was a sound of footsteps on the stairs. Some one came hurriedly down, then went up again. A minute later there was a sound of steps downstairs again; some one stopped near my door and listened.

"Who is there?" I cried.

The door opened. I boldly opened my eyes, and saw my wife. Her face was pale and her eyes were tear-stained.

"You are not asleep, Nikolay Stepanovitch?" she asked.

"What is it? "

"For God's sake, go up and have a look at Liza; there is something the matter with her. . . ."

"Very good, with pleasure," I muttered, greatly relieved at not being alone. "Very good, this minute. . . ."

I followed my wife, heard what she said to me, and was too agitated to understand a word. Patches of light from her candle danced about the stairs, our long shadows trembled. My feet caught in the skirts of my dressing-gown; I gasped for breath, and felt as though something were pursuing me and trying to catch me from behind.

"I shall die on the spot, here on the staircase," I thought. "On the spot. . . ." But we passed the staircase, the dark corridor with the Italian windows, and went into Liza's room. She was sitting on the bed in her nightdress, with her bare feet hanging down, and she was moaning.

"Oh, my God! Oh, my God!" she was muttering, screwing up her eyes at our candle. "I can't bear it."

"Liza, my child," I said, "what is it?"

Seeing me, she began crying out, and flung herself on my neck.

"My kind papa! . . ." she sobbed - "my dear, good

papa . . . my darling, my pet, I don't know what is the matter with me. . . . I am miserable!"

She hugged me, kissed me, and babbled fond words I used to hear from her when she was a child.

"Calm yourself, my child. God be with you," I said. "There is no need to cry. I am miserable, too."

I tried to tuck her in; my wife gave her water, and we awkwardly stumbled by her bedside; my shoulder jostled against her shoulder, and meanwhile I was thinking how we used to give our children their bath together.

"Help her! help her!" my wife implored me. "Do something!"

What could I do? I could do nothing. There was some load on the girl's heart; but I did not understand, I knew nothing about it, and could only mutter:

"It's nothing, it's nothing; it will pass. Sleep, sleep!"

To make things worse, there was a sudden sound of dogs howling, at first subdued and uncertain, then loud, two dogs howling together. I had never attached significance to such omens as the howling of dogs or the shrieking of owls, but on that occasion it sent a pang to my heart, and I hastened to explain the howl to myself.

"It's nonsense," I thought, "the influence of one organism on another. The intensely strained condition of my nerves has infected my wife, Liza, the dog - that is all. . . . Such infection explains presentiments, forebodings. . . ."

When a little later I went back to my room to write a prescription for Liza, I no longer thought I should die at once, but only had such a weight, such a feeling of oppression in my soul that I felt actually sorry that I had not died on the spot. For a long time I stood motionless in the middle of the room, pondering what to prescribe for Liza. But the moans overhead ceased, and I decided to prescribe nothing, and yet I went on standing there. . . .

There was a deathlike stillness, such a stillness, as some author has expressed it, "it rang in one's ears." Time passed slowly; the streaks of moonlight on the window-sill did not shift their position, but seemed as though frozen. . . . It was still some time before dawn.

But the gate in the fence creaked, some one stole in and, breaking a twig from one of those scraggy trees, cautiously tapped on the window with it.

"Nikolay Stepanovitch," I heard a whisper. "Nikolay Stepanovitch."

I opened the window, and fancied I was dreaming: under the window, huddled against the wall, stood a woman in a black dress, with the moonlight bright upon her, looking at me with great eyes. Her face was pale, stern, and weird-looking in the moonlight, like marble, her chin was quivering.

"It is I," she said - " I . . . Katya."

In the moonlight all women's eyes look big and black, all people look taller and paler, and that was probably why I had not recognized her for the first minute.

"What is it?"

"Forgive me! " she said. "I suddenly felt unbearably miserable .. . I couldn't stand it, so came here. There was a light in your window and . . . and I ventured to knock. . . . I beg your pardon. Ah! if you knew how miserable I am! What are you doing just now?"

"Nothing. . . . I can't sleep."

"I had a feeling that there was something wrong, but that is nonsense."

Her brows were lifted, her eyes shone with tears, and her whole face was lighted up with the familiar look of trustfulness which I had not seen for so long.

"Nikolay Stepanovitch," she said imploringly, stretching out both hands to me, "my precious friend, I beg you, I implore you. . . .If you don't despise my affection and respect for you, consent to what I ask of you."

"What is it?"

"Take my money from me!"

"Come! what an idea! What do I want with your money?"

"You'll go away somewhere for your health. . . . You ought to go for your health. Will you take it? Yes? Nikolay Stepanovitch darling, yes?"

She looked greedily into my face and repeated: "Yes, you will take it?"

"No, my dear, I won't take it . . " I said. "Thank you."

She turned her back upon me and bowed her head. Probably I refused her in a tone which made further conversation about money impossible.

"Go home to bed," I said. "We will see each other tomorrow."

"So you don't consider me your friend?" she asked dejectedly.

"I don't say that. But your money would be no use to me now."

"I beg your pardon . . ." she said, dropping her voice a whole octave. "I understand you . . . to be indebted to a person like me . . . a retired actress. . . . But, good-bye. . . ."

And she went away so quickly that I had not time even to say good-bye.

VI

I am in Harkov.

As it would be useless to contend against my present mood and, indeed, beyond my power, I have made up my mind that the last days of my life shall at least be irreproachable externally. If I am unjust in regard to my wife and daughter, which I fully recognize, I will try and do as she wishes; since she wants me to go to Harkov, I go to Harkov. Besides, I have become of late so indifferent to everything that it is really all the same to me where I go, to Harkov, or to Paris, or to Berditchev.

I arrived here at midday, and have put up at the hotel not far from the cathedral. The train was jolting, there were draughts, and now I am sitting on my bed, holding my head and expecting tic douloureux. I ought to have gone today to see some professors of my acquaintance, but I have neither strength nor inclination.

The old corridor attendant comes in and asks whether I have brought my bed-linen. I detain him for five minutes, and put several questions to him about Gnekker, on whose account I have come here. The attendant turns out to be a native of Harkov; he knows the town like the fingers of his hand, but does not remember any household of the surname of Gnekker. I question him about the estate - the same answer.

The clock in the corridor strikes one, then two, then three. . .. These last months in which I am waiting for death seem much longer than the whole of my life. And I have never before been so ready to resign myself to the slowness of time as now. In the old days, when one sat in the station and waited for a train, or presided in an examination-room, a quarter of an hour would seem an eternity. Now I can sit all night on my bed without moving, and quite unconcernedly reflect that tomorrow will be followed by another night as long and colourless, and the day after tomorrow.

In the corridor it strikes five, six, seven. . . . It grows dark.

There is a dull pain in my cheek, the tic beginning. To occupy myself with thoughts, I go back to my old point of view, when I was not so indifferent, and ask myself why I, a distinguished man, a privy councillor, am sitting in this little hotel room, on this bed with the unfamiliar grey quilt. Why am I looking at that cheap tin washing-stand and listening to the whirr of the wretched clock in the corridor? Is all this in keeping with my fame and my lofty position? And I answer these questions with a jeer. I am amused by the naivete with which I used in my youth to exaggerate the value of renown and of the exceptional position which celebrities are supposed to enjoy. I am famous, my name is pronounced with reverence, my portrait has been both in the *Niva* and in the *Illustrated News of the World*; I have read my biography even in a German magazine. And what of all that? Here I am sitting utterly alone in a strange town, on a strange bed, rubbing my aching cheek with my hand. . . . Domestic worries, the hard-heartedness of creditors, the rudeness of the railway servants, the inconveniences of the passport system, the expensive and unwholesome food in the refreshment-rooms, the general rudeness and coarseness in social intercourse - all this, and a great deal more which would take too long to reckon up, affects me as much as any working man who is famous only in his alley. In what way, does my exceptional position find expression? Admitting that I am celebrated a thousand times over, that I am a hero of whom my country is proud. They publish bulletins of my illness in every paper, letters of sympathy come to me by post from my colleagues, my pupils, the general public; but all that does not prevent me from dying in a strange bed, in misery, in utter loneliness. Of course, no one is to blame for that; but I in my foolishness dislike my popularity. I feel as though it had cheated me.

At ten o'clock I fall asleep, and in spite of the tic I sleep soundly, and should have gone on sleeping if I had not been awakened. Soon after one came a sudden knock at the door.

"Who is there?"

"A telegram."

"You might have waited till tomorrow," I say angrily, taking the telegram from the attendant. "Now I shall not get to sleep again."

"I am sorry. Your light was burning, so I thought you were not asleep."

I tear open the telegram and look first at the signature. From my wife.

"What does she want?"

"Gnekker was secretly married to Liza yesterday. Return."

I read the telegram, and my dismay does not last long. I am dismayed, not by what Liza and Gnekker have done, but by the indifference with which I hear of their marriage. They say philosophers and the truly wise are indifferent. It is false: indifference is the paralysis of the soul; it is premature death.

I go to bed again, and begin trying to think of something to occupy my mind. What am I to think about? I feel as though everything had been thought over already and there is nothing which could hold my attention now.

When daylight comes I sit up in bed with my arms round my knees, and to pass the time I try to know myself. "Know thyself" is excellent and useful advice; it is only a pity that the ancients never thought to indicate the means of following this precept.

When I have wanted to understand somebody or myself I have considered, not the actions, in which everything is relative, but the desires.

"Tell me what you want, and I will tell you what manner of man you are."

And now I examine myself: what do I want?

I want our wives, our children, our friends, our pupils, to love in us, not our fame, not the brand and not the label, but to love us as ordinary men. Anything else? I should like to have had helpers and successors. Anything else? I should like to wake up in a hundred years' time and to have just a peep out of one eye at what is happening in science. I should have liked to have lived another ten years. . . What further? Why, nothing further. I think and think, and can think of nothing more. And however much I might think, and however far my thoughts might travel, it is clear to me that there is nothing vital, nothing of great importance in my desires. In my passion for science, in my desire to live, in this sitting on a strange bed, and in this striving to know myself - in all the thoughts, feelings, and ideas I form about everything, there is no common bond to connect it all into one whole. Every feeling and every thought exists apart in me; and in all my criticisms of science, the theatre, literature, my pupils, and in all the pictures my imagination draws, even the most skilful analyst could not find what is called a general idea, or the god of a living man.

And if there is not that, then there is nothing.

In a state so poverty-stricken, a serious ailment, the fear of death, the influences of circumstance and men were enough to turn upside down and scatter in fragments all which I had once looked upon as my theory of life, and in which I had seen the meaning and joy of my existence. So there is nothing surprising in the fact that I have over-shadowed the last months of my life with thoughts and feelings only worthy of a slave and barbarian, and that now I am indifferent and take no heed of the dawn. When a man has not in him what is loftier and mightier than all external impressions a bad cold is really enough to upset his equilibrium and make him begin to see an owl in every bird, to hear a dog howling in every sound. And all his pessimism or optimism with his thoughts great and small have at such times significance as symptoms and nothing more.

I am vanquished. If it is so, it is useless to think, it is useless to talk. I will sit and wait in silence for what is to come.

In the morning the corridor attendant brings me tea and a copy of the local newspaper. Mechanically I read the advertisements on the first page, the leading article, the extracts from the newspapers and journals, the chronicle of events. . . . In the latter I find, among other things, the following paragraph: "Our distinguished savant, Professor Nikolay Stepanovitch So-and-so, arrived yesterday in Harkov, and is staying in the So-and-so Hotel."

Apparently, illustrious names are created to live on their own account, apart from those that bear them. Now my name is promenading tranquilly about Harkov; in another three months, printed in gold letters on my monument, it will shine bright as the sun itself, while I s hall be already under the moss.

A light tap at the door. Somebody wants me.

"Who is there? Come in."

The door opens, and I step back surprised and hurriedly wrap my dressing-gown round me. Before me stands Katya.

"How do you do?" she says, breathless with running upstairs. "You didn't expect me? I have come here, too . . . . I have come, too!"

She sits down and goes on, hesitating and not looking

at me.

"Why don't you speak to me? I have come, too . . . today. . . . I found out that you were in this hotel, and have come to you."

"Very glad to see you," I say, shrugging my shoulders, "but I am surprised. You seem to have dropped from the skies. What have you come for?"

"Oh . . . I've simply come."

Silence. Suddenly she jumps up impulsively and comes to me.

"Nikolay Stepanovitch," she says, turning pale and pressing her hands on her bosom - "Nikolay Stepanovitch, I cannot go on living like this! I cannot! For God's sake tell me quickly, this minute, what I am to do! Tell me, what am I to do?"

"What can I tell you?" I ask in perplexity. "I can do nothing."

"Tell me, I beseech you," she goes on, breathing hard and trembling all over. "I swear that I cannot go on living like this. It's too much for me!"

She sinks on a chair and begins sobbing. She flings her head back, wrings her hands, taps with her feet; her hat falls off and hangs bobbing on its elastic; her hair is ruffled.

"Help me! help me! "she implores me. "I cannot go on!"

She takes her handkerchief out of her travelling-bag, and with it pulls out several letters, which fall from her lap to the floor. I pick them up, and on one of them I recognize the handwriting of Mihail Fyodorovitch and accidentally read a bit of a word "passionat. . ."

"There is nothing I can tell you, Katya," I say.

"Help me!" she sobs, clutching at my hand and kissing it. "You are my father, you know, my only friend! You are clever, educated; you have lived so long; you have been a teacher! Tell me, what am I to do?"

"Upon my word, Katya, I don't know. . . ."

I am utterly at a loss and confused, touched by her sobs, and hardly able to stand.

"Let us have lunch, Katya," I say, with a forced smile. "Give over crying."

And at once I add in a sinking voice:

"I shall soon be gone, Katya. . . ."

"Only one word, only one word!" she weeps, stretching out her hands to me.

"What am I to do?"

"You are a queer girl, really . . ." I mutter. "I don't understand it! So sensible, and all at once crying your eyes out.. . ."

A silence follows. Katya straightens her hair, puts on her hat, then crumples up the letters and stuffs them in

Anton Chekhov

her bag - and all this deliberately, in silence. Her face, her bosom, and her gloves are wet with tears, but her expression now is cold and forbidding. . . . I look at her, and feel ashamed that I am happier than she. The absence of what my philosophic colleagues call a general idea I have detected in myself only just before death, in the decline of my days, while the soul of this poor girl has known and will know no refuge all her life, all her life!

"Let us have lunch, Katya," I say.

"No, thank you," she answers coldly. Another minute passes in silence. "I don't like Harkov," I say; "it's so grey here - such a grey town."

"Yes, perhaps. . . . It's ugly. I am here not for long, passing through. I am going on today."

"Where?"

"To the Crimea . . . that is, to the Caucasus."

"Oh! For long?"

"I don't know."

Katya gets up, and, with a cold smile, holds out her hand without looking at me.

I want to ask her, "Then, you won't be at my funeral?" but she does not look at me; her hand is cold and, as it were, strange. I escort her to the door in silence. She goes out, walks down the long corridor without looking back; she knows that I am looking after her, and most likely she will look back at the turn.

No, she did not look back. I've seen her black dress for the last time: her steps have died away. Farewell, my treasure!

Anton Chekhov

THE PRIVY COUNCILLOR

AT the beginning of April in 1870 my mother, Klavdia Arhipovna, the widow of a lieutenant, received from her brother Ivan, a privy councillor in Petersburg, a letter in which, among other things, this passage occurred: "My liver trouble forces me to spend every summer abroad, and as I have not at the moment the money in hand for a trip to Marienbad, it is very possible, dear sister, that I may spend this summer with you at Kotchuevko. . .."

On reading the letter my mother turned pale and began trembling all over; then an expression of mingled tears and laughter came into her face. She began crying and laughing. This conflict of tears and laughter always reminds me of the flickering and spluttering of a brightly burning candle when one sprinkles it with water. Reading the letter once more, mother called together all the household, and in a voice broken with emotion began explaining to us that there had been four Gundasov brothers: one Gundasov had died as a baby; another had gone to the war, and he, too, was dead; the third, without offence to him be it said, was an actor; the fourth . . .

"The fourth has risen far above us," my mother brought out tearfully. "My own brother, we grew up together; and I am all of a tremble, all of a tremble! . . . A privy councillor with the rank of a general! How shall I meet him, my angel brother? What can I, a foolish, uneducated woman, talk to him about? It's fifteen years since I've seen him! Andryushenka," my mother turned to me, "you must rejoice, little stupid! It's a piece of luck for you that God is sending him to us!"

After we had heard a detailed history of the Gundasovs, there followed a fuss and bustle in the place such as I had been accustomed to see only before Christmas and Easter. The sky above and the water in the river were all that escaped; everything else was subjected to a merciless cleansing, scrubbing, painting. If the sky had been lower and smaller and the river had not flowed so swiftly, they would have scoured them, too, with bath-brick and rubbed them, too, with tow. Our walls were as white as snow, but they were whitewashed; the floors were bright and shining, but they were washed every day. The cat Bobtail (as a small child I had cut off a good quarter of his tail with the knife used for chopping the sugar, and that was why he was called Bobtail) was carried off to the kitchen and put in charge of Anisya; Fedka was told that if any of the dogs came near the front-door "God would punish him." But no one was so badly treated as the poor sofas, easy-chairs, and rugs! They had never, before been so violently beaten as on this occasion in preparation for our visitor. My pigeons took fright at the loud thud of the sticks, and were continually flying up into the sky.

The tailor Spiridon, the only tailor in the whole district who ventured to make for the gentry, came over from Novostroevka. He was a hard-working capable man who did not drink and was not without a certain fancy and feeling for form, but yet he was an atrocious tailor.

Anton Chekhov

His work was ruined by hesitation. . . . The idea that his cut was not fashionable enough made him alter everything half a dozen times, walk all the way to the town simply to study the dandies, and in the end dress us in suits that even a caricaturist would have called *outre* and grotesque. We cut a dash in impossibly narrow trousers and in such short jackets that we always felt quite abashed in the presence of young ladies.

This Spiridon spent a long time taking my measure. He measured me all over lengthways and crossways, as though he meant to put hoops round me like a barrel; then he spent a long time noting down my measurements with a thick pencil on a bit of paper, and ticked off all the measurements with triangular signs. When he had finished with me he set to work on my tutor, Yegor Alexyevitch Pobyedimsky. My beloved tutor was then at the stage when young men watch the growth of their moustache and are critical of their clothes, and so you can imagine the devout awe with which Spiridon approached him. Yegor Alexyevitch had to throw back his head, to straddle his legs like an inverted V, first lift up his arms, then let them fall. Spiridon measured him several times, walking round him during the process like a love-sick pigeon round its mate, going down on one knee, bending double. . . . My mother, weary, exhausted by her exertions and heated by ironing, watched these lengthy proceedings, and said:

"Mind now, Spiridon, you will have to answer for it to God if you spoil the cloth! And it will be the worse for you if you don't make them fit!"

Mother's words threw Spiridon first into a fever, then

into a perspiration, for he was convinced that he would not make them fit. He received one rouble twenty kopecks for making my suit, and for Pobyedimsky's two roubles, but we provided the cloth, the lining, and the buttons. The price cannot be considered excessive, as Novostroevka was about seven miles from us, and the tailor came to fit us four times. When he came to try the things on and we squeezed ourselves into the tight trousers and jackets adorned with basting threads, mother always frowned contemptuously and expressed her surprise:

"Goodness knows what the fashions are coming to nowadays! I am positively ashamed to look at them. If brother were not used to Petersburg I would not get you fashionable clothes!"

Spiridon, relieved that the blame was thrown on the fashion and not on him, shrugged his shoulders and sighed, as though to say:

"There's no help for it; it's the spirit of the age!"

The excitement with which we awaited the arrival of our guest can only be compared with the strained suspense with which spiritualists wait from minute to minute the appearance of a ghost. Mother went about with a sick headache, and was continually melting into tears. I lost my appetite, slept badly, and did not learn my lessons. Even in my dreams I was haunted by an impaient longing to see a general - that is, a man with epaulettes and an embroidered collar sticking up to his ears, and with a naked sword in his hands, exactly like the one who hung over the sofa in the drawing-room and glared with terrible black eyes at everybody who dared to look at him. Pobyedimsky was the only one who felt himself in his element. He was neither terrified nor delighted, and merely from time to time, when he heard the history of the Gundasov family, said:

"Yes, it will be pleasant to have some one fresh to talk to."

My tutor was looked upon among us as an exceptional nature. He was a young man of twenty, with a pimply face, shaggy locks, a low forehead, and an unusually long nose. His nose was so big that when he wanted to look close at anything he had to put his head on one side like a bird. To our thinking, there was not a man in the province cleverer, more cultivated, or more stylish. He had left the high-school in the class next to the top, and had then entered a veterinary college, from which he was expelled before the end of the first half-year. The reason of his expulsion he carefully concealed, which enabled any one who wished to do so to look upon my instructor as an injured and to some extent a mysterious person. He spoke little, and only of intellectual subjects; he ate meat during the fasts, and looked with contempt and condescension on the life going on around him, which did not prevent him, however, from taking presents, such as suits of clothes, from my mother, and drawing funny faces with red teeth on my kites. Mother disliked him for his "pride," but stood in awe of his cleverness.

Our visitor did not keep us long waiting. At the beginning of May two wagon-loads of big boxes arrived from the station. These boxes looked so majestic that the drivers instinctively took off their hats as they lifted them down.

"There must be uniforms and gunpowder in those boxes," I thought.

Why "gunpowder"? Probably the conception of a general was closely connected in my mind with cannons and gunpowder.

When I woke up on the morning of the tenth of May, nurse told me in a whisper that "my uncle had come." I dressed rapidly, and, washing after a fashion, flew out of my bedroom without saying my prayers. In the vestibule I came upon a tall, solid gentleman with fashionable whiskers and a foppish-looking overcoat. Half dead with devout awe, I went up to him and, remembering the ceremonial mother had impressed upon me, I scraped my foot before him, made a very low bow, and craned forward to kiss his hand; but the gentleman did not allow me to kiss his hand: he informed me that he was not my uncle, but my uncle's footman, Pyotr. The appearance of this Pyotr, far better dressed than Pobyedimsky or me, excited in me the utmost astonishment, which, to tell the truth, has lasted to this day. Can such dignified, respectable people with stern and intellectual faces really be footmen? And what for?

Pyotr told me that my uncle was in the garden with my mother. I rushed into the garden.

Nature, knowing nothing of the history of the Gundasov family and the rank of my uncle, felt far more at ease and unconstrained than I. There was a clamour going on in the garden such as one only bears at fairs. Masses of starlings flitting through the air and hopping about the walks were noisily chattering as they hunted for cockchafers. There were swarms of sparrows in the lilac-bushes, which threw their tender, fragrant blossoms straight in one's face. Wherever one turned, from every direction came the note of the golden oriole and the shrill cry of the hoopoe and the red-legged falcon. At any other time I should have begun chasing dragon-flies or throwing stones at a crow which was sitting on a low mound under an aspen-tree, with his blunt beak turned away; but at that moment I was in no mood for mischief. My heart was throbbing, and I felt a cold sinking at my stomach; I was preparing myself to confront a gentleman with epaulettes, with a naked sword, and with terrible eyes!

But imagine my disappointment! A dapper little foppish gentleman in white silk trousers, with a white cap on his head, was walking beside my mother in the garden. With his hands behind him and his head thrown back, every now and then running on ahead of mother, he looked quite young. There was so much life and movement in his whole figure that I could only detect the treachery of age when I came close up behind and saw beneath his cap a fringe of close-cropped silver hair. Instead of the staid dignity and stolidity of a general, I saw an almost schoolboyish nimbleness; instead of a collar sticking up to his ears, an ordinary light blue necktie. Mother and my uncle were walking in the avenue talking together. I went softly up to them from behind, and waited for one of them to look round.

"What a delightful place you have here, Klavdia!" said my uncle. "How charming and lovely it is! Had I known before that you had such a charming place, nothing would have induced me to go abroad all these years."

My uncle stooped down rapidly and sniffed at a tulip. Everything he saw moved him to rapture and excitement, as though he had never been in a garden on a sunny day before. The queer man moved about as though he were on springs, and chattered incessantly, without allowing mother to utter a single word. All of a sudden Pobyedimsky came into sight from behind an elder-tree at the turn of the avenue. His appearance was so unexpected that my uncle positively started and stepped back a pace. On this occasion my tutor was attired in his best Inverness cape with sleeves, in which, especially back-view, he looked remarkably like a windmill. He had a solemn and majestic air. Pressing his hat to his bosom in Spanish style, he took a step towards my uncle and made a bow such as a marquis makes in a melodrama, bending forward, a little to one side.

"I have the honour to present myself to your high excellency," he said aloud: "the teacher and instructor of your nephew, formerly a pupil of the veterinary institute, and a nobleman by birth, Pobyedimsky!"

This politeness on the part of my tutor pleased my mother very much. She gave a smile, and waited in thrilled suspense to hear what clever thing he would say next; but my tutor, expecting his dignified address to be answered with equal dignity - that is, that my uncle would say "H'm!" like a general and hold out two fingers - was greatly confused and abashed when the latter laughed genially and shook hands with him. He muttered something incoherent, cleared his throat, and walked away.

"Come! isn't that charming?" laughed my uncle. "Just look! he has made his little flourish and thinks he's a very clever fellow! I do like that - upon my soul I do! What youthful aplomb, what life in that foolish flourish! And what boy is this?" he asked, suddenly turning and looking at me.

"That is my Andryushenka," my mother introduced me, flushing crimson. "My consolation. . ."

I made a scrape with my foot on the sand and dropped a low bow.

"A fine fellow . . . a fine fellow . . ." muttered my uncle, taking his hand from my lips and stroking me on the head. "So your name is Andrusha? Yes, yes. . . . H'm! . . . upon my soul! . . . Do you learn lessons?"

My mother, exaggerating and embellishing as all mothers do, began to describe my achievements in the sciences and the excellence of my behaviour, and I walked round my uncle and, following the ceremonial laid down for me, I continued making low bows. Then my mother began throwing out hints that with my remarkable abilities it would not be amiss for me to get a government nomination to the cadet school; but at the point when I was to have burst into tears and begged for my uncle's protection, my uncle suddenly stopped and flung up his hands in amazement.

"My goo-oodness! What's that?" he asked.

Tatyana Ivanovna, the wife of our bailiff, Fyodor Petrovna, was coming towards us. She was carrying a starched white petticoat and a long ironing-board. As she passed us she looked shyly at the visitor through her eyelashes and flushed crimson.

"Wonders will never cease . . ." my uncle filtered through his teeth, looking after her with friendly interest. "You have a fresh surprise at every step, sister . . . upon my soul!"

"She's a beauty . . ." said mother. "They chose her as a bride for Fyodor, though she lived over seventy miles from here. . . ."

Not every one would have called Tatyana a beauty. She was a plump little woman of twenty, with black eyebrows and a graceful figure, always rosy and attractive-looking, but in her face and in her whole person there was not one striking feature, not one bold line to catch the eye, as though nature had lacked inspiration and confidence when creating her. Tatyana Ivanovna was shy, bashful, and modest in her behaviour; she moved softly and smoothly, said little, seldom laughed, and her whole life was as regular as her face and as flat as her smooth, tidy hair. My uncle screwed up his eyes looking after her, and smiled. Mother looked intently at his smiling face and grew serious.

"And so, brother, you've never married!" she sighed.

"No; I've not married."

"Why not?" asked mother softly.

"How can I tell you? It has happened so. In my youth I was too hard at work, I had no time to live, and when I longed to live - I looked round - and there I had fifty years on my back already. I was too late! However, talking about it . . . is depressing."

Anton Chekhov

My mother and my uncle both sighed at once and walked on, and I left them and flew off to find my tutor, that I might share my impressions with him. Pobyedimsky was standing in the middle of the yard, looking majestically at the heavens.

"One can see he is a man of culture!" he said, twisting his head round. "I hope we shall get on together."

An hour later mother came to us.

"I am in trouble, my dears!" she began, sighing. "You see brother has brought a valet with him, and the valet, God bless him, is not one you can put in the kitchen or in the hall; we must give him a room apart. I can't think what I am to do! I tell you what, children, couldn't you move out somewhere - to Fyodor's lodge, for instance - and give your room to the valet? What do you say?"

We gave our ready consent, for living in the lodge was a great deal more free than in the house, under mother's eye.

"It's a nuisance, and that's a fact!" said mother. "Brother says he won't have dinner in the middle of the day, but between six and seven, as they do in Petersburg. I am simply distracted with worry! By seven o'clock the dinner will be done to rags in the oven. Really, men don't understand anything about housekeeping, though they have so much intellect. Oh, dear! we shall have to cook two dinners every day! You will have dinner at midday as before, children, while your poor old mother has to wait till seven, for the sake of her brother."

Then my mother heaved a deep sigh, bade me try and please my uncle, whose coming was a piece of luck for me for which we must thank God, and hurried off to the kitchen. Pobyedimsky and I moved into the lodge the same day. We were installed in a room which formed the passage from the entry to the bailiff's bedroom.

Contrary to my expectations, life went on just as before, drearily and monotonously, in spite of my uncle's arrival and our move into new quarters. We were excused lessons "on account of the visitor. "Pobyedimsky, who never read anything or occupied himself in any way, spent most of his time sitting on his bed, with his long nose thrust into the air, thinking. Sometimes he would get up, try on his new suit, and sit down again to relapse into contemplation and silence. Only one thing worried him, the flies, which he used mercilessly to squash between his hands. After dinner he usually "rested," and his snores were a cause of annoyance to the whole household. I ran about the garden from morning to night, or sat in the lodge sticking my kites together. For the first two or three weeks we did not see my uncle often. For days together he sat in his own room working, in spite of the flies and the heat. His extraordinary capacity for sitting as though glued to his table produced upon us the effect of an inexplicable conjuring trick. To us idlers, knowing nothing of systematic work, his industry seemed simply miraculous. Getting up at nine, he sat down to his table, and did not leave it till dinner-time; after dinner he set to work again, and went on till late at night. Whenever I peeped through the keyhole I invariably saw the same thing: my uncle sitting at the table working. The work consisted in his writing with one hand while he turned over the leaves of a book with the other, and, strange to say, he kept moving all over - swinging his leg as though it were a pendulum, whistling, and nodding his head in time. He had an extremely careless and frivolous expression all the while, as though he were not working, but playing at noughts and crosses. I always saw him wearing a smart short jacket and a jauntily tied cravat, and he always smelt, even through the keyhole, of delicate feminine perfumery. He only left his room for dinner, but he ate little.

"I can't make brother out!" mother complained of him. "Every day we kill a turkey and pigeons on purpose for him, I make a *compote* with my own hands, and he eats a plateful of broth and a bit of meat the size of a finger and gets up from the table. I begin begging him to eat; he comes back and drinks a glass of milk. And what is there in that, in a glass of milk? It's no better than washing up water! You may die of a diet like that. . . . If I try to persuade him, he laughs and makes a joke of it. . . . No; he does not care for our fare, poor dear!"

We spent the evenings far more gaily than the days. As a rule, by the time the sun was setting and long shadows were lying across the yard, we - that is, Tatyana Ivanovna, Pobyedimsky, and I - were sitting on the steps of the lodge. We did not talk till it grew quite dusk. And, indeed, what is one to talk of when every subject has been talked over already? There was only one thing new, my uncle's arrival, and even that subject was soon exhausted. My tutor never took his eyes off Tatyana Ivanovna 's face, and frequently heaved deep sighs. . . . At the time I did not understand those sighs, and did not try to fathom their significance; now they explain a great deal to me.

When the shadows merged into one thick mass of shade, the bailiff Fyodor would come in from shooting or from the field. This Fyodor gave me the impres sion of being a fierce and even a terrible man. The son of a Russianized gipsy from Izyumskoe, swarthy-faced and curly-headed, with big black eyes and a matted beard, he was never called among our Kotchuevko peasants by any name but "The Devil." And, indeed, there was a great deal of the gipsy about him apart from his appearance. He could not, for instance, stay at home, and went off for days together into the country or into the woods to shoot. He was gloomy, ill-humoured, taciturn, was afraid of nobody, and refused to recognize any authority. He was rude to mother, addressed me familiarly, and was contemptuous of Pobyedimsky's learning. All this we forgave him, looking upon him as a hot-tempered and nervous man; mother liked him because, in spite of his gipsy nature, he was ideally honest and industrious. He loved his Tatyana Ivanovna passionately, like a gipsy, but this love took in him a gloomy form, as though it cost him suffering. He was never affectionate to his wife in our presence, but simply rolled his eyes angrily at her and twisted his mouth.

When he came in from the fields he would noisily and angrily put down his gun, would come out to us on the steps, and sit down beside his wife. After resting a little, he would ask his wife a few questions about household matters, and then sink into silence.

"Let us sing," I would suggest.

My tutor would tune his guitar, and in a deep deacon's bass strike up "In the midst of the valley." We would begin singing. My tutor took the bass, Fyodor sang in a hardly audible tenor, while I sang soprano in unison with Tatyana Ivanovna.

When the whole sky was covered with stars and the frogs had left off croaking, they would bring in our supper from the kitchen. We went into the lodge and sat down to the meal. My tutor and the gipsy ate greedily, with such a sound that it was hard to tell whether it was the bones crunching or their jaws, and Tatyana Ivanovna and I scarcely succeeded in getting our share. After supper the lodge was plunged in deep sleep.

One evening, it was at the end of May, we were sitting on the steps, waiting for supper. A shadow suddenly fell across us, and Gundasov stood before us as though he had sprung out of the earth. He looked at us for a long time, then clasped his hands and laughed gaily.

"An idyll!" he said. "They sing and dream in the moonlight! It's charming, upon my soul! May I sit down and dream with you?"

We looked at one another and said nothing. My uncle sat down on the bottom step, yawned, and looked at the sky. A silence followed. Pobyedimsky, who had for a long time been wanting to talk to somebody fresh, was delighted at the opportunity, and was the first to break the silence. He had only one subject for intellectual conversation, the epizootic diseases. It sometimes happens that after one has been in an immense crowd, only some one countenance of the thousands remains long imprinted on the memory; in the same way, of all that Pobyedimsky had heard, during his six months at the veterinary institute, he remembered only one passage:

"The epizootics do immense damage to the stock of the country. It is the duty of society to work hand in hand with the government in waging war upon them."

Before saying this to Gundasov, my tutor cleared his throat three times, and several times, in his excitement, wrapped himself up in his Inverness. On hearing about the epizootics, my uncle looked intently at my tutor and made a sound between a snort and a laugh.

"Upon my soul, that's charming!" he said, scrutinizing us as though we were mannequins. "This is actually life. . . . This is really what reality is bound to be. Why are you silent, Pelagea Ivanovna?" he said, addressing Tatyana Ivanovna.

She coughed, overcome with confusion.

"Talk, my friends, sing . . . play! . . . Don't lose time. You know, time, the rascal, runs away and waits for no man! Upon my soul, before you have time to look round, old age is upon you. . . . Then it is too late to live! That's how it is, Pelagea Ivanovna. . . . We mustn't sit still and be silent. . . ."

At that point supper was brought out from the kitchen. Uncle went into the lodge with us, and to keep us company ate five curd fritters and the wing of a duck. He ate and looked at us. He was touched and delighted by us all. Whatever silly nonsense my precious tutor talked, and whatever Tatyana Ivanovna did, he thought charming and delightful. When after supper Tatyana Ivanovna sat quietly down and took up her knitting, he kept his eyes fixed on her fingers and chatted away without ceasing.

"Make all the haste you can to live, my friends. . ." he said. "God forbid you should sacrifice the present for the future! There is youth, health, fire in the present; the future is smoke and deception! As soon as you are twenty begin to live."

Tatyana Ivanovna dropped a knitting-needle. My uncle jumped up, picked up the needle, and handed it to Tatyana Ivanovna with a bow, and for the first time in my life I learnt that there were people in the world more refined than Pobyedimsky.

"Yes . . ." my uncle went on, "love, marry, do silly things. Foolishness is a great deal more living and healthy than our straining and striving after rational life."

My uncle talked a great deal, so much that he bored us; I sat on a box listening to him and dropping to sleep. It distressed me that he did not once all the evening pay attention to me. He left the lodge at two o'clock, when, overcome with drowsiness, I was sound asleep.

From that time forth my uncle took to coming to the lodge every evening. He sang with us, had supper with us, and always stayed on till two o'clock in the morning, chatting incessantly, always about the same subject. His evening and night work was given up, and by the end of June, when the privy councillor had learned to eat mother's turkey and *compote*, his work by day was abandoned too. My uncle tore himself away from his table and plunged into "life." In the daytime he walked up and down the garden, he whistled to the workmen and hindered them from working, making them tell him their various histories. When his eye fell on Tatyana Ivanovna he ran up to her, and, if she were carrying anything, offered his assistance, which embarrassed her dreadfully.

As the summer advanced my uncle grew more and more frivolous, volatile, and careless. Pobyedimsky was completely disillusioned in regard to him.

"He is too one-sided," he said. "There is nothing to show that he is in the very foremost ranks of the service. And he doesn't even know how to talk. At every word it's 'upon my soul.' No, I don't like him!"

From the time that my uncle began visiting the lodge there was a noticeable change both in Fyodor and my tutor. Fyodor gave up going out shooting, came home early, sat more taciturn than ever, and stared with particular ill-humour at his wife. In my uncle's presence my tutor gave up talking about epizootics, frowned, and even laughed sarcastically.

"Here comes our little bantam cock!" he growled on one occasion when my uncle was coming into the lodge.

I put down this change in them both to their being offended with my uncle. My absent-minded uncle mixed up their names, and to the very day of his departure failed to distinguish which was my tutor and which was Tatyana Ivanovna's husband. Tatyana Ivanovna herself he sometimes called Nastasya, sometimes Pelagea, and sometimes Yevdokia. Touched and delighted by us, he laughed and behaved exactly as though in the company of small children. . . . All this, of course, might well offend young men. It was not a case of offended pride, however, but, as I realize now, subtler feelings.

I remember one evening I was sitting on the box struggling with sleep. My eyelids felt glued together and my body, tired out by running about all day, drooped sideways. But I struggled against sleep and tried to look on. It was about midnight. Tatyana Ivanovna, rosy and unassuming as always, was sitting at a little table sewing at her husband's shirt. Fyodor, sullen and gloomy, was staring at her from one corner, and in the other sat Pobyedimsky, snorting angrily and retreating into the high collar of his shi rt. My uncle was walking up and down the room thinking. Silence reigned; nothing was to be heard but the rustling of the linen in Tatyana Ivanovna's hands. Suddenly my uncle stood still before Tatyana Ivanovna, and said:

"You are all so young, so fresh, so nice, you live so peacefully in this quiet place, that I envy you. I have become attached to your way of life here; my heart aches when I remember I have to go away. . . . You may believe in my sincerity!"

Sleep closed my eyes and I lost myself. When some sound waked me, my uncle was standing before Tatyana Ivanovna, looking at her with a softened expression. His cheeks were flushed.

"My life has been wasted," he said. "I have not lived! Your young face makes me think of my own lost youth, and I should be ready to sit here watching you to the day of my death. It would be a pleasure to me to take you with me to Petersburg."

"What for?" Fyodor asked in a husky voice.

"I should put her under a glass case on my work-table. I should admire her and show her to other people. You know, Pelagea Ivanovna, we have no women like you there. Among us there is wealth, distinction, sometimes beauty, but we have not this true sort of life, this healthy serenity. . . ."

My uncle sat down facing Tatyana Ivanovna and took her by the hand.

"So you won't come with me to Petersburg?" he laughed. "In that case give me your little hand. . . . A charming little hand! . . . You won't give it? Come, you miser! let me kiss it, anyway. . .."

At that moment there was the scrape of a chair. Fyodor jumped up, and with heavy, measured steps went up to his wife. His face was pale, grey, and quivering. He brought his fist down on the table with a bang, and said in a hollow voice:

"I won't allow it!

At the same moment Pobyedimsky jumped up from his chair. He, too, pale and angry, went up to Tatyana Ivanovna, and he, too, struck the table with his fist.

"I . . . I won't allow it!" he said.

"What, what's the matter?" asked my uncle in surprise.

"I won't allow it!" repeated Fyodor, banging on the table.

My uncle jumped up and blinked nervously. He tried to speak, but in his amazement and alarm could not utter a word; with an embarrassed smile, he shuffled out of the lodge with the hurried step of an old man, leaving his hat behind. When, a little later, my mother ran into the lodge, Fyodor and Pobyedimsky were still hammering on the table like blacksmiths and repeating, "I won't allow it!"

"What has happened here?" asked mother. "Why has my brother been taken ill? What's the matter?"

Looking at Tatyana's pale, frightened face and at her infuriated husband, mother probably guessed what was the matter. She sighed and shook her head.

"Come! give over banging on the table!" she said. "Leave off, Fyodor! And why are you thumping, Yegor Alexyevitch? What have you got to do with it?"

Pobyedimsky was startled and confused. Fyodor looked intently at him, then at his wife, and began walking about the room. When mother had gone out of the lodge, I saw what for long afterwards I looked upon as a dream. I saw Fyodor seize my tutor, lift him up in the air, and thrust him out of the door.

When I woke up in the morning my tutor's bed was empty. To my question where he was nurse told me in a whisper that he had been taken off early in the morning to the hospital, as his arm was broken. Distressed at this intelligence and remembering the scene of the previous evening, I went out of doors. It was a grey day. The sky was covered with storm-clouds and there was a wind blowing dust, bits of paper, and feathers along the ground. . . .It felt as though rain were coming. There was a look of boredom in the servants and in the animals. When I went into the house I was told not to make such a noise with my feet, as mother was ill and in bed with a migraine. What was I to do? I went outside the gate, sat down on the little bench there, and fell to trying to discover the meaning of what I had seen and heard the day before. From our gate there was a road which, passing the forge and the pool which never dried up, ran into the main road. I looked at the telegraph-posts, about which clouds of dust were whirling, and at the sleepy birds sitting on the wires, and I suddenly felt so dreary that I began to cry.

A dusty wagonette crammed full of townspeople, probably going to visit the shrine, drove by along the main road. The wagonette was hardly out of sight when a light chaise with a pair of horses came into view. In it was Akim Nikititch, the police inspector, standing up and holding on to the coachman's belt. To my great surprise, the chaise turned into our road and flew by me in at the gate. While I was puzzling why the police inspector had come to see us, I heard a noise, and a carriage with three horses came into sight on the road. In the carriage stood the police captain, directing his coachman towards our gate.

"And why is he coming?" I thought, looking at the dusty police captain. "Most probably Pobyedimsky has complained of Fyodor to him, and they have come to take him to prison."

But the mystery was not so easily solved. The police inspector and the police captain were only the first instalment, for five minutes had scarcely passed when a coach drove in at our gate. It dashed by me so swiftly that I could only get a glimpse of a red beard.

Lost in conjecture and full of misgivings, I ran to the house. In the passage first of all I saw mother; she was

Anton Chekhov

pale and looking with horror towards the door, from which came the sounds of men's voices. The visitors had taken her by surprise in the very throes of migraine.

"Who has come, mother?" I asked.

"Sister," I heard my uncle's voice, "will you send in something to eat for the governor and me?"

"It is easy to say 'something to eat,' " whispered my mother, numb with horror. "What have I time to get ready now? I am put to shame in my old age!"

Mother clutched at her head and ran into the kitchen. The governor's sudden visit stirred and overwhelmed the whole household. A ferocious slaughter followed. A dozen fowls, five turkeys, eight ducks, were killed, and in the fluster the old gander, the progenitor of our whole flock of geese and a great favourite of mother's, was beheaded. The coachmen and the cook seemed frenzied, and slaughtered birds at random, without distinction of age or breed. For the sake of some wretched sauce a pair of valuable pigeons, as dear to me as the gander was to mother, were sacrificed. It was a long while before I could forgive the governor their death.

In the evening, when the governor and his suite, after a sumptuous dinner, had got into their carriages and driven away, I went into the house to look at the remains of the feast. Glancing into the drawing-room from the passage, I saw my uncle and my mother. My uncle, with his hands behind his back, was walking nervously up and down close to the wall, shrugging his shoulders. Mother, exhausted and looking much thinner, was sitting on the sofa and watching his movements with heavy eyes.

"Excuse me, sister, but this won't do at all," my uncle grumbled, wrinkling up his face. "I introduced the governor to you, and you didn't offer to shake hands. You covered him with confusion, poor fellow! No, that won't do. . . . Simplicity is a very good thing, but there must be limits to it. . . . Upon my soul! And then that dinner! How can one give people such things? What was that mess, for instance, that they served for the fourth course?"

"That was duck with sweet sauce . . ." mother answered softly.

"Duck! Forgive me, sister, but . . . but here I've got heartburn! I am ill!"

My uncle made a sour, tearful face, and went on:

"It was the devil sent that governor! As though I wanted his visit! Pff! . . . heartburn! I can't work or sleep . . . I am completely out of sorts. . . . And I can't understand how you can live here without anything to do . . . in this boredom! Here I've got a pain coming under my shoulder-blade! . . ."

My uncle frowned, and walked about more rapidly than ever.

"Brother," my mother inquired softly, "what would it cost to go abroad?"

"At least three thousand . . ." my uncle answered in a te arful voice. "I would go, but where am I to get it? I

Anton Chekhov

haven't a farthing. Pff! . . . heartburn!"

My uncle stopped to look dejectedly at the grey, overcast prospect from the window, and began pacing to and fro again.

A silence followed. . . . Mother looked a long while at the ikon, pondering something, then she began crying, and said:

"I'll give you the three thousand, brother. . . ."

Three days later the majestic boxes went off to the station, and the privy councillor drove off after them. As he said good-bye to mother he shed tears, and it was a long time before he took his lips from her hands, but when he got into his carriage his face beamed with childlike pleasure. . . . Radiant and happy, he settled himself comfortably, kissed his hand to my mother, who was crying, and all at once his eye was caught by me. A look of the utmost astonishment came into his face.

"What boy is this?" he asked.

My mother, who had declared my uncle's coming was a piece of luck for which I must thank God, was bitterly mortified at this question. I was in no mood for questions. I looked at my uncle's happy face, and for some reason I felt fearfully sorry for him. I could not resist jumping up to the carriage and hugging that frivolous man, weak as all men are. Looking into his face and wanting to say something pleasant, I asked:

"Uncle, have you ever been in a battle?"

"Ah, the dear boy . . ." laughed my uncle, kissing me. "A charming boy, upon my soul! How natural, how living it all is, upon my soul! . . ."

The carriage set off. . . . I looked after him, and long afterwards that farewell "upon my soul" was ringing in my ears.

THE MAN IN A CASE

AT the furthest end of the village of Mironositskoe some belated sportsmen lodged for the night in the elder Prokofy's barn. There were two of them, the veterinary surgeon Ivan Ivanovitch and the schoolmaster Burkin. Ivan Ivanovitch had a rather strange double-barrelled surname - Tchimsha-Himalaisky - which did not suit him at all, and he was called simply Ivan Ivanovitch all over the province. He lived at a stud-farm near the town, and had come out shooting now to get a breath of fresh air. Burkin, the high-school teacher, stayed every summer at Count P ---'s, and had been thoroughly at home in this district for years.

They did not sleep. Ivan Ivanovitch, a tall, lean old fellow with long moustaches, was sitting outside the door, smoking a pipe in the moonlight. Burkin was lying within on the hay, and could not be seen in the darkness.

They were telling each other all sorts of stories. Among other things, they spoke of the fact that the elder's wife, Mavra, a healthy and by no means stupid woman, had never been beyond her native village, had never seen a town nor a railway in her life, and had spent the last ten years sitting behind the stove, and only at night going out into the street.

"What is there wonderful in that!" said Burkin. "There are plenty of people in the world, solitary by temperament, who try to retreat into their shell like a hermit crab or a snail. Perhaps it is an instance of atavism, a return to the period when the ancestor of man was not yet a social animal and lived alone in his den, or perhaps it is only one of the diversities of human character - who knows? I am not a natural science man, and it is not my business to settle such questions; I only mean to say that people like Mavra are not uncommon. There is no need to look far; two months ago a man called Byelikov, a colleague of mine, the Greek master, died in our town. You have heard of him, no doubt. He was remarkable for always wearing goloshes and a warm wadded coat, and carrying an umbrella even in the very finest weather. And his umbrella was in a case, and his watch was in a case made of grey chamois leather, and when he took out his penknife to sharpen his pencil, his penknife, too, was in a little case; and his face seemed to be in a case too, because he always hid it in his turned-up collar. He wore dark spectacles and flannel vests, stuffed up his ears with cotton-wool, and when he got into a cab always told the driver to put up the hood. In short, the man displayed a constant and insurmountable impulse to wrap himself in a covering, to make himself, so to speak, a case which would isolate him and protect him from external influences. Reality irritated him, frightened him, kept him in continual agitation, and, perhaps to justify his timidity, his aversion for the actual, he always praised the past and what had never existed; and even the classical languages which he taught were in reality for him goloshes and umbrellas in which he sheltered himself from real life.

" 'Oh, how sonorous, how beautiful is the Greek language!' he would say, with a sugary expression; and as though to prove his words he would screw up his eyes and, raising his finger, would pronounce 'Anthropos!'

"And Byelikov tried to hide his thoughts also in a case. The only things that were clear to his mind were government circulars and newspaper articles in which something was forbidden. When some proclamation prohibited the boys from going out in the streets after nine o'clock in the evening, or some article declared carnal love unlawful, it was to his mind clear and definite; it was forbidden, and that was enough. For him there was always a doubtful element, something vague and not fully expressed, in any sanction or permission. When a dramatic club or a reading-room or a tea-shop was licensed in the town, he would shake his head and say softly:

"It is all right, of course; it is all very nice, but I hope it won't lead to anything!"

"Every sort of breach of order, deviation or departure from rule, depressed him, though one would have thought it was no business of his. If one of his colleagues was late for church or if rumours reached him of some prank of the high-school boys, or one of the mistresses was seen late in the evening in the company of an officer, he was much disturbed, and said he hoped that nothing would come of it. At the teachers' meetings he simply oppressed us with his caution, his circumspection, and his characteristic reflection on the ill-behaviour of the young people in both male and female high-schools, the uproar in the classes.

"Oh, he hoped it would not reach the ears of the authorities; oh, he hoped nothing would come of it; and he thought it would be a very good thing if Petrov were expelled from the second class and Yegorov from the fourth. And, do you know, by his sighs, his despondency, his black spectacles on his pale little face, a little face like a pole-cat's, you know, he crushed us all, and we gave way, reduced Petrov's and Yegorov's marks for conduct, kept them in, and in the end expelled them both. He had a strange habit of visiting our lodgings. He would come to a teacher's, would sit down, and remain silent, as though he were carefully inspecting something. He would sit like this in silence for an hour or two and then go away. This he called 'maintaining good relations with his colleagues'; and it was obvious that coming to see us and sitting there was tiresome to him, and that he came to see us simply because he considered it his duty as our colleague. We teachers were afraid of him. And even the headmaster was afraid of him. Would you believe it, our teachers were all intellectual, right-minded people, brought up on Turgenev and Shtchedrin, yet this little chap, who always went about with goloshes and an umbrella, had the whole high-school under his thumb for fifteen long years! High-school, indeed - he had the whole town under his thumb! Our ladies did not get up private theatricals on Saturdays for fear he should hear of it, and the clergy dared not eat meat or play cards in his presence. Under the influence of people like Byelikov we have got into the way of being afraid of everything in our town for the last ten or fifteen years. They are afraid to speak aloud, afraid to send letters, afraid to make acquaintances, afraid to read books, afraid to help the poor, to teach people to read and write. . . ."

Ivan Ivanovitch cleared his throat, meaning to say something, but first lighted his pipe, g azed at the moon, and then said, with pauses:

"Yes, intellectual, right minded people read Shtchedrin and Turgenev, Buckle, and all the rest of them, yet they knocked under and put up with it. . . that's just how it is."

"Byelikov lived in the same house as I did," Burkin went on, "on the same storey, his door facing mine; we often saw each other, and I knew how he lived when he was at home. And at home it was the same story: dressing-gown, nightcap, blinds, bolts, a perfect succession of prohibitions and restrictions of all sorts, and - 'Oh, I hope nothing will come of it!' Lenten fare was bad for him, yet he could not eat meat, as people might perhaps say Byelikov did not keep the fasts, and he ate freshwater fish with butter - not a Lenten dish, yet one could not say that it was meat. He did not keep a female servant for fear people might think evil of him, but had as cook an old man of sixty, called Afanasy, half-witted and given to tippling, who had once been an officer's servant and could cook after a fashion. This Afanasy was usually standing at the door with his arms folded; with a deep sigh, he would mutter always the same thing:

" 'There are plenty of *them* about nowadays!'

"Byelikov had a little bedroom like a box; his bed had curtains. When he went to bed he covered his head over; it was hot and stuffy; the wind battered on the closed doors; there was a droning noise in the stove and a sound of sighs from the kitchen - ominous sighs. . . . And he felt frightened under the bed-clothes. He was afraid that something might happen, that Afanasy might murder him, that thieves might break in, and so he had troubled dreams all night, and in the morning, when we went together to the high-school, he was depressed and pale, and it was evident that the high-school full of people excited dread and aversion in his whole being, and that to walk beside me was irksome to a man of his solitary temperament.

" 'They make a great noise in our classes,' he used to say, as though trying to find an explanation for his depression. 'It's beyond anything.'

"And the Greek master, this man in a case - would you believe it? - almost got married."

Ivan Ivanovitch glanced quickly into the barn, and said:

"You are joking!"

"Yes, strange as it seems, he almost got married. A new teacher of history and geography, Milhail Savvitch Kovalenko, a Little Russian, was appointed. He came, not alone, but with his sister Varinka. He was a tall, dark young man with huge hands, and one could see from his face that he had a bass voice, and, in fact, he had a voice that seemed to come out of a barrel - 'boom, boom, boom!' And she was not so young, about thirty, but she, too, was tall, well-made, with black eyebrows and red cheeks - in fact, she was a regular sugar-plum, and so sprightly, so noisy; she was always singing Little Russian songs and laughing. For the least thing she would go off into a ringing laugh - 'Ha-ha-ha!' We made our first thorough acquaintance with the Kovalenkos at the headmaster's name-day party. Among the glum and intensely bored teachers who came even to the name-day party as a duty we suddenly saw a new Aphrodite risen from the waves; she walked with her arms akimbo, laughed, sang, danced. . . . She sang with feeling 'The Winds do Blow,' then another song, and another, and she fascinated us all - all, even Byelikov. He sat down by her and said with a honeyed smile:

" 'The Little Russian reminds one of the ancient Greek in its softness and agreeable resonance.'

"That flattered her, and she began telling him with feeling and earnestness that they had a farm in the Gadyatchsky district, and that her mamma lived at the farm, and that they had such pears, such melons, such *kabaks*! The Little Russians call pumpkins *kabaks* (i.e., pothouses), while their pothouses they call *shinki*, and they make a beetroot soup with tomatoes and aubergines in it, 'which was so nice - awfully nice!'

"We listened and listened, and suddenly the same idea dawned upon us all:

" 'It would be a good thing to make a match of it,' the headmaster's wife said to me softly.

"We all for some reason recalled the fact that our friend Byelikov was not married, and it now seemed to us strange that we had hitherto failed to observe, and had in fact completely lost sight of, a detail so important in his life. What was his attitude to woman? How had he settled this vital question for himself? This had not interested us in the least till then; perhaps we had not even admitted the idea that a man who went out in all weathers in goloshes and slept under curtains could be in love.

" 'He is a good deal over forty and she is thirty,' the headmaster's wife went on, developing her idea. 'I believe she would marry him.'

"All sorts of things are done in the provinces through boredom, all sorts of unnecessary and nonsensical things! And that is because what is necessary is not done at all. What need was there for instance, for us to make a match for this Byelikov, whom one could not even imagine married? The headmaster's wife, the inspector's wife, and all our high-school ladies, grew livelier and even better-looking, as though they had suddenly found a new object in life. The headmaster's wife would take a box at the theatre, and we beheld sitting in her box Varinka, with such a fan, beaming and happy, and beside her Byelikov, a little bent figure, looking as though he had been extracted from his house by pincers. I would give an evening party, and the ladies would insist on my inviting Byelikov and Varinka. In short, the machine was set in motion. It appeared that Varinka was not averse to matrimony. She had not a very cheerful life with her brother; they could do nothing but quarrel and scold one another from morning till night. Here is a scene, for instance. Kovalenko would be coming along the street, a tall, sturdy young ruffian, in an embroidered shirt, his love-locks falling on his forehead under his cap, in one hand a bundle of books, in the other a thick knotted stick, followed by his sister, also with books in her hand.

" 'But you haven't read it, Mihalik!' she would be arguing loudly. 'I tell you, I swear you have not read it at all!'

" 'And I tell you I have read it,' cries Kovalenko, thumping his stick on the pavement.

" 'Oh, my goodness, Mihalik! why are you so cross? We are arguing about principles.'

" 'I tell you that I have read it!' Kovalenko would shout, more loudly than ever.

"And at home, if there was an outsider present, there was sure to be a skirmish. Such a life must have been wearisome, and of course she must have longed for a home of her own. Besides, there was her age to be considered; there was no time left to pick and choose; it was a case of marrying anybody, even a Greek master. And, indeed, most of our young ladies don't mind whom they marry so long as they do get married. However that may be, Varinka began to show an unmistakable partiality for Byelikov.

"And Byelikov? He used to visit Kovalenko just as he did us. He would arrive, sit down, and remain silent. He would sit quiet, and Varinka would sing to him 'The Winds do Blow,' or would look pensively at him with her dark eyes, or would suddenly go off into a peal - 'Ha-ha-ha!'

"Suggestion plays a great part in love affairs, and still more in getting married. Everybody - both his colleagues and the ladies - began assuring Byelikov that he ought to get married, that there was nothing left for him in life but to get married; we all congratulated him, with solemn countenances delivered ourselves of various platitudes, such as 'Marriage is a serious step.' Besides, Varinka was good-looking and interesting; she was the daughter of a civil councillor, and had a farm; and what was more, she was the first woman who had been warm and friendly in her manner to him. His head was turned, and he decided that he really ought to get married."

"Well, at that point you ought to have taken away his goloshes and umbrella," said Ivan Ivanovitch.

"Only fancy! that turned out to be impossible. He put Varinka's portrait on his table, kept coming to see me and talking about Varinka, and home life, saying marriage was a serious step. He was frequently at Kovalenko's, but he did not alter his manner of life in the least; on the contrary, indeed, his determination to get married seemed to have a depressing effect on him. He grew thinner and paler, and seemed to retreat further and further into his case.

" 'I like Varvara Savvishna,' he used to say to me, with a faint and wry smile, 'and I know that every one ought to get married, but . . . you know all this has happened so suddenly. . . . One must think a little.'

" 'What is there to think over?' I used to say to him. 'Get married - that is all.'

" 'No; marriage is a serious step. One must first weigh the duties before one, the responsibilities . . . that nothing may go wrong afterwards. It worries me so much that I don't sleep at night. And I must confess I am afraid: her brother and she have a strange way of thinking; they look at things strangely, you know, and her disposition is very impetuous. One may get married, and then, there is no knowing, one may find oneself in an unpleasant position.'

"And he did not make an offer; he kept putting it off, to the great vexation of the headmaster's wife and all our ladies; he went on weighing his future duties and responsibilities, and meanwhile he went for a walk with Varinka almost every day - possibly he thought that this was necessary in his position - and came to see me to talk about family life. And in all probability in the end he would have proposed to her, and would have made one of those unnecessary, stupid marriages such as are made by thousands among us from being bored and having nothing to do, if it had not been for a *kolossalische scandal*. I must mention that Varinka's brother, Kovalenko, detested Byelikov from the first day of their acquaintance, and could not endure him.

" 'I don't understand,' he used to say to us, shrugging his shoulders - 'I don't understand how you can put up with that sneak, that nasty phiz. Ugh! how can you live here! The atmosphere is stifling and unclean! Do you call yourselves schoolmasters, teachers? You are paltry government clerks. You keep, not a temple of science, but a department for red tape and loyal behaviour, and it smells as sour as a police-station. No, my friends; I will stay with you for a while, and then I will go to my farm and there catch crabs and teach the Little Russians. I shall go, and you can stay here with your Judas - damn his soul!'

"Or he would laugh till he cried, first in a loud bass, then in a shrill, thin laugh, and ask me, waving his hands:

" 'What does he sit here for? What does he want? He sits and stares.'

"He even gave Byelikov a nickname, 'The Spider.' And

it will readily be understood that we avoided talking to him of his sister's being about to marry 'The Spider.'

"And on one occasion, when the headmaster's wife hinted to him what a good thing it would be to secure his sister's future with such a reliable, universally respected man as Byelikov, he frowned and muttered:

" 'It's not my business; let her marry a reptile if she likes. I don't like meddling in other people's affairs.'

"Now hear what happened next. Some mischievous person drew a caricature of Byelikov walking along in his goloshes with his trousers tucked up, under his umbrella, with Varinka on his arm; below, the inscription 'Anthropos in love.' The expression was caught to a marvel, you know. The artist must have worked for more than one night, for the teachers of both the boys' and girls' high-schools, the teachers of the seminary, the government officials, all received a copy. Byelikov received one, too. The caricature made a very painful impression on him.

"We went out together; it was the first of May, a Sunday, and all of us, the boys and the teachers, had agreed to meet at the high-school and then to go for a walk together to a wood beyond the town. We set off, and he was green in the face and gloomier than a storm-cloud.

'What wicked, ill-natured people there are!' he said, and his lips quivered.

"I felt really sorry for him. We were walking along, and all of a sudden - would you believe it? - Kovalenko came bowling along on a bicycle, and after him, also on a bicycle, Varinka, flushed and exhausted, but good-humoured and gay.

" 'We are going on ahead,' she called. 'What lovely weather! Awfully lovely!'

"And they both disappeared from our sight. Byelikov turned white instead of green, and seemed petrified. He stopped short and stared at me. . . .

" 'What is the meaning of it? Tell me, please!' he asked. 'Can my eyes have deceived me? Is it the proper thing for high-school masters and ladies to ride bicycles?'

" 'What is there improper about it?' I said. 'Let them ride and enjoy themselves.'

" 'But how can that be?' he cried, amazed at my calm. 'What are you saying?'

"And he was so shocked that he was unwilling to go on, and returned home.

"Next day he was continually twitching and nervously rubbing his hands, and it was evident from his face that he was unwell. And he left before his work was over, for the first time in his life. And he ate no dinner. Towards evening he wrapped himself up warmly, though it was quite warm weather, and sallied out to the Kovalenkos'. Varinka was out; he found her brother, however.

" 'Pray sit down,' Kovalenko said coldly, with a frown. His face looked sleepy; he had just had a nap after dinner, and was in a very bad humour.

"Byelikov sat in silence for ten minutes, and then began:

" 'I have come to see you to relieve my mind. I am very, very much troubled. Some scurrilous fellow has drawn an absurd caricature of me and another person, in whom we are both deeply interested. I regard it as a duty to assure you that I have had no hand in it. . . . I have given no sort of ground for such ridicule - on the contrary, I have always behaved in every way like a gentleman.'

"Kovalenko sat sulky and silent. Byelikov waited a little, and went on slowly in a mournful voice:

" 'And I have something else to say to you. I have been in the service for years, while you have only lately entered it, and I consider it my duty as an older colleague to give you a warning. You ride on a bicycle, and that pastime is utterly unsuitable for an educator of youth.'

" 'Why so?' asked Kovalenko in his bass.

" 'Surely that needs no explanation, Mihail Savvitch - surely you can understand that? If the teacher rides a bicycle, what can you expect the pupils to do? You will have them walking on their heads next! And so long as there is no formal permission to do so, it is out of the question. I was horrified yesterday! When I saw your sister everything seemed dancing before my eyes. A lady or a young girl on a bicycle - it's awful!'

" 'What is it you want exactly?'

" 'All I want is to warn you, Mihail Savvitch. You are a

young man, you have a future before you, you must be very, very careful in your behaviour, and you are so careless - oh, so careless! You go about in an embroidered shirt, are constantly seen in the street carrying books, and now the bicycle, too. The headmaster will learn that you and your sister ride the bicycle, and then it will reach the higher authorities . . . . Will that be a good thing?'

" 'It's no business of anybody else if my sister and I do bicycle!' said Kovalenko, and he turned crimson. 'And damnation take any one who meddles in my private affairs!'

"Byelikov turned pale and got up.

" 'If you speak to me in that tone I cannot continue,' he said. 'And I beg you never to express yourself like that about our superiors in my presence; you ought to be respectful to the authorities.'

" 'Why, have I said any harm of the authorities?' asked Kovalenko, looking at him wrathfully. 'Please leave me alone. I am an honest man, and do not care to talk to a gentleman like you. I don't like sneaks!'

"Byelikov flew into a nervous flutter, and began hurriedly putting on his coat, with an expression of horror on his face. It was the first time in his life he had been spoken to so rudely.

" 'You can say what you please,' he said, as he went out from the entry to the landing on the staircase. 'I ought only to warn you: possibly some on e may have overheard us, and that our conversation may not be misunderstood and harm come of it, I shall be compelled to inform our headmaster of our conversation . . . in its main features. I am bound to do so.'

" 'Inform him? You can go and make your report!'

"Kovalenko seized him from behind by the collar and gave him a push, and Byelikov rolled downstairs, thudding with his goloshes. The staircase was high and steep, but he rolled to the bottom unhurt, got up, and touched his nose to see whether his spectacles were all right. But just as he was falling down the stairs Varinka came in, and with her two ladies; they stood below staring, and to Byelikov this was more terrible than anything. I believe he would rather have broken his neck or both legs than have been an object of ridicule. 'Why, now the whole town would hear of it; it would come to the headmaster's ears, would reach the higher authorities - oh, it might lead to something! There would be another caricature, and it would all end in his being asked to resign his post. . . .

"When he got up, Varinka recognized him, and, looking at his ridiculous face, his crumpled overcoat, and his goloshes, not understanding what had happened and supposing that he had slipped down by accident, could not restrain herself, and laughed loud enough to be heard by all the flats:

" 'Ha-ha-ha!'

"And this pealing, ringing 'Ha-ha-ha!' was the last straw that put an end to everything: to the proposed match and to Byelikov's earthly existence. He did not hear what Varinka said to him; he saw nothing. On reaching home, the first thing he did was to remove her portrait from the table; then he went to bed, and he never got up again.

"Three days later Afanasy came to me and asked whether we should not send for the doctor, as there was something wrong with his master. I went in to Byelikov. He lay silent behind the curtain, covered with a quilt; if one asked him a question, he said 'Yes' or 'No' and not another sound. He lay there while Afanasy, gloomy and scowling, hovered about him, sighing heavily, and smelling like a pothouse.

"A month later Byelikov died. We all went to his funeral - that is, both the high-schools and the seminary. Now when he was lying in his coffin his expression was mild, agreeable, even cheerful, as though he were glad that he had at last been put into a case which he would never leave again. Yes, he had attained his ideal! And, as though in his honour, it was dull, rainy weather on the day of his funeral, and we all wore goloshes and took our umbrellas. Varinka, too, was at the funeral, and when the coffin was lowered into the grave she burst into tears. I have noticed that Little Russian women are always laughing or crying - no intermediate mood.

"One must confess that to bury people like Byelikov is a great pleasure. As we were returning from the cemetery we wore discreet Lenten faces; no one wanted to display this feeling of pleasure - a feeling like that we had experienced long, long ago as children when our elders had gone out and we ran about the garden for an hour or two, enjoying complete freedom. Ah, freedom, freedom! The merest hint, the faintest hope of its possibility gives wings to the soul, does it not?

"We returned from the cemetery in a good humour. But not more than a week had passed before life went on as in the past, as gloomy, oppressive, and senseless - a life not forbidden by government prohibition, but not fully permitted, either: it was no better. And, indeed, though we had buried Byelikov, how many such men in cases were left, how many more of them there will be!"

"That's just how it is," said Ivan Ivanovitch and he lighted his pipe.

"How many more of them there will be!" repeated Burkin.

The schoolmaster came out of the barn. He was a short, stout man, completely bald, with a black beard down to his waist. The two dogs came out with him.

"What a moon!" he said, looking upwards.

It was midnight. On the right could be seen the whole village, a long street stretching far away for four miles. All was buried in deep silent slumber; not a movement, not a sound; one could hardly believe that nature could be so still. When on a moonlight night you see a broad village street, with its cottages, haystacks, and slumbering willows, a feeling of calm comes over the soul; in this peace, wrapped away from care, toil, and sorrow in the darkness of night, it is mild, melancholy, beautiful, and it seems as though the stars look down upon it kindly and with tenderness, and as though there were no evil on earth and all were well. On the left the open country began from the end of the village; it could be seen stretching far away to the horizon, and there was no movement, no sound in that whole expanse bathed in moonlight.

"Yes, that is just how it is," repeated Ivan Ivanovitch; "and isn't our living in town, airless and crowded, our writing useless papers, our playing *vint* - isn't that all a sort of case for us? And our spending our whole lives among trivial, fussy men and silly, idle women, our talking and our listening to all sorts of nonsense - isn't that a case for us, too? If you like, I will tell you a very edifying story."

"No; it's time we were asleep," said Burkin. "Tell it tomorrow."

They went into the barn and lay down on the hay. And they were both covered up and beginning to doze when they suddenly heard light footsteps - patter, patter. . . . Some one was walking not far from the barn, walking a little and stopping, and a minute later, patter, patter again. . . . The dogs began growling.

"That's Mavra," said Burkin.

The footsteps died away.

"You see and hear that they lie," said Ivan Ivanovitch, turning over on the other side, "and they call you a fool for putting up with their lying. You endure insult and humiliation, and dare not openly say that you are on the side of the honest and the free, and you lie and smile yourself; and all that for the sake of a crust of bread, for the sake of a warm corner, for the sake of a wretched little worthless rank in the service. No, one can't go on living like this."

"Well, you are off on another tack now, Ivan

Ivanovitch," said the schoolmaster. "Let us go to sleep!

And ten minutes later Burkin was asleep. But Ivan Ivanovitch kept sighing and turning over from side to side; then he got up, went outside again, and, sitting in the doorway, lighted his pipe.

GOOSEBERRIES

THE whole sky had been overcast with rain-clouds from early morning; it was a still day, not hot, but heavy, as it is in grey dull weather when the clouds have been hanging over the country for a long while, when one expects rain and it does not come. Ivan Ivanovitch, the veterinary surgeon, and Burkin, the high-school teacher, were already tired from walking, and the fields seemed to them endless. Far ahead of them they could just see the windmills of the village of Mironositskoe; on the right stretched a row of hillocks which disappeared in the distance behind the village, and they both knew that this was the bank of the river, that there were meadows, green willows, homesteads there, and that if one stood on one of the hillocks one could see from it the same vast plain, telegraph-wires, and a train which in the distance looked like a crawling caterpillar, and that in clear weather one could even see the town. Now, in still weather, when all nature seemed mild and dreamy, Ivan Ivanovitch and Burkin were filled with love of that countryside, and both thought how great, how beautiful a land it was.

"Last time we were in Prokofy's barn," said Burkin, "you were about to tell me a story."

"Yes; I meant to tell you about my brother."

Ivan Ivanovitch heaved a deep sigh and lighted a pipe to begin to tell his story, but just at that moment the rain began. And five minutes later heavy rain came down, covering the sky, and it was hard to tell when it would be over. Ivan Ivanovitch and Burkin stopped in hesitation; the dogs, already drenched, stood with their tails between their legs gazing at them feelingly.

"We must take shelter somewhere," said Burkin. "Let us go to Alehin's; it's close by."

"Come along."

They turned aside a nd walked through mown fields, sometimes going straight forward, sometimes turning to the right, till they came out on the road. Soon they saw poplars, a garden, then the red roofs of barns; there was a gleam of the river, and the view opened on to a broad expanse of water with a windmill and a white bath-house: this was Sofino, where Alehin lived.

The watermill was at work, drowning the sound of the rain; the dam was shaking. Here wet horses with drooping heads were standing near their carts, and men were walking about covered with sacks. It was damp, muddy, and desolate; the water looked cold and malignant. Ivan Ivanovitch and Burkin were already conscious of a feeling of wetness, messiness, and discomfort all over; their feet were heavy with mud, and when, crossing the dam, they went up to the barns, they were silent, as though they were angry with one another.

In one of the barns there was the sound of a winnowing machine, the door was open, and clouds of dust were coming from it. In the doorway was standing Alehin

Anton Chekhov

himself, a man of forty, tall and stout, with long hair, more like a professor or an artist than a landowner. He had on a white shirt that badly needed washing, a rope for a belt, drawers instead of trousers, and his boots, too, were plastered up with mud and straw. His eyes and nose were black with dust. He recognized Ivan Ivanovitch and Burkin, and was apparently much delighted to see them.

"Go into the house, gentlemen," he said, smiling; "I'll come directly, this minute."

It was a big two-storeyed house. Alehin lived in the lower storey, with arched ceilings and little windows, where the bailiffs had once lived; here everything was plain, and there was a smell of rye bread, cheap vodka, and harness. He went upstairs into the best rooms only on rare occasions, when visitors came. Ivan Ivanovitch and Burkin were met in the house by a maid-servant, a young woman so beautiful that they both stood still and looked at one another.

"You can't imagine how delighted I am to see you, my friends," said Alehin, going into the hall with them. "It is a surprise! Pelagea," he said, addressing the girl, "give our visitors something to change into. And, by the way, I will change too. Only I must first go and wash, for I almost think I have not washed since spring. Wouldn't you like to come into the bath-house? and meanwhile they will get things ready here."

Beautiful Pelagea, looking so refined and soft, brought them towels and soap, and Alehin went to the bath-house with his guests.

"It's a long time since I had a wash," he said,

undressing. "I have got a nice bath-house, as you see - my father built it - but I somehow never have time to wash."

He sat down on the steps and soaped his long hair and his neck, and the water round him turned brown.

"Yes, I must say," said Ivan Ivanovitch meaningly, looking at his head.

"It's a long time since I washed . . ." said Alehin with embarrassment, giving himself a second soaping, and the water near him turned dark blue, like ink.

Ivan Ivanovitch went outside, plunged into the water with a loud splash, and swam in the rain, flinging his arms out wide. He stirred the water into waves which set the white lilies bobbing up and down; he swam to the very middle of the millpond and dived, and came up a minute later in another place, and swam on, and kept on diving, trying to touch the bottom.

"Oh, my goodness!" he repeated continually, enjoying himself thoroughly. "Oh, my goodness!" He swam to the mill, talked to the peasants there, then returned and lay on his back in the middle of the pond, turning his face to the rain. Burkin and Alehin were dressed and ready to go, but he still went on swimming and diving. "Oh, my goodness! . . ." he said. "Oh, Lord, have mercy on me! . . ."

"That's enough!" Burkin shouted to him.

They went back to the house. And only when the lamp was lighted in the big drawing-room upstairs, and Burkin and Ivan Ivanovitch, attired in silk dressing-

Anton Chekhov

gowns and warm slippers, were sitting in arm-chairs; and Alehin, washed and combed, in a new coat, was walking about the drawing-room, evidently enjoying the feeling of warmth, cleanliness, dry clothes, and light shoes; and when lovely Pelagea, stepping noiselessly on the carpet and smiling softly, handed tea and jam on a tray - only then Ivan Ivanovitch began on his story, and it seemed as though not only Burkin and Alehin were listening, but also the ladies, young and old, and the officers who looked down upon them sternly and calmly from their gold frames.

"There are two of us brothers," he began -"I, Ivan Ivanovitch, and my brother, Nikolay Ivanovitch, two years younger. I went in for a learned profession and became a veterinary surgeon, while Nikolay sat in a government office from the time he was nineteen. Our father, Tchimsha-Himalaisky, was a kantonist, but he rose to be an officer and left us a little estate and the rank of nobility. After his death the little estate went in debts and legal expenses; but, anyway, we had spent our childhood running wild in the country. Like peasant children, we passed our days and nights in the fields and the woods, looked after horses, stripped the bark off the trees, fished, and so on. . . . And, you know, whoever has once in his life caught perch or has seen the migrating of the thrushes in autumn, watched how they float in flocks over the village on bright, cool days, he will never be a real townsman, and will have a yearning for freedom to the day of his death. My brother was miserable in the government office. Years passed by, and he went on sitting in the same place, went on writing the same papers and thinking of one and the same thing - how to get into the country. And this yearning by degrees passed into a definite desire, into a dream of buying himself a little farm somewhere on the banks of a river or a lake.

"He was a gentle, good-natured fellow, and I was fond of him, but I never sympathized with this desire to shut himself up for the rest of his life in a little farm of his own. It's the correct thing to say that a man needs no more than six feet of earth. But six feet is what a corpse needs, not a man. And they say, too, now, that if our intellectual classes are attracted to the land and yearn for a farm, it's a good thing. But these farms are just the same as six feet of earth. To retreat from town, from the struggle, from the bustle of life, to retreat and bury oneself in one's farm - it's not life, it's egoism, laziness, it's monasticism of a sort, but monasticism without good works. A man does not need six feet of earth or a farm, but the whole globe, all nature, where he can have room to display all the qualities and peculiarities of his free spirit.

"My brother Nikolay, sitting in his government office, dreamed of how he would eat his own cabbages, which would fill the whole yard with such a savoury smell, take his meals on the green grass, sleep in the sun, sit for whole hours on the seat by the gate gazing at the fields and the forest. Gardening books and the agricultural hints in calendars were his delight, his favourite spiritual sustenance; he enjoyed reading newspapers, too, but the only things he read in them were the advertisements of so many acres of arable land and a grass meadow with farm-houses and buildings, a river, a garden, a mill and millponds, for sale. And his imagination pictured the garden-paths, flowers and fruit, starling cotes, the carp in the pond, and all that sort of thing, you know. These imaginary pictures were of different kinds according to the advertisements which he came across, but for some reason in every one of them he had always to have gooseberries. He could not imagine a homestead, he could not picture an idyllic nook, without gooseberries.

" 'Country life has its conveniences,' he would sometimes say. 'You sit on the verandah and you drink tea, while your ducks swim on the pond, there is a delicious smell everywhere, and . . . and the gooseberries are growing.'

"He used to draw a map of his property, and in every map there were the same things - (a) house for the family, (b) servants' quarters, (c) kitchen-ga rden, (d) gooseberry-bushes. He lived parsimoniously, was frugal in food and drink, his clothes were beyond description; he looked like a beggar, but kept on saving and putting money in the bank. He grew fearfully avaricious. I did not like to look at him, and I used to give him something and send him presents for Christmas and Easter, but he used to save that too. Once a man is absorbed by an idea there is no doing anything with him.

"Years passed: he was transferred to another province. He was over forty, and he was still reading the adver-tisements in the papers and saving up. Then I heard he was married. Still with the same object of buying a farm and having gooseberries, he married an elderly and ugly widow without a trace of feeling for her, simply because she had filthy lucre. He went on living frugally after marrying her, and kept her short of food, while he put her money in the bank in his name.

"Her first husband had been a postmaster, and with him she was accustomed to pies and home-made wines, while with her second husband she did not get enough black bread; she began to pine away with this sort of life, and three years later she gave up her soul to God. And I need hardly say that my brother never for one moment imagined that he was responsible for her death. Money, like vodka, makes a man queer. In our town there was a merchant who, before he died, ordered a plateful of honey and ate up all his money and lottery tickets with the honey, so that no one might get the benefit of it. While I was inspecting cattle at a railway-station, a cattle-dealer fell under an engine and had his leg cut off. We carried him into the waiting-room, the blood was flowing - it was a horrible thing - and he kept asking them to look for his leg and was very much worried about it; there were twenty roubles in the boot on the leg that had been cut off, and he was afraid they would be lost."

"That's a story from a different opera," said Burkin.

"After his wife's death," Ivan Ivanovitch went on, after thinking for half a minute, "my brother began looking out for an estate for himself. Of course, you may look about for five years and yet end by making a mistake, and buying something quite different from what you have dreamed of. My brother Nikolay bought through an agent a mortgaged estate of three hundred and thirty acres, with a house for the family, with servants' quarters, with a park, but with no orchard, no gooseberry-bushes, and no duck-pond; there was a river, but the water in it was the colour of coffee, because on one side of the estate there was a brickyard and on the other a factory for burning bones. But Nikolay Ivanovitch did not grieve much; he ordered twenty gooseberry-bushes, planted them, and began living as a country gentleman.

"Last year I went to pay him a visit. I thought I would go and see what it was like. In his letters my brother called his estate 'Tchumbaroklov Waste, alias Himalaiskoe.' I reached 'alias Himalaiskoe' in the afternoon. It was hot. Everywhere there were ditches, fences, hedges, fir-trees planted in rows, and there was no knowing how to get to the yard, where to put one's horse. I went up to the house, and was met by a fat red dog that looked like a pig. It wanted to bark, but it was too lazy. The cook, a fat, barefooted woman, came out of the kitchen, and she, too, looked like a pig, and said that her master was resting after dinner. I went in to see my brother. He was sitting up in bed with a quilt over his legs; he had grown older, fatter, wrinkled; his cheeks, his nose, and his mouth all stuck out - he looked as though he might begin grunting into the quilt at any moment.

"We embraced each other, and shed tears of joy and of sadness at the thought that we had once been young and now were both grey-headed and near the grave. He dressed, and led me out to show me the estate.

" 'Well, how are you getting on here?' I asked.

" 'Oh, all right, thank God; I am getting on very well.'

"He was no more a poor timid clerk, but a real landowner, a gentleman. He was already accustomed to it, had grown used to it, and liked it. He ate a great deal, went to the bath-house, was growing stout, was already at law with the village commune and both factories, and was very much offended when the peasants did not call him 'Your Honour.' And he concerned himself with the salvation of his soul in a substantial, gentlemanly manner, and performed deeds of charity, not simply, but with an air of consequence. And what deeds of charity! He treated the peasants for every sort of disease with soda and castor oil, and on his name-day had a thanksgiving service in the middle of the village, and then treated the peasants to a gallon of vodka - he thought that was the thing to do. Oh, those horrible gallons of vodka! One day the fat landowner hauls the peasants up before the district captain for trespass, and next day, in honour of a holiday, treats them to a gallon of vodka, and they drink and shout 'Hurrah!' and when they are drunk bow down to his feet. A change of life for the better, and being well-fed and idle develop in a Russian the most insolent self-conceit. Nikolay Ivanovitch, who at one time in the government office was afraid to have any views of his own, now could say nothing that was not gospel truth, and uttered such truths in the tone of a prime minister. 'Education is essential, but for the peasants it is premature.' 'Corporal punishment is harmful as a rule, but in some cases it is necessary and there is nothing to take its place.'

" 'I know the peasants and understand how to treat them,' he would say. 'The peasants like me. I need only to hold up my little finger and the peasants will do anything I like.'

"And all this, observe, was uttered with a wise, benevolent smile. He repeated twenty times over 'We noblemen,' 'I as a noble'; obviously he did not remember that our grandfather was a peasant, and our father a soldier. Even our surname Tchimsha-Himalaisky, in reality so incongruous, seemed to him now melodious, distinguished, and very agreeable.

"But the point just now is not he, but myself. I want to

tell you about the change that took place in me during the brief hours I spent at his country place. In the evening, when we were drinking tea, the cook put on the table a plateful of gooseberries. They were not bought, but his own gooseberries, gathered for the first time since the bushes were planted. Nikolay Ivanovitch laughed and looked for a minute in silence at the gooseberries, with tears in his eyes; he could not speak for excitement. Then he put one gooseberry in his mouth, looked at me with the triumph of a child who has at last received his favourite toy, and said:

" 'How delicious!'

"And he ate them greedily, continually repeating, 'Ah, how delicious! Do taste them!'

"They were sour and unripe, but, as Pushkin says:

" 'Dearer to us the falsehood that exalts
Than hosts of baser truths.'

"I saw a happy man whose cherished dream was so obviously fulfilled, who had attained his object in life, who had gained what he wanted, who was satisfied with his fate and himself. There is always, for some reason, an element of sadness mingled with my thoughts of human happiness, and, on this occasion, at the sight of a happy man I was overcome by an oppressive feeling that was close upon despair. It was particularly oppressive at night. A bed was made up for me in the room next to my brother's bedroom, and I could hear that he was awake, and that he kept getting up and going to the plate of gooseberries and taking one. I reflected how many satisfied, happy people there really are! 'What a suffocating force it is! You look at life: the insolence and idleness of the strong, the ignorance and brutishness of the weak, incredible poverty all about us, overcrowding, degeneration, drunkenness, hypocrisy, lying. . . . Yet all is calm and stillness in the houses and in the streets; of the fifty thousand living in a town, there is not one who would cry out, who would give vent to his indignation aloud. We see the people going to market for provisions, eating by day, sleeping by night, talking their silly nonse nse, getting married, growing old, serenely escorting their dead to the cemetery; but we do not see and we do not hear those who suffer, and what is terrible in life goes on somewhere behind the scenes. . . . Everything is quiet and peaceful, and nothing protests but mute statistics: so many people gone out of their minds, so many gallons of vodka drunk, so many children dead from malnutrition. . . . And this order of things is evidently necessary; evidently the happy man only feels at ease because the unhappy bear their burdens in silence, and without that silence happiness would be impossible. It's a case of general hypnotism. There ought to be behind the door of every happy, contented man some one standing with a hammer continually reminding him with a tap that there are unhappy people; that however happy he may be, life will show him her laws sooner or later, trouble will come for him - disease, poverty, losses, and no one will see or hear, just as now he neither sees nor hears others. But there is no man with a hammer; the happy man lives at his ease, and trivial daily cares faintly agitate him like the wind in the aspen-tree - and all goes well.

"That night I realized that I, too, was happy and contented," Ivan Ivanovitch went on, getting up. "I, too, at dinner and at the hunt liked to lay down the law on life and religion, and the way to manage the peasantry. I, too, used to say that science was light, that culture was essential, but for the simple people reading and writing was enough for the time. Freedom is a blessing, I used to say; we can no more do without it than without air, but we must wait a little. Yes, I used to talk like that, and now I ask, 'For what reason are we to wait?' " asked Ivan Ivanovitch, looking angrily at Burkin. "Why wait, I ask you? What grounds have we for waiting? I shall be told, it can't be done all at once; every idea takes shape in life gradually, in its due time. But who is it says that? Where is the proof that it's right? You will fall back upon the natural order of things, the uniformity of phenomena; but is there order and uniformity in the fact that I, a living, thinking man, stand over a chasm and wait for it to close of itself, or to fill up with mud at the very time when perhaps I might leap over it or build a bridge across it? And again, wait for the sake of what? Wait till there's no strength to live? And meanwhile one must live, and one wants to live!

"I went away from my brother's early in the morning, and ever since then it has been unbearable for me to be in town. I am oppressed by its peace and quiet; I am afraid to look at the windows, for there is no spectacle more painful to me now than the sight of a happy family sitting round the table drinking tea. I am old and am not fit for the struggle; I am not even capable of hatred; I can only grieve inwardly, feel irritated and vexed; but at night my head is hot from the rush of ideas, and I cannot sleep. . . . Ah, if I were young!"

Ivan Ivanovitch walked backwards and forwards in excitement, and repeated: "If I were young!"

He suddenly went up to Alehin and began pressing first one of his hands and then the other.

"Pavel Konstantinovitch," he said in an imploring voice, "don't be calm and contented, don't let yourself be put to sleep! While you are young, strong, confident, be not weary in well-doing! There is no happiness, and there ought not to be; but if there is a meaning and an object in life, that meaning and object is not our happiness, but something greater and more rational. Do good!"

And all this Ivan Ivanovitch said with a pitiful, imploring smile, as though he were asking him a personal favour.

Then all three sat in arm-chairs at different ends of the drawing-room and were silent. Ivan Ivanovitch's story had not satisfied either Burkin or Alehin. When the generals and ladies gazed down from their gilt frames, looking in the dusk as though they were alive, it was dreary to listen to the story of the poor clerk who ate gooseberries. They felt inclined, for some reason, to talk about elegant people, about women. And their sitting in the drawing-room where everything - the chandeliers in their covers, the arm-chairs, and the carpet under their feet - reminded them that those very people who were now looking down from their frames had once moved about, sat, drunk tea in this room, and the fact that lovely Pelagea was moving noiselessly about was better than any story.

Alehin was fearfully sleepy; he had got up early, before three o'clock in the morning, to look after his work, and now his eyes were closing; but he was afraid his visitors might tell some interesting story after he had gone, and he lingered on. He did not go into the question whether what Ivan Ivanovitch had just said was right and true. His visitors did not talk of groats, nor of hay, nor of tar, but of something that had no direct bearing on his life, and he was glad and wanted them to go on.

"It's bed-time, though," said Burkin, getting up. "Allow me to wish you good-night."

Alehin said good-night and went downstairs to his own domain, while the visitors remained upstairs. They were both taken for the night to a big room where there stood two old wooden beds decorated with carvings, and in the corner was an ivory crucifix. The big cool beds, which had been made by the lovely Pelagea, smelt agreeably of clean linen.

Ivan Ivanovitch undressed in silence and got into bed.

"Lord forgive us sinners!" he said, and put his head under the quilt.

His pipe lying on the table smelt strongly of stale tobacco, and Burkin could not sleep for a long while, and kept wondering where the oppressive smell came from.

The rain was pattering on the window-panes all night.

ABOUT LOVE

AT lunch next day there were very nice pies, crayfish, and mutton cutlets; and while we were eating, Nikanor, the cook, came up to ask what the visitors would like for dinner. He was a man of medium height, with a puffy face and little eyes; he was close-shaven, and it looked as though his moustaches had not been shaved, but had been pulled out by the roots. Alehin told us that the beautiful Pelagea was in love with this cook. As he drank and was of a violent character, she did not want to marry him, but was willing to live with him without. He was very devout, and his religious convictions would not allow him to "live in sin"; he insisted on her marrying him, and would consent to nothing else, and when he was drunk he used to abuse her and even beat her. Whenever he got drunk she used to hide upstairs and sob, and on such occasions Alehin and the servants stayed in the house to be ready to defend her in case of necessity.

We began talking about love.

"How love is born," said Alehin, "why Pelagea does not love somebody more like herself in her spiritual and external qualities, and why she fell in love with Nikanor, that ugly snout - we all call him 'The Snout' - how far questions of personal happiness are of consequence in love - all that is known; one can take

Anton Chekhov

what view one likes of it. So far only one incontestable truth has been uttered about love: 'This is a great mystery.' Everything else that has been written or said about love is not a conclusion, but only a statement of questions which have remained unanswered. The explanation which would seem to fit one case does not apply in a dozen others, and the very best thing, to my mind, would be to explain every case individually without attempting to generalize. We ought, as the doctors say, to individualize each case."

"Perfectly true," Burkin assented.

"We Russians of the educated class have a partiality for these questions that remain unanswered. Love is usually poeticized, decorated with roses, nightingales; we Russians decorate our loves with these momentous questions, and select the most uninteresting of them, too. In Moscow, when I was a student, I had a friend who shared my life, a charming lady, and every time I took her in my arms she was thinking what I would allow her a month for housekeeping and what was the price of beef a pound. In the same way, when we are in love we are never tired of asking ourselves questi ons: whether it is honourable or dishonourable, sensible or stupid, what this love is leading up to, and so on. Whether it is a good thing or not I don't know, but that it is in the way, unsatisfactory, and irritating, I do know."

It looked as though he wanted to tell some story. People who lead a solitary existence always have something in their hearts which they are eager to talk about. In town bachelors visit the baths and the restaurants on purpose to talk, and sometimes tell the most interesting things to bath attendants and waiters;

in the country, as a rule, they unbosom themselves to their guests. Now from the window we could see a grey sky, trees drenched in the rain; in such weather we could go nowhere, and there was nothing for us to do but to tell stories and to listen.

"I have lived at Sofino and been farming for a long time," Alehin began, "ever since I left the University. I am an idle gentleman by education, a studious person by disposition; but there was a big debt owing on the estate when I came here, and as my father was in debt partly because he had spent so much on my education, I resolved not to go away, but to work till I paid off the debt. I made up my mind to this and set to work, not, I must confess, without some repugnance. The land here does not yield much, and if one is not to farm at a loss one must employ serf labour or hired labourers, which is almost the same thing, or put it on a peasant footing - that is, work the fields oneself and with one's family. There is no middle path. But in those days I did not go into such subtleties. I did not leave a clod of earth unturned; I gathered together all the peasants, men and women, from the neighbouring villages; the work went on at a tremendous pace. I myself ploughed and sowed and reaped, and was bored doing it, and frowned with disgust, like a village cat driven by hunger to eat cucumbers in the kitchen-garden. My body ached, and I slept as I walked. At first it seemed to me that I could easily reconcile this life of toil with my cultured habits; to do so, I thought, all that is necessary is to maintain a certain external order in life. I established myself upstairs here in the best rooms, and ordered them to bring me there coffee and liquor after lunch and dinner, and when I went to bed I read every night the *Yyesnik Evropi*. But one day our priest, Father Ivan, came and drank up all my liquor at one sitting; and the

Yyesnik Evropi went to the priest's daughters; as in the summer, especially at the haymaking, I did not succeed in getting to my bed at all, and slept in the sledge in the barn, or somewhere in the forester's lodge, what chance was there of reading? Little by little I moved downstairs, began dining in the servants' kitchen, and of my former luxury nothing is left but the servants who were in my father's service, and whom it would be painful to turn away.

"In the first years I was elected here an honourary justice of the peace. I used to have to go to the town and take part in the sessions of the congress and of the circuit court, and this was a pleasant change for me. When you live here for two or three months without a break, especially in the winter, you begin at last to pine for a black coat. And in the circuit court there were frock-coats, and uniforms, and dress-coats, too, all lawyers, men who have received a general education; I had some one to talk to. After sleeping in the sledge and dining in the kitchen, to sit in an arm-chair in clean linen, in thin boots, with a chain on one's waistcoat, is such luxury!

"I received a warm welcome in the town. I made friends eagerly. And of all my acquaintanceships the most intimate and, to tell the truth, the most agreeable to me was my acquaintance with Luganovitch, the vice-president of the circuit court. You both know him: a most charming personality. It all happened just after a celebrated case of incendiarism; the preliminary investigation lasted two days; we were exhausted. Luganovitch looked at me and said:

" 'Look here, come round to dinner with me.'

"This was unexpected, as I knew Luganovitch very little, only officially, and I had never been to his house. I only just went to my hotel room to change and went off to dinner. And here it was my lot to meet Anna Alexyevna, Luganovitch's wife. At that time she was still very young, not more than twenty-two, and her first baby had been born just six months before. It is all a thing of the past; and now I should find it difficult to define what there was so exceptional in her, what it was in her attracted me so much; at the time, at dinner, it was all perfectly clear to me. I saw a lovely young, good, intelligent, fascinating woman, such as I had never met before; and I felt her at once some one close and already familiar, as though that face, those cordial, intelligent eyes, I had seen somewhere in my childhood, in the album which lay on my mother's chest of drawers.

"Four Jews were charged with being incendiaries, were regarded as a gang of robbers, and, to my mind, quite groundlessly. At dinner I was very much excited, I was uncomfortable, and I don't know what I said, but Anna Alexyevna kept shaking her head and saying to her husband:

" 'Dmitry, how is this?'

"Luganovitch is a good-natured man, one of those simple-hearted people who firmly maintain the opinion that once a man is charged before a court he is guilty, and to express doubt of the correctness of a sentence cannot be done except in legal form on paper, and not at dinner and in private conversation.

" 'You and I did not set fire to the place,' he said softly, 'and you see we are not condemned, and not in prison.'

"And both husband and wife tried to make me eat and drink as much as possible. From some trifling details, from the way they made the coffee together, for instance, and from the way they understood each other at half a word, I could gather that they lived in harmony and comfort, and that they were glad of a visitor. After dinner they played a duet on the piano; then it got dark, and I went home. That was at the beginning of spring.

"After that I spent the whole summer at Sofino without a break, and I had no time to think of the town, either, but the memory of the graceful fair-haired woman remained in my mind all those days; I did not think of her, but it was as though her light shadow were lying on my heart.

"In the late autumn there was a theatrical performance for some charitable object in the town. I went into the governor's box (I was invited to go there in the interval); I looked, and there was Anna Alexyevna sitting beside the governor's wife; and again the same irresistible, thrilling impression of beauty and sweet, caressing eyes, and again the same feeling of nearness. We sat side by side, then went to the foyer.

" 'You've grown thinner,' she said; 'have you been ill?'

" 'Yes, I've had rheumatism in my shoulder, and in rainy weather I can't sleep.'

" 'You look dispirited. In the spring, when you came to dinner, you were younger, more confident. You were full of eagerness, and talked a great deal then; you were very interesting, and I really must confess I was a little carried away by you. For some reason you often came back to my memory during the summer, and when I was getting ready for the theatre today I thought I should see you.'

"And she laughed.

" 'But you look dispirited today,' she repeated; 'it makes you seem older.'

"The next day I lunched at the Luganovitchs'. After lunch they drove out to their summer villa, in order to make arrangements there for the winter, and I went with them. I returned with them to the town, and at midnight drank tea with them in quiet domestic surroundings, while the fire glowed, and the young mother kept going to see if her baby girl was asleep. And after that, every time I went to town I never failed to visit the Luganovitchs. They grew used to me, and I grew used to them. As a rule I went in unannounced, as though I were one of the family.

" 'Who is there?' I would hear from a faraway room, in the drawling voice that seemed to me so lovely.

" 'It is Pavel Konstantinovitch,' answered the maid or the nurse.

"Anna Alexyevna would come out to me with an anxious face, and would ask every time:

" 'Why is it so long since you have been? Has anything happened?'

"Her eyes, the elegant refined hand she gave me, her indoor dress, the way she did her hair, her voice, her step, always produced the same impression on me of something new and extraordinary in my life, and very important. We talked together for hours, were silent, thinking each our own thoughts, or she played for hours to me on the piano. If there were no one at home I stayed and waited, talked to the nurse, played with the child, or lay on the sofa in the study and read; and when Anna Alexyevna came back I met her in the hall, took all her parcels from her, and for some reason I carried those parcels every time with as much love, with as much solemnity, as a boy.

"There is a proverb that if a peasant woman has no troubles she will buy a pig. The Luganovitchs had no troubles, so they made friends with me. If I did not come to the town I must be ill or something must have happened to me, and both of them were extremely anxious. They were worried that I, an educated man with a knowledge of languages, should, instead of devoting myself to science or literary work, live in the country, rush round like a squirrel in a rage, work hard with never a penny to show for it. They fancied that I was unhappy, and that I only talked, laughed, and ate to conceal my sufferings, and even at cheerful moments when I felt happy I was aware of their searching eyes fixed upon me. They were particularly touching when I really was depressed, when I was being worried by some creditor or had not money enough to pay interest on the proper day. The two of them, husband and wife, would whisper together at the window; then he would come to me and say with a grave face:

" 'If you really are in need of money at the moment, Pavel Konstantinovitch, my wife and I beg you not to hesitate to borrow from us.'

"And he would blush to his ears with emotion. And it would happen that, after whispering in the same way at the window, he would come up to me, with red ears, and say:

" 'My wife and I earnestly beg you to accept this present.'

"And he would give me studs, a cigar-case, or a lamp, and I would send them game, butter, and flowers from the country. They both, by the way, had considerable means of their own. In early days I often borrowed money, and was not very particular about it - borrowed wherever I could - but nothing in the world would have induced me to borrow from the Luganovitchs. But why talk of it?

"I was unhappy. At home, in the fields, in the barn, I thought of her; I tried to understand the mystery of a beautiful, intelligent young woman's marrying some one so uninteresting, almost an old man (her husband was over forty), and having children by him; to understand the mystery of this uninteresting, good, simple-hearted man, who argued with such wearisome good sense, at balls and evening parties kept near the more solid people, looking listless and superfluous, with a submissive, uninterested expression, as though he had been brought there for sale, who yet believed in his right to be happy, to have children by her; and I kept trying to understand why she had met him first and not me, and why such a terrible mistake in our lives need have happened.

"And when I went to the town I saw every time from her eyes that she was expecting me, and she would confess to me herself that she had had a peculiar feeling all that day and had guessed that I should come. We talked a long time, and were silent, yet we did not confess our love to each other, but timidly and jealously concealed it. We were afraid of everything that might reveal our secret to ourselves. I loved her tenderly, deeply, but I reflected and kept asking myself what our love could lead to if we had not the strength to fight against it. It seemed to be incredible that my gentle, sad love could all at once coarsely break up the even tenor of the life of her husband, her children, and all the household in which I was so loved and trusted. Would it be honourable? She would go away with me, but where? Where could I take her? It would have been a different matter if I had had a beautiful, interesting life - if, for instance, I had been struggling for the emancipation of my country, or had been a celebrated man of science, an artist or a painter; but as it was it would mean taking her from one everyday humdrum life to another as humdrum or perhaps more so. And how long would our happiness last? What would happen to her in case I was ill, in case I died, or if we simply grew cold to one another?

"And she apparently reasoned in the same way. She thought of her husband, her children, and of her mother, who loved the husband like a son. If she abandoned herself to her feelings she would have to lie, or else to tell the truth, and in her position either would have been equally terrible and inconvenient. And she was tormented by the question whether her love would bring me happiness - would she not complicate my life, which, as it was, was hard enough and full of all sorts of trouble? She fancied she was not young enough for me, that she was not industrious nor energetic enough to begin a new life, and she often talked to her husband of the importance of my marrying a girl of intelligence and merit who would be a capable housewife and a help to me - and she would immediately add that it would be difficult to find such a girl in the whole town.

"Meanwhile the years were passing. Anna Alexyevna already had two children. When I arrived at the Luganovitchs' the servants smiled cordially, the children shouted that Uncle Pavel Konstantinovitch had come, and hung on my neck; every one was overjoyed. They did not understand what was passing in my soul, and thought that I, too, was happy. Every one looked on me as a noble being. And grown-ups and children alike felt that a noble being was walking about their rooms, and that gave a peculiar charm to their manner towards me, as though in my presence their life, too, was purer and more beautiful. Anna Alexyevna and I used to go to the theatre together, always walking there; we used to sit side by side in the stalls, our shoulders touching. I would take the opera-glass from her hands without a word, and feel at that minute that she was near me, that she was mine, that we could not live without each other; but by some strange misunderstanding, when we came out of the theatre we always said good-bye and parted as though we were strangers. Goodness knows what people were saying about us in the town already, but there was not a word of truth in it all!

"In the latter years Anna Alexyevna took to going away for frequent visits to her mother or to her sister; she began to suffer from low spirits, she began to recognize that her life was spoilt and unsatisfied, and at times she did not care to see her husband nor her children. She was already being treated for neurasthenia.

"We were silent and still silent, and in the presence of outsiders she displayed a strange irritation in regard to me; whatever I talked about, she disagreed with me, and if I had an argument she sided with my opponent. If I dropped anything, she would say coldly:

" 'I congratulate you.'

"If I forgot to take the opera-glass when we were going to the theatre, she would say afterwards:

" 'I knew you would forget it.'

"Luckily or unluckily, there is nothing in our lives that does not end sooner or later. The time of parting came, as Luganovitch was appointed president in one of the western provinces. They had to sell their furniture, their horses, their summer villa. When they drove out to the villa, and afterwards looked back as they were going away, to look for the last time at the garden, at the green roof, every one was sad, and I realized that I had to say goodbye not only to the villa. It was arranged that at the end of August we should see Anna Alexyevna off to the Crimea, where the doctors were sending her, and that a little later Luganovitch and the children would set off for the western province.

"We were a great crowd to see Anna Alexye vna off. When she had said good-bye to her husband and her children and there was only a minute left before the third bell, I ran into her compartment to put a basket, which she had almost forgotten, on the rack, and I had to say good-bye. When our eyes met in the compartment our spiritual fortitude deserted us both; I took her in my arms, she pressed her face to my breast, and tears flowed from her eyes. Kissing her face, her shoulders, her hands wet with tears - oh, how unhappy we were! - I confessed my love for her, and with a burning pain in my heart I realized how unnecessary, how petty, and how deceptive all that had hindered us from loving was. I understood that when you love you must either, in your reasonings about that love, start from what is highest, from what is more important than happiness or unhappiness, sin or virtue in their accepted meaning, or you must not reason at all.

"I kissed her for the last time, pressed her hand, and parted for ever. The train had already started. I went into the next compartment - it was empty - and until I reached the next station I sat there crying. Then I walked home to Sofino. . . ."

While Alehin was telling his story, the rain left off and the sun came out. Burkin and Ivan Ivanovitch went out on the balcony, from which there was a beautiful view over the garden and the mill-pond, which was shining now in the sunshine like a mirror. They admired it, and at the same time they were sorry that this man with the kind, clever eyes, who had told them this story with such genuine feeling, should be rushing round and round this huge estate like a squirrel on a wheel instead of devoting himself to science or something else which would have made his life more pleasant; and they thought what a sorrowful face Anna Alexyevna must have had when he said good-bye to her in the railway-carriage and kissed her face and shoulders. Both of them had met her in the town, and Burkin knew her and thought her beautiful.

Anton Chekhov

THE LOTTERY TICKET

IVAN DMITRITCH, a middle-class man who lived with his family on an income of twelve hundred a year and was very well satisfied with his lot, sat down on the sofa after supper and began reading the newspaper.

"I forgot to look at the newspaper today," his wife said to him as she cleared the table. "Look and see whether the list of drawings is there."

"Yes, it is," said Ivan Dmitritch; "but hasn't your ticket lapsed?"

"No; I took the interest on Tuesday."

"What is the number?"

"Series 9,499, number 26."

"All right . . . we will look . . . 9,499 and 26."

Ivan Dmitritch had no faith in lottery luck, and would not, as a rule, have consented to look at the lists of winning numbers, but now, as he had nothing else to do and as the newspaper was before his eyes, he passed his finger downwards along the column of numbers. And immediately, as though in mockery of his scepticism, no further than the second line from the top, his eye was caught by the figure 9,499! Unable to believe his eyes, he hurriedly dropped the paper on his knees without looking to see the number of the ticket, and, just as though some one had given him a douche of cold water, he felt an agreeable chill in the pit of the stomach; tingling and terrible and sweet!

"Masha, 9,499 is there!" he said in a hollow voice.

His wife looked at his astonished and panic-stricken face, and realized that he was not joking.

"9,499?" she asked, turning pale and dropping the folded tablecloth on the table.

"Yes, yes . . . it really is there!"

"And the number of the ticket?"

"Oh, yes! There's the number of the ticket too. But stay . . .wait! No, I say! Anyway, the number of our series is there! Anyway, you understand. . . ."

Looking at his wife, Ivan Dmitritch gave a broad, senseless smile, like a baby when a bright object is shown it. His wife smiled too; it was as pleasant to her as to him that he only mentioned the series, and did not try to find out the number of the winning ticket. To torment and tantalize oneself with hopes of possible fortune is so sweet, so thrilling!

"It is our series," said Ivan Dmitritch, after a long silence. "So there is a probability that we have won. It's only a probability, but there it is!"

"Well, now look!"

Anton Chekhov

"Wait a little. We have plenty of time to be disappointed. It's on the second line from the top, so the prize is seventy-five thousand. That's not money, but power, capital! And in a minute I shall look at the list, and there - 26! Eh? I say, what if we really have won?"

The husband and wife began laughing and staring at one another in silence. The possibility of winning bewildered them; they could not have said, could not have dreamed, what they both needed that seventy-five thousand for, what they would buy, where they would go. They thought only of the figures 9,499 and 75,000 and pictured them in their imagination, while somehow they could not think of the happiness itself which was so possible.

Ivan Dmitritch, holding the paper in his hand, walked several times from corner to corner, and only when he had recovered from the first impression began dreaming a little.

"And if we have won," he said - "why, it will be a new life, it will be a transformation! The ticket is yours, but if it were mine I should, first of all, of course, spend twenty-five thousand on real property in the shape of an estate; ten thousand on immediate expenses, new furnishing . . . travelling . . .paying debts, and so on. . . . The other forty thousand I would put in the bank and get interest on it."

"Yes, an estate, that would be nice," said his wife, sitting down and dropping her hands in her lap.

"Somewhere in the Tula or Oryol provinces. . . . In the first place we shouldn't need a summer villa, and besides, it would always bring in an income."

And pictures came crowding on his imagination, each more gracious and poetical than the last. And in all these pictures he saw himself well-fed, serene, healthy, felt warm, even hot! Here, after eating a summer soup, cold as ice, he lay on his back on the burning sand close to a stream or in the garden under a lime-tree. . . . It is hot. . . . His little boy and girl are crawling about near him, digging in the sand or catching ladybirds in the grass. He dozes sweetly, thinking of nothing, and feeling all over that he need not go to the office today, tomorrow, or the day after. Or, tired of lying still, he goes to the hayfield, or to the forest for mushrooms, or watches the peasants catching fish with a net. When the sun sets he takes a towel and soap and saunters to the bathing-shed, where he undresses at his leisure, slowly rubs his bare chest with his hands, and goes into the water. And in the water, near the opaque soapy circles, little fish flit to and fro and green water-weeds nod their heads. After bathing there is tea with cream and milk rolls. . . . In the evening a walk or *vint* with the neighbours.

"Yes, it would be nice to buy an estate," said his wife, also dreaming, and from her face it was evident that she was enchanted by her thoughts.

Ivan Dmitritch pictured to himself autumn with its rains, its cold evenings, and its St. Martin's summer. At that season he would have to take longer walks about the garden and beside the river, so as to get thoroughly chilled, and then drink a big glass of vodka and eat a salted mushroom or a soused cucumber, and then - drink another. . . . The children would come running from the kitchen-garden, bringing a carrot and a radish smelling of fresh earth. . . . And then, he would lie stretched full length on the sofa, and in leisurely fashion turn over the pages of some illustrated magazine, or, covering his face with it and unbuttoning his waistcoat, give himself up to slumber.

The St. Martin's summer is followed by cloudy, gloomy weather. It rains day and night, the bare trees weep, the wind is damp and cold. The dogs, the horses, the fowls - all are wet, depressed, downcast. There is nowhere to walk; one can't go out for days together; one has to pace up and down the room, looking despondently at the grey window. It is dreary!

Ivan Dmitritch stopped and looked at his wife.

"I should go abro ad, you know, Masha," he said.

And he began thinking how nice it would be in late autumn to go abroad somewhere to the South of France . . . to Italy . . . . to India!

"I should certainly go abroad too," his wife said. "But look at the number of the ticket!"

"Wait, wait! . . ."

He walked about the room and went on thinking. It occurred to him: what if his wife really did go abroad? It is pleasant to travel alone, or in the society of light, careless women who live in the present, and not such as think and talk all the journey about nothing but their children, sigh, and tremble with dismay over every farthing. Ivan Dmitritch imagined his wife in the train with a multitude of parcels, baskets, and bags; she would be sighing over something, complaining that the train made her head ache, that she had spent so much money. . . . At the stations he would continually be having to run for boiling water, bread and butter. . . . She wouldn't have dinner because of its being too dear. . . .

"She would begrudge me every farthing," he thought, with a glance at his wife. "The lottery ticket is hers, not mine! Besides, what is the use of her going abroad? What does she want there? She would shut herself up in the hotel, and not let me out of her sight. . . . I know!"

And for the first time in his life his mind dwelt on the fact that his wife had grown elderly and plain, and that she was saturated through and through with the smell of cooking, while he was still young, fresh, and healthy, and might well have got married again.

"Of course, all that is silly nonsense," he thought; "but . . . why should she go abroad? What would she make of it? And yet she would go, of course. . . . I can fancy . . . In reality it is all one to her, whether it is Naples or Klin. She would only be in my way. I should be dependent upon her. I can fancy how, like a regular woman, she will lock the money up as soon as she gets it. . . . She will hide it from me. . . . She will look after her relations and grudge me every farthing."

Ivan Dmitritch thought of her relations. All those wretched brothers and sisters and aunts and uncles would come crawling about as soon as they heard of the winning ticket, would begin whining like beggars, and fawning upon them with oily, hypocritical smiles. Wretched, detestable people! If they were given anything, they would ask for more; while if they were refused, they would swear at them, slander them, and wish them every kind of misfortune.

Ivan Dmitritch remembered his own relations, and their faces, at which he had looked impartially in the past, struck him now as repulsive and hateful.

"They are such reptiles!" he thought.

And his wife's face, too, struck him as repulsive and hateful. Anger surged up in his heart against her, and he thought malignantly:

"She knows nothing about money, and so she is stingy. If she won it she would give me a hundred roubles, and put the rest away under lock and key."

And he looked at his wife, not with a smile now, but with hatred. She glanced at him too, and also with hatred and anger. She had her own daydreams, her own plans, her own reflections; she understood perfectly well what her husband's dreams were. She knew who would be the first to try and grab her winnings.

"It's very nice making daydreams at other people's expense!" is what her eyes expressed. "No, don't you dare!"

Her husband understood her look; hatred began stirring again in his breast, and in order to annoy his wife he glanced quickly, to spite her at the fourth page on the newspaper and read out triumphantly:

"Series 9,499, number 46! Not 26!"

Hatred and hope both disappeared at once, and it began

immediately to seem to Ivan Dmitritch and his wife that their rooms were dark and small and low-pitched, that the supper they had been eating was not doing them good, but lying heavy on their stomachs, that the evenings were long and wearisome. . . .

"What the devil's the meaning of it?" said Ivan Dmitritch, beginning to be ill-humoured. "Wherever one steps there are bits of paper under one's feet, crumbs, husks. The rooms are never swept! One is simply forced to go out. Damnation take my soul entirely! I shall go and hang myself on the first aspen-tree!"

Anton Chekhov